DREAM of AFRICA

Chaos Before Order

Mukii Gachugu

Publisher:
Australian Self Publishing Group, Pty. Ltd. / Inspiring Publishers
PO Box 159, Calwell, ACT 2905, Australia.
Phone: 61-(0) 2 6291-2904
http://australianselfpublishinggroup.com

National Library of Australia Prepublication Data Service

A catalogue record for this book is available from the National Library of Australia

Author: Mukii Gachugu

Title: **Dream of Africa: Chaos Before Order**

Genre: Fiction - Historical Fiction/Thriller

ISBN: 978-1-923449-40-4 (print)

To all the people who dream of a better tomorrow, this book is for you.

My sincere thanks to my family who without fail, have supported my dream of writing and publishing this book. My heartfelt thanks to my wife Myra Mukii for her enduring support. I am most grateful to my daughter Mimo Mukii who took time to go through my early drafts. Her editorial skills and inputs are greatly appreciated. And to all my friends, who enriched and influenced this story, many thanks.

Chapter 1:
Chaos Before Order

"Speak softly but carry a big stick"
(African saying)

"Without a leader, black ants get confused."
(African proverb)

Dr. Fungai looked around the conference table to his colleagues. Two years after escaping from Onim's men in Oko, he had set up his headquarters in Zimai, the capital city of Mpula Republic. He had built *Antu*, a formidable organization, with representatives from all over Africa.

He cleared his throat, a sign that the meeting had started. 'As the old saying goes, "Speak softly but carry a big stick."' Fungai spoke with a gentleness that belied his strength of body and character. He was a big man with a big dream and a will to carry it through.

'What if Africa is one nation, one economy, had one armed force? How great would we be?' Fungai paused, allowing a moment for the question to sink in before continuing. 'Our objective is clear and simple. It is to make Africa great and truly independent. To be great, Africa must first unite; it must be one nation. Our actions are, therefore, not aimed at grabbing leadership but uniting our people into one people.' He looked for agreement around the table. All six members nodded.

'Then we are in agreement that I institute *Project Africa*? We will shock the world, create a power vacuum, then provide the way forward,' he continued, eyeing each one of Project Africa's leaders. He was looking out for any apprehension, doubts, fear, or potential for betrayal. What he saw pleased him ... total commitment.

'What we're doing is right! Our despicable, despotic and corrupt heads of African states have made us weak. To the world, we're a pathetic and inferior race. It's our obligation ... no, our duty to change this. A new era demands a new leadership. You ... us. It has all been arranged.'

He felt the vibration in his breast pocket. Forewarned, Fungai hit the floor in one smooth motion, sliding under the solid mahogany table. What followed was pure nightmare. A slight change of pressure, then a tremor, followed by loud whining sound. He knew exactly what was coming.

Caught unawares, their fists raised high in the process of saluting their leader, affirming his decision, his six colleagues seemed bewildered as if wondering, what the hell is happening?

Still under the table, he saw a helicopter, a huge metallic-coloured bird hovering outside the window of their fifth-floor meeting room. Then, hell rained down on them.

'Get down, get down!' Fungai shouted as bullets shuttered the large windows. Shards of glass and wooden splinters sliced at his friends' skin.

Amidst the chaos of shattering glass and timber, Fungai heard the screams of his comrades. Suddenly, the helicopter lifted off, climbing and banking to the right. The loud noise gave way to an eerie silence. For a moment, the air was still. Nothing moved. The smell of gunpowder, dust and burning timber filled the air around him.

'Is everyone okay?' Fungai shouted, immediately realizing how ridiculous his question was. No answer. He dared to peep above the table, and that's when he saw the carnage. His comrades were torn to pieces. Mangled, bloody bodies, contorted into unrecognisable shapes. He felt grief overpower him but knew he had no time to spare. As though on cue, he heard gunshots and realised his security team were taking heavy fire. He knew then that it had to be the government behind the assault. It was time to leave. He had to leave his dead comrades behind and flee if he was to keep the dream alive. It was all up to him now.

From the fifth-floor boardroom, he looked through the shattered window to see a paramilitary platoon cross the street heading to the front of his building. They wore special army issue uniforms. He knew this notorius lot well. Clearly, they were after the Seven. He turned back and ran across the room, jumping over his fallen friends and out into the corridor.

'Get down, sir,' he heard one of his men manning the corridor shout. Gunfire was coming from the other end of the corridor. Soldiers from the *Republic of Zonga? Onim's men? What are they doing operating in Impula?* Fungai wondered as he made his way towards his men. His security team had done well, they had retreated to protect the office and blockaded the corridor with tables and chairs, restricting the approach by Onim's men.

'Hey, give me a rifle, I will hold them off,' Fungai shouted. 'In the conference room, there's an escape door. Change into civilian clothes in the cabinet, then run. Now go, go!' He commanded.

From their stance and determined faces, he could see they were not going to listen.

'Now! Move out, that's an order!' He shouted again, his voice commanding.

They looked at him with concern. 'Goodbye, sir.' One of them shouted as they turned and ran to the office. He turned back to face Onim's soldiers, their red berets with the Zonga special forces insignia now clear from his riffle scope. Now even more motivated after seeing his men run off. Tap, tap, tap, he returned fire. He heard one soldier shout in pain, the rest ducked. He knew it was his turn to move. He crawled back into the board room, closing the door behind him. He surveyed the room again, noticing papers scattered around the mahogany desk and the floor. Quickly picking up as many of the pages as he could, he sprinted through a trap door at the far end of the board room. It led to a secret lift. The lift descended to the basement car park. Coming out of the lift, he turned left into a narrow corridor that was almost clogged with office waste bins. He squeezed through the bins towards what appeared to be a dead end. He took a quick glance behind him before opening what looked like a cleaner's closet. On his left, mopes and brooms dangled off the hooks, a power meter box above them. To his right was a shelf full of cleaning detergents, brushes, clothes and the like. He felt around for a button hidden in the cornice above the meter box. He pushed it. A trap door slid open on the far side of the closet. He slid through the small gap into a dimly lit corridor that mirrored the one he had just left behind.

With a mop in one hand and an empty bucket in the other, he walked, limping and hunched like an old cleaner beat up by hard work and too much homemade brew. As he reached the end of the corridor, he scanned his surroundings. There was no one around in the basement parking. 'Almost there,' he said to himself.

He straightened up and lost the limp, transforming into someone late for an appointment. He walked quickly to a white Peugeot 404 with dark-tinted windows and quickly reached out for the key under the driver's seat. As he exited the car park, he scanned the street. Fifty meters to his right, a group of soldiers in all black fatigues were talking animatedly to each other. They did not notice the white Peugeot exiting from the adjacent building. He drove a short distance and parked the car on the sidewalk, opened the window and pressed the red button of a gadget that looked like a walkie-talkie, then he drove off. *Chaos and confusion are your friends*, he remembered his military training.

Behind him there was a loud *boom!* Followed by a surge of air which shook his car violently one hundred paces away. The rigged grenades and a room packed with gasoline containers quickly set the office block on fire. Hopefully, his security team had left the building. *Leave no evidence*, his sergeant in the military's intelligence unit would say.

'Rest in peace, my friends,' he said to himself as he quickly glanced at his rearview mirror, seeing the flames take hold of his office—the Meridian building would be no more.

He took a left into the main street, leaving the ensuing chaos behind him. A sign to his left pointed towards the harbour. At the main entrance of the harbour he took a left turn and headed out of town.

Fungai had hoped it would never come to this but he was always the pragmatist and a strategist, he had planned for this very scenario when they had started their clandestine meetings.

Across from the office, a beggar in tattered clothes had watched as the military cars took position. Urgently, he had removed what looked like a transistor radio and pressed a button, this had transmitted a radio wave, causing a vibration to another similar gadget in the pocket of his boss, Mr. Fungai. From his position, he had witnessed everything. He heard, then saw, the helicopter hover outside the window of the fifth-floor office and fire machine guns. He had seen the soldiers in black military uniforms go through the front door. He had heard the firefight and had seen a white Peugeot exit from the adjacent building. 'Thank God,' he had whispered as he rushed away from the inferno and chaos that he knew was about to unfold.

As Fungai drove away, police cars, ambulances and a fire truck raced towards the now blazing building.

What happened? Who betrayed us? He wondered. He had built an intelligence system and network that rivalled any that he knew, yet it had been compromised. He had been caught unawares, it had to be an inside job. He was not safe.

He remembered what his grandpa Ramla once told him, 'A river may change course but it always flows to its destination.' His destiny was elsewhere. *It's time to change course, time to execute a vanishing act,* he decided.

✦

Chapter 2:
Change Course, Same Destination

***A river may change course,
but it always flows to its destination.***

My destiny is elsewhere; it's time to change course. He started driving up the escarpment, turning and twisting, following the narrow road heading west towards the border. The neighbouring Democratic Republic of Tanga would be a good place to lay low while he planned for his next move. Using his rearview mirror, he took a last glance at the city, remembering the people he was leaving behind. His fiancé, loving, caring and carrying his baby; his unborn child about to grow up without a father. He knew she would survive but he was worried it would be a tough life. At a distance, the city, bright with the afternoon sun, looked peaceful, almost serene. He noticed the cranes, insect-like mechanical contractions, moving in slow motion, loading and unloading cargo at the harbour. *One day, I will be back,* he vowed as he focused on the way ahead.

He noticed the car begin to overheat, now high up in the hills. He passed a group of girls, each balancing a clay pot full of water on their heads. He parked his car on the side of the road and stepped out as the girls approached the car.

'Good afternoon, girls.'

'Good afternoon, older brother,' one of them responded politely while the others looked at him with suspicious eyes.

'I need water. Can I buy two pots from you? I will pay for it. I forgot to add water into my car.' The more daring one looked at the car, noticing the steam spilling from under the bonnet. A smile on her face indicated she understood.

'No problem, older brother, we give you two pots and in return, you give us a lift to our village up the hill. No need to pay.'

As he added water to the radiator, he could hear the girls giggling and chatting excitedly, not a worry in their lives. The future must be assured for the girls. *Full of life and hope,* he thought.

With the engine of the Peugeot now cool, he drove back to the river with the girls. They filled up the two pots, and then he drove up the hill, dropping them and their pots of water at the small settlement overlooking the city. An old woman was selling an assortment of fruits and vegetables on the side of the road. On seeing the ripe bananas and mangos, his stomach rumbled, reminding him he hadn't eaten since breakfast. It was now almost three in the afternoon.

'Good afternoon, Auntie, please sell me a bunch of bananas, a piece of sugarcane, four mangoes and a bag of peanuts,' he said, pointing to the items he wanted. The woman broke into a huge smile, though toothless, it was warm and endearing.

'My son, your politeness tells me you are a good person. May your journey be fruitful,' she said, wishing him well. As she accepted his coins, she spit on her chest, blessing him and showing gratitude at the same time.

'And may your lovely smile continue to lighten the hearts of your customers,' he responded with a smile of his own.

Provisioned, he hit the road, climbing higher and higher up into the mountain range, which gradually opened up to a vista of earthy browns and green, the blue and ash white of the skies. The beauty of the high-country plateau eased his mind from the happenings of the day. He stopped on the roadside and got out of the car to enjoy the air, the smells of the countryside and the beauty of his country. Here, the air was clean and crisp; the skies were clear and blue. Looking into the horizon he saw herds of cattle grazing side by side with zebras, wildebeest and gazelles of various descriptions. High in the sky, a lone bird glided effortlessly. *What a beautiful country,* he thought. *My friends died for this. I must not fail them,* he reminded himself.

For six hours, Fungai drove, only stopping once to go behind a bush, as they say, 'to visit my uncle.' In the distance, he saw the lights. He was approaching the border town of Iyaka. In thirty minutes, he could be there if he used the highway. But Fungai knew the police and militia would be on the lookout given the events of the day. There would be several checkpoints, and he was not prepared to explain why he was headed to the border.

Upfront, he knew there was a dirt track that threaded through tribal homesteads just outside town. He turned into the dirt road and drove slowly, aware that many animals used the thorny bushes that enclosed the narrow track. As he turned a corner, a pride of six lions lay in the middle of the track, soaking up the heat of the dry dirt hardened by vehicles.

'Well, what have we here? Let's see how daring you guys are,' he said aloud. He pushed the gas pedal, revving the engine of the small car. One of the lions growled, visibly angry at the disturbance. A big male stood up slowly and deliberately, showing off his impressive silver-grey mane covering his thick neck, shoulders and chest. As though competing with the whining engine, he heaved out a deep, voluminous roar, so loud that it felt like it moved the air around him. Fungai could feel the vibrations inside his car thirty meters away. 'Hi, big guy, I have no quarrel with you. Just move off the road,' he said, as if the lion could hear him. He released the clutch pedal and gradually rolled the car forward, approaching the now agitated pride.

The arrogant male was not yet done—clearly. He focused, locking eyes with Fungai as it slowly raised itself to its full height, then crouched again and lowered his head. At that moment, Fungai realised his intent, and a bit of fear crept in.

'Damn, he's coming for me,' Fungai spoke to himself. All of a sudden, the alpha male made a tentative step, then burst into full flight, leaping high in the air, swift and frightening. Intent to kill. In a split second, the huge beast was about to land on his windscreen. Fungai pushed the accelerator hard to the floor. The Peugeot, like the lion, leapt forward. The lion flew high over the car, landing on the boot. Looking at the rearview mirror, Fungai saw the huge lion fall awkwardly, tumbling over itself before turning around with amazing speed to face its foe once more. Ahead of him, the other lions looked alarmed and a bit bemused, as if they were enjoying the contest.

What are you going to do now? The other lions seemed to be asking their mate. Fungai shifted his gaze back to the rearview mirror, this time ready to maneuver the car the instant the lion made his move. The lion crouched again. One … two steps and then it lunged forwards once more, heading straight for the small car at a terrifying pace. Then it was airborne, like a huge bird. Fungai, a difficult man to scare, felt his hands trembling as his grip on the steering wheel tightened. He knew he only had seconds to respond. *Speed and surprise*—he remembered his army training. Waiting until the lion was above the car, he slammed his foot down on the gas pedal, aggressively reversing the car. The large cat landed on the bonnet, before toppling off, landing on the road with a thud, dust-clouds swirling around him. The lion, momentarily stunned, shook himself vigorously. He eyed Fungai, his tongue hanging out, dripping saliva, breathing heavily. He focused again, crouching low like a rugby player ready to tackle an opponent, this time more wary of his adversary. Fungai noticed a huge lioness out of the corner of his eye, most likely the matriarch of the pride, walking briskly towards the big male. Sensing her, he shifted his sight to the lioness who came to his side, snuggling lovingly against him as though trying to tell him, *boss, chill out*. She licked the side of his nose, removing some of the dirt .

The huge male growled, whisked his tail left and right, looked at Fungai again before turning and slowly moving away to a nearby bush. He lay down and started licking his bruised foreleg. The large female and the others followed him.

His heart was beating like an African bongo drum as he rolled the car past the pride, making as little engine noise as possible, respecting the king of the jungle.

Thirty minutes later, he was weaving through pastoral homesteads, each marked by a circular cattle kraal and a cluster of small circular mud and grass-thatched huts. Young men sat around bonfires, no doubt telling fibs of their day and reminiscing about their hunting and fighting prowess.

As he approached the border town from the back route, he spotted a bar to his right and to his left, a car wreckers' compound.

A good place to ditch the Peugeot, he decided. He came out, poured a bottle of water into the petrol tank. Anyone watching would think he had run out of gas and was just refilling. He had removed the car number plates just before entering town. He knew that by morning, the car would be a shell, cannibalized for spares by the wreckers.

He retrieved his backpack and headed for the bar across the road, entering as though he was a local.

✦

Chapter 3:
Pub Trouble

**"If you want to go fast, go alone.
If you want to go far, go together."**
(African proverb)

The lights were dim, making the place seem cozy. In contrast, the music was loud, the mob boisterous and the smell of piss and stale beer overwhelming. Nothing unexpected. This was the standard of a bar in a small town awash with cash from mostly illegal cross-border trade. And it was a Friday, the end of the month and a market day. No one but a waiter at the counter noticed him as he headed through the back door to the long-drop toilets. The stench was suffocating, but he needed to do his business; it had been a long, eventful day.

'Cattle trading was intense today with the big buyers from the city getting ready for Ramadan.' He heard a man outside his cubicle say.

'Did you see those illiterate pastoralists?' The man continued, 'the way they are drinking and throwing money at the girls? They must have done well today.'

'I was thinking exactly the same, brother. Perhaps we should help them lose it. What do you think?' A second man added with a laugh. 'Anyway, what do they do with the money in the bush?'

Inside the cubicle, Fungai listened quietly as the two strangers plotted. Fungai's instincts were screaming at him: *this is not right, I need to do something, but what? I cannot get involved in anything that would attract the attention of the police. I am a wanted man, not just by anyone, but by President Onim and his puppet President Nima.* Fungai contemplated. *But I am who I am,* he concluded.

Fungai stepped out of the toilet and quietly slipped past as the two men continued plotting. He headed quickly to the main bar. From the style of their dress, he identified the young warriors—cattle keepers. Hanging from their ears were their snuff containers made of bamboo stem. The red and black striped calico cloth was wrapped around their left shoulders. The five young men were drinking beer while chatting with three young women who were no doubt expecting a big pay-night. One of them, slightly older and seated at the head of the wooden plank bench-like table, obviously their leader, was not drinking, nor did he have a girl sitting next to him.

Fungai approached him. 'Good day, brother, watch out, you are about to be robbed.' Fungai whispered. The leader looked at Fungai with questioning eyes as though asking ... *what?* Fungai pointed towards the toilets just as the two thugs were approaching the group.

The leader saw them, immediately understanding. He stood up and, in a flashing moment, pulled out a long knife, brandishing it with his left hand just as one of the thieves pulled out a gun. What happened next was at such speed that few except Fungai noticed. With one swift movement, the cattleman threw a knobbed throwing stick at the thief with the gun, hitting him hard on the chest. The thief staggered back, screaming with pain from the blow, but managed to stay standing.

'You stupid cow dung! You're dead.' He shouted as he lifted his gun, aiming at the young man not more than ten meters away. Fungai knew the young man had no chance. He had to act, and fast. From his position slightly to the right, he dived headlong, crashing into the man's chest. He heard the ribs snap followed by the scream of a man in extreme pain. Before the thug could recover, Fungai pinned him face-down. He reached out to the hand still gripping the gun and jacked it upwards with all his strength. He heard the popping of the man's shoulder. Another agonising scream followed as the the gun fell from his limp fingers.

'You're done, man. Stay down, or I will break your neck.' Fungai spoke to the thug, in a calm but commanding voice.

He looked over his shoulder to see the other thug down on his knees begging, 'please don't kill me. He's the one who wanted to rob you.' One of the young cattlemen whacked the man's face with the flat side of his long knife, breaking his jaw in the process. The thug screamed in pain. 'Please forgive me,' he cried out. 'Don't kill me.'

The man Fungai was holding pushed back with all of his force, trying to get away. Fungai punched him hard on the side of the neck. The man went down, unconscious.

'We have to go before the police arrive,' Fungai shouted to the leader of the cattlemen. Better not to be here when they arrive.'

'Let's go,' the leader shouted as he rushed towards a side door that led to a dusty backstreet and into a back gate of a small motel. Quickly, the young men gathered their belongings from one of the rooms. Within minutes, they were out of the motel, heading into the pastoral community that he had driven through only an hour ago.

'Thank you for warning me. The situation would have been worse otherwise. My name is Morani, by the way.' The leader of the small band of warriors informed Fungai as he opened the door of an old Land Rover pickup parked in one of the homesteads.

'Come in. I see you have your luggage,' he said before continuing. 'Who are you, and where are you headed?'

The other younger warriors got into the back of the Land Rover as their leader engaged gears and drove off at speed, following the backtrack Fungai had used earlier. 'You fought like a soldier and risked your life for me. I owe you one.' Morani continued.

'Who am I? That is a long story; where am I going? As far away as possible from this country,' Fungai responded.

Morani glanced at him sideways, a smile spreading across his face. 'I understand,' he said as he continued driving west.

'Where are we going?' Fungai asked as the Land Rover roughed it through a rocky stretch of the road.

'As far away as possible from that bar.' Morani responded, laughing with humour. 'Just joking, John, we are approaching a settlement where we can rest for the night.'

'Did you just give me a name?'

Morani gave a slight shrug. 'You don't want to advertise your name. For this reason, your name, to my warriors, is John.'

'Yes, my name is John. Thank you for understanding but why John?'

'Apparently, John means God has been gracious. The thugs could have taken all the money that my people have worked for these past months, or worse. That, according to me is a blessing.'

It was almost midnight when they reached the settlement. Morani weaved his way through homesteads, stopping in the middle of a cluster of round mud huts. The young men at the back jumped out, silent, not wanting to disturb the sleeping village. One of the men entered the nearest hut. Fungai and the rest followed him—his torch, the only light.

From the torchlight, Fungai could tell this was a bachelor's pad. It was empty except for five foam mattresses scattered around the floor. An earthen water pot sat on three fire stones next to the door.

'John here will take the king's bed,' Morani announced, holding his shoulder and pointing to a mattress at the far end of the room covered with a coarse grey blanket.

One of the men dipped a calabash scoop into the pot.

'John, have a drink first before you sleep.'

'Thank you,' Fungai responded, taking the calabash scoop and having a long drink. He felt the water course through his system, hydrating and reinvigorating his body.

Another young man reached into his goatskin bag, digging out strips of goat biltong, dry and chewy.

'You are a warrior John, you fear no one, even a thug with a gun,' the young man said as he passed the biltong to Fungai.

'Thank you,' Fungai responded again, accepting the meat. 'I am no warrior and I was terrified. I didn't have any other option. I am sure you would have done the same if you were in my position.'

All the young men surrounded him, slapping his shoulders appreciatively, praising him for knocking the thug down and out.

He knew then—he was safe. His body was demanding rest; he needed to lay down.

'*This is one of the few days I will never forget,*' he reflected before falling into a deep but disturbed slumber.

Chapter 4:
Onim The Crocodile

**A crocodile hides under the surface
of the water until it's ready to strike.**

'So, what do you know about President Onim?' Fumi asked Matadi as they sat at the kitchen table having a coffee.

Matadi was a natural storyteller. 'Who is Onim?' He asked rhetorically before clearing his throat, as practiced orators do. Fumi pulled his seat closer to the table, keen to learn as much as possible about his enemy.

It is said that Onim enjoys telling his own story. His story starts in Sukuta, a small village on the southern edge of the great desert. He was born Kora el Sukuta before he became Onim or the Crocodile. As was usual, Kora, a boy of about 13 years, was awakened at sunrise when the family rooster crowed, courtesy of his dear mother. She fed him with warm sour sorghum and millet porridge, handed him a piece of charcoal-roasted cassava and sent him off to graze the family cows, goats, sheep and camels. 'Now off you go, you rascal and be careful,' she had said endearingly. 'I don't want you back here with swollen limbs from your sword fighting practice that you and your brothers are so fond of,' his mother had reminded him as she had done every morning.

Kora, a nickname given to him by the village boys because of his love for the eight-stringed musical instrument, drove his father's herd up towards the high steppes that surrounded Sukuta. After an hour of navigating through rocky slopes and across dry ravines, he reached the top of an atoll jutting out of the flat plain. Shrouded by the morning mist, he could just make out his village to the east. Far to the west, he made out the slopes of the upper steppe. He felt at home in these serene surroundings. He heard the sound of cowbells across the ridge, no doubt other boys and young men grazing their families' livestock.

After the hard climb, his herd settled down, nibbling on the grass scrub now softened by overnight dew. He saw some of his goats standing on their hind legs, trying to reach up to the leaves of the thorny acacia trees. The vegetation in this desolate landscape was scarce but the animals somehow found enough to sustain themselves. *Now that the herd is settled, I can rest a bit,* Kora thought. He sat down and focused on the beautiful morning reflections and shadows out to the west.

As the sun continued to make its majestic rise, Kora immersed himself into the landscape, hypnotised by its beauty—the changing colours, the fresh air and the numerous sounds of birds and insects. Far to the west, almost out of his eyesight, he thought he noticed a faint column of cloud rising from the surface of the vast wadi. *That's odd, the rains are not in another three moons,* he contemplated.

He wrapped his rough handwoven shawl tightly around his shoulders to avoid the sharp, cold wind coming from the north. As he continued to watch, he noticed that it was actually a cloud of dust, and it seemed like it was coming closer and closer every minute. He looked more keenly and noticed what looked like men riding fast towards their village. He noted the way they rode—high on the saddle of their horses. This spooked him. He counted twenty of them. They looked like the *djinis*—supernatural creatures said to be the spirits from the dead that roamed the desert, pouncing and feeding on human souls. He could see them more clearly now. The leader looked like a lion on horseback, his head that of a ferocious lion with a thick mane dropping to his shoulders. The others looked like different animals. There was the oryx, the addax, the wolf and even a humongous scorpion. They all carried spears and swords.

Kora was scared to his bones now. *This is not good*, he decided. He had heard stories of the raiders from the northern wilderness but he had never encountered them. His father had told him of his encounters with the *djinis*. 'They come from Berber tribes who live deep in the desert. They steal our camels and horses, take our young girls and boys to be wives and slaves, they kill everyone and everything else. They are the scourge of the desert, a curse to our people,' his father had told him and the other boys. He had spoken with such venom that the message was imprinted in his mind forever.

'Raiders! Raiders! *Djini!*'... he shouted, then he blew his horn made from the horn of a ram, hoping the boys on the other ridge would hear him. He blew a sharp and sustained whistle. His horse heard him. It galloped to his side. He had been training the mare for some time now. With one swift motion, Kora jumped onto the bare back of the horse, which took off galloping down towards his village at the foothill of the steppe. He hoped he would not be too late.

Kora saw the smoke first, then heard the screams. *I'm too late*, he realised. He saw the women and children running out of the village towards the hills, raiders high on their heels, slashing them with their scimitar-shaped swords. There was nothing he could do. Guiding his horse behind a rocky outcrop, he watched the carnage.

At a distance, he saw his father and older brother standing shoulder to shoulder with their short swords in one hand and spears in the other, facing two Berber warriors on horses. They stood up straight and brave, knowing they had little chance of coming out alive but preferring to die while fighting. His father took off as though running to his right. The biggest of the Berber warriors galloped after him. The rider raised his sword, readying to strike. His father turned around abruptly and planted his spear in the ground, the spearhead skywards. The Berber tried to stop but it was too late. The horse skidded, stood on its hind legs, then came down as though trying to trample his father. In a fraction, his father adjusted the angle of the spear and rolled it to the side in one motion. The spear penetrated the chest of the horse, burying itself deep into the heart of the beast. The horse whined, a loud, ghastly sound as it collapsed, rolling forward head first, crushing the Berber rider.

On seeing this, another rider rode straight towards his father, a big mistake. In his anger and disgust, he had forgotten my brother, who swiftly, in one motion raised his spear as he arched backwards, aiming for the man's back. The spear was true to its mark, driving deep into the man's torso and straight into his heart.

The man froze before collapsing on the dusty ground as his horse took off in panic. By this time, the other Berber warriors had noticed and came rushing into the fight. His father and brother fought bravely, bringing down two more warriors before they were overpowered. Kora saw them being hacked to death. Yet he could do nothing.

He saw three warriors rush into his family hut. They came out, dragging along the women and girls—his sisters and aunties. Even at that distance, Kora heard the scream of his mother as she saw her husband and son's bodies lying next to each other. One of the Berber warriors approached her. Kneeling next to her husband and son, she started chanting: 'when we go, we be together, but not without a fight,' with a sad voice she chanted, over and over. She seemed to be oblivious to the Berber warrior who lifted his scimitar-shaped sword, ready to strike. Like a snake, she uncoiled, striking hard and fast, driving a hidden knife deep into the warrior's belly. At that moment, the sword made contact, slashing deep into her neck. Kora saw his mother collapse next to his father and brother. The warrior came down, seeming to kneel next to her, before toppling over on top of her. His two sisters went into hysteria, screaming and scratching at their captors and murderers, but the men were too strong. The warriors tied them up like slaves and dragged them off on foot, heading north and west into the desert. The screams continued from the wounded, the captured and those moaning for their dead. Kora could not stop crying from the pain, anger and hatred he was experiencing.

He felt a firm hand on his shoulder. He screamed in panic, thinking he had been found. He looked over his shoulder, ready to see a sword coming down to slice his neck, but it was the familiar face of one of the older boys. 'All we can do now is hide until the Berbers go,' the boy told him in a shaky, high-pitched voice. He shook his head in agreement—this was the only course of action.

The two boys retreated back into the hills, careful not to be seen. Both sat silently under the cliff overhang, overlooking their village. Still in shock, reliving the grisly actions of the Berbers and the deaths of their families. In his head, Kora heard the screams of the dying, the excited ululation of the raiders as they retreated with their prize. He had one last glance at the village he called home, all the grass-thatched huts now ablaze. Against the mid-morning glare of the sun, smoke billowed high into the sky as though announcing the carnage afoot while escorting the spirits of the dead into the afterlife.

Kora was annoyed with himself for being a coward. *I could have gone out there to fight and die with my brother, father and other men of the village*, he told himself. His shame turned to anger, then to sadness, then back to anger. At that point, he vowed he would take revenge for his family and his people. He swore he would never be caught unawares again. 'Never again!' He shouted. 'Let's get out of here, it saddens me,' he told his friend.

'Do you think the Berbers will come back?' Kora asked his friend as they stopped on a dry riverbed and started scooping away the sand to get water under the shallow sand. They had been riding for close to an hour, heading towards the secret caves hidden deep in the slopes of the steppe.

'They want our cattle. They normally send a second party to search for all the cattle they can get. We had better go to the secret caves where we will find other survivors.' So, they continued, riding through ravines, climbing, sometimes forced to maneuver the horses on foot, up the steep and rocky shoulder of the escarpment.

They reached the caves in the late afternoon. They were among the first to arrive. Their Chief was already there. 'Good to see you, Kora, and so sorry about your family, but life must go on. Rest a bit, then go with the men to hunt for food for the clan. We will need to feed everyone.'

The hunting team had hoped to get at least one addax or an oryx that were common in the hillslopes of the escarpment, but they only managed a single mountain goat. The women and girls had gathered wild berries, edible leaves and tubers. The food was barely enough for the survivors.

As darkness fell, bats came out from the deeper chambers of the cave, flying low, making sharp screeching noises as though annoyed by the human invasion of their home. A communal fire was lit to warm the cave. Kora lay down next to one of his older cousins, who had also lost his family. 'I have to find my sisters,' Kora had whispered to his cousin. 'I will track the raiders and get my sisters back. I don't want them to be slaves to those savages,' he declared.

'Just let it be, Kora, what good will it do if you died in the desert or, even worse, those *djinis* captured you and sold you as a slave? It is the gods' will what happened,' his cousin had rationalised. Kora just looked at him, scorning him for his cowardice. He decided not to talk about it with his cousin any more. Going to sleep, his only thought was of how he would take revenge. He would kill every Berber he came across. *One day, all of you will pay for what you have done to my family* this was his last resolution before he dozed off into a sleep full of nightmares.

The next morning, Kora was nowhere to be seen. It is said that on that day, the young boy became a man, a man possessed. For two days, he had tracked the raiders deep into the desert. He was found almost dead by salt merchants going south to Sukuta.

'I beg you, my friend and saviour, to take me with you. My father, mother and older brother have been killed, my sisters taken into the desert, there is nothing for me in this place. Please allow me to accompany you to the big city.' Kora had begged the old man with a face scarred and grizzled by war, desert sand and the harsh sun.

The old man looked at him with his cloudy one-eye. After a long pause, he blinked his eye, a slight nod saying okay. He spoke softly, almost imperceptible in his rather rough Kuta dialect. 'I will take you with me but on one condition, you work for me for six moons. No pay.' Kora nodded, accepting the offer.

It is said that after six moons, the trader had demanded that Kora continue working for him. 'Why would I let you go? You are my slave.'

'I am free to go. I have served you as we agreed, and I am out of your bondage.' Kora had shouted at the old man.

The old man had stood up, approached and backhanded Kora's face. A second backhand got him on the right ear. Kora saw stars. His head rang like an empty drum. Dazed, he collapsed to the ground and was out for some seconds. He woke up to find the old man standing on top of him, a knife in his hand.

'You will do as I say, slave. Otherwise, I will not only kill you. I will also buy your sisters off those Berbers and kill them myself,' the one-eyed man shouted at Kora.

Kora was boiling with anger and was about to fight back. Then he remembered his father's advice: 'a crocodile hides under the surface of the water until it's ready to strike.'

'Okay, okay,' Kora had said, nodding his head vigorously. When he was upright, he raised his hands in submission. 'I will do as you say, Ahmed. Another six months,' Kora conceded.

For six moons, Kora had been a servant, more like a slave to Ahmed, the one-eyed man. He had attended errands in the main market. He had come to know some traders and other shady characters, one of whom was *the Warkara*, the shaman, an old man from his tribe. Warkara as he was called by everyone was said to have the powers of the spirits, that he could exorcise demons that seemed to favour many people of the desert.

The morning after he had conceded to Ahmed's enslavement, Kora visited the old man. He had but a few valuable possessions that he could use as payment for Warkara's services. Before leaving his home in Sukuta, he had managed to unearth a metal box containing his mother's jewellery and coins that had been buried under the dusty floor of their outdoor kitchen. One such jewel was a heavy silver necklace with traditional markings of lines, dots and animal shapes that were unique to her clan.

Kora entered the small dark room home to Warkara, the traditional healer. At mid-morning, the room was still nice and cool. After a moment, he saw the figure of the old man at the far end of the dark room.

'You are Kora from Sukuta, of the Sus clan,' the old man said in a calm, sonorous voice. The voice was almost familiar, as though he had heard it before. He felt like his father was talking to him from the other side. How could the old man, who sounded so much like his father, know where he was from?

'Is it not revenge that you seek?' The old man continued.

Now, Kora was convinced this witch was a seer otherwise, how could he know what he wanted before he had spoken a word?

'You need not tell me what you need. That I know, but how will you pay for this very expensive service, my son?'

Kora produced the heavy, very old and very special necklace as he walked the few steps to the old man, handing him the necklace. 'This belonged to my mother. It is the only item I possess of any worth.'

The old man held the heavy necklace for a long time, fingering the engraved grooves, marks and curves in the semi-darkness. It was as though he was harnessing the spirits from the necklace. Then suddenly, he cleared his throat loudly.

His eyes closed, face contorted as he concentrated on feeling the necklace, the traditional healer spoke in a high-pitched voice—that of a girl of ten years. 'Malika Bi Demba el Sukuta, your mother. Her spirits say she loves you, they beg me not to accept this necklace, the last remaining item that connects you to her.'

What the hell! How could he possibly know not only his mother's name but also his father and where she came from? This was truly a great wizard, Kora concluded.

The old man relaxed now, looked at the necklace greedily, then hesitatingly handed it back to Kora.

'I go against the wish of the spirits? I wish I could, but I cannot. Take the necklace with you, it will be your good fortune charm. As long as you have it, your mother will protect you.' Warkara told Kora.

Warkara stood up, took a few steps to an old bench that was packed with all kinds of bizarre items and found what he was looking for: a whisk made of a bull's tail. Then he unlocked a drawer that was packed with bottles with all sorts of concoctions. Opening a bottle, he took out what looked like dry biscuits the size of a big coin. He placed the dry cakes into a bowl, then he added an ash-coloured powder, then a brownish-red liquid from yet another bottle.

'Now we wait,' the old man said as though talking to himself. 'You know, I am from the village of Mansu, a bit to the north and east of your village. In fact, we're related. Your father, the son of my father's brother, was destined to be a healer, like our grandfather, but he met your mother, the most beautiful girl from the village.

'He had a choice,' Warkara continued. 'To marry Malika or to be a *warkara*.' The choice could not have been simpler. He decided to marry Malika, and soon he had a family.'

'So, you see, I am not such a great wizard, I just gather a lot of knowledge and use it to predict events or to impress my clients such as you.' *Warkara* explained in an easy tone while all along grinning like a toothless toddler.

In the meantime, the mixture in the ceramic bowl had turned into a brownish putty. The healer spooned it into a small bamboo container, commonly used to contain tobacco snuff. He closed it with a wooden stopper.

'I gather you are a domestic help in the house of Ahmed, the trader. I hear he will not release you from your bondage. I don't want to know what you want to do with this but know this: it will kill in ten minutes,' Warkara warned Kora. He continued, 'if you must use it, be prepared for your next move. And remember your father's words ... 'a crocodile hides under the surface of the water until it's ready to strike.'

This old man is full of surprises, Kora thought to himself. *How did he know what my father taught me?*

The next day, the bodies of Ahmed the trader, his two wives and five children were found lying on the rich carpets of their living room. It looked like they were having dinner when they died, though what killed them was unclear. The boy, Kora el Sukuta, as the trader used to call him, had disappeared. It was said with a sack full of money and jewellery.

I need to be as far as possible come morning, Kora reasoned as he galloped out of town, now asleep using Ahmed's strongest stallion. *Come morning, they will be sending out search parties and mercenaries. I figure they will not even bother to bring me back alive.* He rode hard, heading south and east following the river they called Kogi Nijere. He had heard there were many big towns to the south, some with so many people that you could disappear and no one would ever find you. That is where he needed to be. He rode the whole night, finding himself in the next town at day break. He let his horse loose as he approached the town. Slapping its rump, 'be on your way, horse,' he urged it to go. This early in the morning, the streets were yet to be busy. He breathed heavily and straightened up. Pushing his chest out, a confident young man walked towards the hooting and the shouts of bus touts. As he approached the bus station, he heard the touts shouting destinations he had never heard of, and the fares for various destinations. *Money? Not a problem*, he thought; destination, south.

'Which bus is heading south?' he asked one of the touts.

'That one, the one with a red line. It is going to Oko,' pointing to a rather rugged-looking bus. Kora boarded even though he didn't have a clue where Oko was.

They travelled the whole day, heading south and east. The bus would stop at every town, village and settlement, dropping off passengers and picking up new ones. It seemed like he was the only one who was not getting off. Whenever the bus stopped in a town or village, vendors would converge around it, pushing through the windows all types of food, sweet drinks and fruits. He bought himself a roasted purple yam, a bunch of fruits and a sweet drink they called kokakola. The bus continued south, following a rough road that seemed to meander with the big river. The next morning, they arrived in a huge city that seemed to be full of people. They had arrived in Niami.

Over the next three days, using his stolen wealth, he travelled further south, crossing huge rivers and entering new countries he never knew existed. The further he went southwards, the more people there were, it seemed. Each town with more people than the previous one. He was determined to go as far south as the road would take him.

On the sixth day, he looked out of the bus window and saw a huge body of water to his right. After living in the arid lands of the north all his young life, he could not fathom how there could be so much water. A lake that had no end, that seemed to converge with the blue skies far to the south. He realised he had reached the end. He could go no further, at least not by road.

A young man alighted the bus, not as Kora el Sukuta, but as Onim, the Crocodile—that must wait and strike at the right moment. He quickly found he was in Oko, the largest city he had seen. His final destination.

This will be home for now, but I can never forget Sukuta, my home, my mother, father, brother and sisters and the revenge they deserve. Vengeance will be my driver, Onim committed.

The cruelty of mankind and the greediness of those he trusted would shape his life. Onim the Crocodile, as he came to be known, survived and thrived in the big city of Oko. Without family and real friends, he initially lived off the streets. From picking pockets, he became a leader of gangs, sought after by businessmen and politicians to do their dirty work. Like those who slaughtered and enslaved his family, he became single-minded, ruthless, and without conscience. 'Never again,' he promised himself, 'would I be weak.'

'Wow!... what a story. Now I understand who I am dealing with,' Fumi responded as he stood up, stretched, thanked Matadi for dinner, then headed back to Mr. Fungai's house.

Chapter 5:
The Conference

Beautiful woolen silver clouds bring no rain.
Dark, menacing clouds, thunder and
lightning that is sure rain.

Across Europe, Africa was a hot topic of discussion over many dinner tables. 'The blacks are demanding independence.' 'What would the poor Africans do if we left them alone?' 'How can we change the game so that we continue to control their resources after we give them independence?' These were questions that concerned many European leaders. In the last century, the fathers and grandfathers of these same leaders had met in Berlin to divide the African continent. They had extracted gold, diamonds, ivory, slaves, timber and other untold wealth. They had plundered the continent and colonised its people. Countries and territories had been created from clans, tribes and ancient kingdoms. Like slavery, colonialism and imperialism were at an end. A new era was in the making. Hope and optimism for a free and prosperous people drove the African leaders at the African Heads of States conference.

Many of these leaders had experienced the big war, fighting for one side or the other. Exposed to the world, new languages and knowledge they had learned … the white man does bleed, just like the black or brown men. They have advanced knowledge? Yes! Killing machines? Yes! They are divided and greedy, just like black people. The war had awoken their understanding of what it meant to be free. To have free choice—to be able to govern themselves. 'We are going to be truly free!' they said behind closed doors at the African Leaders conference. What could possibly go wrong?

The conference hall was packed, optimism in the air, smiles all around. The future looked bright. Amongst the many dignitaries: Kwame Nkurumah stood out with his green and gold gown; Patrice Lumumba, the vocal leader from the Kongo, was silent, observant, and aloof; Kenneth Kaunda, donning a well-groomed Afro hair-do and wearing his trademark tailor-made suit, sat next to his friend Hastings Kamuzu Banda from Nyasaland, a rather short man who looked out of place next to the giants of Africa; and finally, Holden Roberto, who preferred to be called Rui Ventura from Angola, the land of the Ovimbundu people, looked at his watch. He seemed impatient with the waiting.

A stout figure with strong Berber and Arabic features, dressed in a flowing and flamboyant savannah green jubba robe and a corresponding keffiyeh that sat on his rather big head, started speaking. Like Nkuruma before him, he used lofty, flamboyant language, articulating the wrongs occasioned to the African continent and its people and the path that 'we must chart.' He was highly animated, always moving, his arms up and down, reminiscent of a military commander, extolling his troops to fight and die as heroes for a greater good. A most powerful performance.

'Great minds have come before us,' he said. 'Our journey, from slavery to colonisation, has been hard. We pay our respect and learn from the great leaders such as Kwame Nkurumah, who brought light and awoke the people of Ghana.' He looked directly at Kwame, nodding in respect. 'We remember the likes of Leopold Senghor and Sekou Touré, who told us, "there is no dignity without freedom ... we prefer freedom in poverty to opulence in slavery." From the ashes of our history, we must build. From the failures of our past, we have learned the only way our children will have true freedom is if we work together—as one.' He paused to a loud applause that echoed throughout the hall. 'If we fail ... our children shall be doomed to be subservient to others, as we have been since the slave days.'

What kind of camel dung is this? Talking big words, gesticulating like a monkey swatting at flies. What do these guys know of the real Africa, the people on the streets? Onim thought to himself. He was sitting next to his President, and he was getting worked up by the Berber. His enemy. 'This guy reminds me of the thugs who killed my family and took my sisters,' he muttered to himself.

He got even more agitated as he listened to the lofty ideas of more men who, according to him, seemed to be out of touch with reality. And yet he could not leave his President's side, another one with 'floating clouds' in his head. Onim remembered his father. He used to say, 'beautiful woolen floating clouds bring no rain; dark, menacing clouds, thunder and lightning, that is sure rain.' *Heads full of woolen clouds, these men have, and they call themselves leaders? Thank God the session is finished, I need to piss,* he thought as he stood up.

Holding his walkie-talkie close to his mouth, Onim gave discreetly instructions to his security men. 'Excuse me, Mr. President, I will be back in a minute. One of my men will be with you shortly.' He stood up and left as a young man approached and took his place.

Great speech by the speaker wearing the jubba who reminisced on Africa's leaders' aspirations and frustrations, Fungai thought. Calling for action, creating one nation with many states … that is a big idea and the only way forward if we have to be equal with the great nations of the world. Fungai removed his headphones and, like many of the other participants, headed out of the auditorium towards the toilets.

'What a man? He is my kind of man. He speaks like a commander and looks like a movie star.' Fungai heard a young man shout boisterously, dissecting the keynote speech. As he walked back to his seat, another young man came to him, hand outstretched.

'Hi, I saw you in the toilet, how are you? My name is Onim, I am from Africa,' the stranger said breaking out in laughter at his own joke. 'Can I invite you for a drink? On my president's account, of course.'

Later that night, Fungai bade farewell to Onim. 'I will be finishing my studies in about eight months. I promise I will find you, and perhaps then, I will be in a position to buy the scotch that I noticed you prefer. Maybe by then, I will be drinking with a minister!' Fungai said to Onim with a smile as he crept into a rather beat-up taxi. That was the start of a friendship that lasted until they became major adversaries.

Chapter 6:
Fallout

'It's unbelievable!' Onim shouted excitedly as he vigorously shook hands with Fungai. 'Three fucking years since the conference. I thought you said you would be back in eight months.

'I didn't know you were a seer. You know, your prediction came through. You're looking at the Minister responsible for internal security. How do you like that eh? And tomorrow! Who knows?' Onim said excitedly as they met in a darkly lit bar in downtown Oko.

'Well, my friend, you look great! Congratulations are in order, big man.' Fungai responded in kind, with a vigorous handshake and a broad grin on his face. 'I decided to do some work after finishing my studies. I needed the money. Now, it is time to enjoy Africa.'

'You've come to the right person,' Onim responded. 'If you want money, I can make you rich just like that!' Onim said, clicking his thumb and middle finger for emphasis. 'I know all the deals happening in Africa. Mining, construction, factories, people smuggling, American money, Soviet money, Arab money and even Chinese money. You name it, I am in it.'

Fungai looked at his friend closely. He was indeed serious about what he was saying. He had become one of them leaders whose sole purpose was to grab from their people. 'I would love to talk more about this, but now, it's beer time, my friend.'

After a few drinks, Onim turned to politics and his conviction, that everyone else but him were wrong. 'I understand the mind of the poor. I was one of them.' He was talking about how to deal with street protests, riots and looting that were occurring on a daily basis in many towns in his country. 'Our politicians are greedy and put self-interest above all else,' he continued, seeming to have conveniently forgotten that he had just told him about making him rich in an instant. 'I am the man for the top job. I will deal with the politicians one by one. Those that I cannot convince with money, I will use threats and, if need be, other extreme measures.'

'Now wait. There is no need for that, my friend. Perhaps it is better to have your peers on your side. This way, your leadership will be benevolent,' Fungai advised his friend, hoping to moderate his views.

'No, my friend, you have been away for too long. Africans understand only one language—violence. They respect one currency, absolute power.' Onim retorted, shaking his huge hands as though he was about to hit an enemy. 'This, my friend, is the African way. I tell you what, I will be president very soon. You wait and see.'

At that moment, a young woman entered. She was stunning, her beauty mesmerising. Heads turned, as did those of Onim and Fungai. Tall, dark, shiny skin, a rather long neck, a distinct tribal line—a mark of pride and belonging, was prominent on her forehead. An elaborate African scarf sat on her head, adding to her royal posture and beauty. Everyone seemed enthralled by this young woman, with measured, confident steps, a straight back, her walk—that of a noble upbringing. *A daughter of a chief or something like that,* Fungai thought.

'What a beautiful Olof girl,' Onim commented as the woman passed by, heading to the far side of the bar.

'I wouldn't have a clue from what country, let alone tribe, she is from, but she sure is beautiful,' Fungai responded.

As she passed next to their table, Fungai couldn't resist looking up, a smile on his face, hoping she would notice him. A wisp of fragrance, jasmine-like, drifted around the woman, captivating Fungai even more. For a moment, he felt dizzy, confused by her presence. Their eyes locked, just for a moment, as a bartender approached her.

'Madam Beki, let me take you to your table.' As she followed the waiter, she turned, eyeing Fungai. On her face, a suggestive smile. Her eyes caught a ray of light from the low-voltage bulb, like hot coal, heating Fungai from the inside out—a meltdown. *I have to talk to her,* he decided. At that point, he noticed his friend Onim looking at him, then the girl. His face cringing, the smile that had been on his face a few moments before gone. Fungai sensed a dark shadow invading their table, as he normally did when danger was lurking. He knew the feeling well, he could sense things that others couldn't. 'Are you okay, my friend?' he asked Onim politely.

Onim did not bother to answer. Suddenly, Onim stood up and headed towards the woman's table. 'Hey you, Beki, was it? Why did you eye him and not me? Am I not good enough?' He was fuming. An enraged buffalo. A young man sitting at an adjacent table stood up. 'Hey man, leave the lady alone.' But before he could move another step, Onim turned, stepped and punched the young man. He folded and slumped to the floor, groaning in pain. The punch to the stomach had done its job.

'Hey Onim, what is the matter with you?' Fungai asked as he approached his friend, hoping to diffuse the situation. Onim shifted his gaze and swung a fist at Fungai so fast it almost caught Fungai in the face. Fungai ducked and stepped back, realising he was about to have a brawl with his friend.

'You think you're better than me?' Onim shouted with such venom that Fungai was taken aback.

'Now I know, you're the one the Warkara warned me about. You pretend to be my friend, yet you plan to kill me! The one who will take my woman, give me nothing but grief and nightmares, then finish me?' Lately, Onin had been having a recurring dream of the shaman.

'Wait a minute, brother, what are you talking about?' Fungai responded, raising both hands placatingly, hoping to buy time, allowing his friend to cool down. Onim did not seem to hear him, instead, he threw a body shot at Fungai. Fungai was ready this time. 'Sometimes, the way of war is to be passive, let your enemy think they are winning.' He remembered his grandfather's many training sessions up in the eastern mountains. He allowed the punch to connect. It was both powerful and painful. He fell backwards, hitting the floor with a thud.

Onim stepped over him. 'Fuck you, man. You and your fancy clothes, you think you are better than me ... eh?'

'Hey, stop it, you brute.' Fungai heard the young woman screaming.

Onim backhanded her. She slumped to the floor and blacked out.

'Beating a woman? That is too much, even for you,' Fungai shouted at his friend as he stood up. This time, he would not pull any punches. *Enough is enough*, he thought. *I have to teach this idiot a lesson.* He tapped Onim's shoulder. Onim swung. Fungai had anticipated this, he ducked, kicked his leg out—a kung-fu move he had learned recently—connecting with Onim's knee. Onim went down, screaming. He made an effort to stand with his good leg. Fungai swiped that leg, too. He collapsed on the floor, screaming with pain but more with shame.

'You will know who I am, Fungai. No place will be safe for you. You are a dead man.'

'Let's get out of here.' Fungai heard a soft voice behind him. He turned to see the young lady, with a red eye and blood oozing from a split lip. She took his hand, urging him to hurry up and leave the scene. Onim continued to shout abuse at their backs.

Following the young man who had tried to protect Beki, they left through a back door just as a large group of men in dark suits entered the bar.

'Follow them and let me know where they go. Don't let them see you.' Onim ordered the men in dark suits.

'Yes sir,' a senior officer responded. 'Hey, you three, with me.' The group of four left the bar in haste, using the back door, following Fungai and Beki.

'We're being followed, please head to the Hilton hotel,' Fungai told the young man. He realised he was her driver and bodyguard.

'Everyone knows he is a bully but I didn't expect him to behave like that,' said Beki.

As the driver dropped them in front of the hotel, Fungai watched the car that had been following them park across the road. He made a mental note: car registration GZ 290, four men.

'What do you think your friend is going to do now?' Beki asked.

'It looks like he's given instructions to observe us, not to hurt us. He wants to deal with us himself. I don't take his threats lightly. He is a psycho who will do almost anything to get what he wants. And you, my dear, are in great danger. He has his eyes on you.' Fungai had heard that Onim had 'cleaned up', as they called it, a whole village that had dared to support one of his enemies. Fungai had not believed this at first but having seen him tonight, he now knew this to be true.

'I humiliated him in public. I am sure he will want to redeem himself. The question is, how? Better not to find out. I am leaving this place and so should you.'

'But where can I go? My mother is here.' Beki responded.

'It is either you disappear or face him,' Fungai surmised. He saw Beki thinking, overwhelmed by her predicament.

'I think you need to know me first, then we can decide what to do next.' Fungai suggested. He gave a short version of his life story, concluding with the fact that he was a Post-doctotal fellow at Harvard University, Massachusetts, 'See, this is my passport and my Harvard ID. Why did I tell you who I am?' He asked rhetorically. 'Because I am going to propose that you disappear with me. I had plans to leave for Zimai tomorrow but I suspect he will try to stop me.'

'Before you go any further, Dr. Fungai, you need to know something about me too.' Beki interjected. 'I know who you are. Our meeting was not a coincidence. Let me ask you, who suggested that you reconnect with Africa?'

Fungai took a moment, thinking before he connected the dots. 'You? You! you don't say!' Looking at her more closely. 'Of course, Professor Osman el Nijere.' Fungai said excitedly.

'Shoosh, not too loud, handsome,' she responded, smiling, her index finger on her lips.

'I am Bekizeli Zendi. You can call me Beki.' She came close to him, whispering in his ear. 'You may also know me as Aminata binti Osman el Nijere. But you don't, okay?' She said winking a conspiratorial smile on her face. 'So, yes to whatever you're going to propose, no matter how dangerous—for my father, the Organisation and for Africa.' She said this in a rather serious tone. 'My instructions are to, ah ... give you complete cooperation.'

Fungai was fleetingly entranced by her closeness, perfume, even her sweet, minty breath. She was breathtakingly desirable, and she knew it.

Pull yourself together, an inner voice told him. *Women are tricky.*

'So, daughter of Osman of Nijere, I can see the resemblance with the brilliant professor. If I may ask, what is his favourite saying, especially when he has had a drink?'

'Ah ... I see you don't trust me. Good, because I am dangerous. I would have been worried if you didn't ask for evidence,' she responded amiably. 'When he is happy, with good friends, he will reminisce of boys hanging out on the banks of the Kogi Nijere, village girls walking by, jerrycans of water balancing on their heads, hips swinging side to side to get the attention of the boys, one of those girls being my mother.

'He tells of how boys would talk about her beauty but none would bring themselves to speak to her. Why? Because she was the daughter of the village chief, known for his strict nature. "Even then, I was smart enough to know I needed help." He would tell his friends. "I went to my grandmother to ask how to get to this beautiful girl."

'"Listen, my child," she said, "a man who hangs around a beautiful girl, without saying a word, ends up fetching water for the guests at her wedding,"' quoting an old African adage. Does that satisfy you? What's the plan?' Beki asked.

Fungai looked at the beautiful woman before him again. He remembered the professor who had convinced him that he was too good for economics only, arguing, 'your lineage is great, Fungai. You see patterns in numbers, you perceive things that others cannot, your destiny is written. You need to be prepared, understand how the world works and how to make money. Study finance and computers. Your brain can handle that, believe me.'

'What is the plan, you ask?' Fungai reiterated the question as he resolved their next move. 'I saw you have a two-way radio. Alert your driver to park near but opposite Onim's guys.'

'Delta ... Delta ... over,' Beki called the driver. 'Yes. Bravo. Over.'

'Park the car near and across the Charlie goons, confirm please.'

'Understood, over and out.'

'I have a commercial flight to Zimai tomorrow but that's now useless. Onim has that information. Any ideas on how to charter, say to Baju?' Fungai asked Beki, hoping she knew her way around.

'Today, my new friend, is your lucky day. I, *moi*, am the sole owner of a Cessna twin-engine, courtesy of my father and the Futures Group.' Beki responded with a smile. 'See, you need me. Not just my body, eh! I deliver medical supplies to a few hospitals and humanitarian organisations, including in Jola, so it shouldn't be a problem getting there. I presume you know how to deal with the goons watching us?'

Fungai looked at the woman afresh with new understanding. *She is indeed the daughter of my friend Prof Osman*, Fungai thought. The Professor had helped him set up the Africa Futures Group.

'Neutralise the enemy before they neutralise you. Deception buys you time.' Fungai mimicked his grandfather. 'That is what we do.' He explained his plan to Beki.

Beki headed to the hotel bar, still busy on a Friday evening. Fungai heard her order four Cokes as he went past the bar towards the kitchen. The kitchen staff, busy cleaning up, took no notice of him as he walked towards the back door, exiting into a dark, deserted lane. Hugging the walls, he hobbled along, a homeless person looking for a place to lay down. As he exited the darkly lit lane, he noted the car belonging to Onim's men had not moved. He headed towards Beki's car, parked directly across from Onim's car but facing the opposite way. He tapped lightly at the passenger window. The driver wound it down.

'Be ready to move,' he told the driver as Beki came out of the hotel, balancing a tray with four Coke bottles in her hand, very much like a trained waiter. She crossed the road directly, heading for Onim's men.

'Look at that woman. What is she doing?' The driver's voice rang out. 'She's heading this way with drinks, is she mad?'

'I know this is a tough drill, gentlemen,' she said jovially as she passed the drinks to the driver. The driver looked at her, seeming amused but he accepted the drinks anyway. He turned around to pass the drink to the others.

'Here, gentlemen,' he said mimicking Beki. 'Drinks from the beautiful lady.' Neither of them saw a sachet slip from Beki's hand on the side of the driver's door.

'Enjoy,' she said jovially as she turned and headed back towards the hotel entrance.

'Now we wait, ten minutes should be enough.' Fungai told the driver.

Beki turned to look at the driver. He raised the bottle of Coke in appreciation, then shut the dark-tinted windows. She checked her watch as she headed to the ladies. It was 10.50 pm. *Ten minutes, Fungai had said, let's hope this works; otherwise, we are in deep shit*, she thought to herself.

Fungai checked his watch: 11 pm on the hour, ten minutes since Beki dropped the sachet. It's time. Crossing the road, he approached Onim's car from the back. Through the tinted windows, he did not see any movement. He tapped lightly on the passenger-side window ... no movement. He tapped again, this time a bit harder, like it was urgent but again, there was no response. The sleeping powder had done its work, he concluded, remembering Professor Osman's experiment. 'Fungai, watch this,' he had said as he had dropped the sachet into an enclosed glass cage with two German shepherds. In five minutes, the dogs had meekly folded their legs, heads had drooped and were out without a whimper. Seven minutes,

Fungai had noted. After four hours, they were still sleeping. 'Carry a box of the powder with you, you never know when you need a bit of magic,' he had said. *You could not be more correct, Professor,* Fungai thought.

He saw Beki standing next to her car, waiting. 'Where to Ms. Beki?' the driver asked politely as soon as Fungai entered the car. 'To the hangar, please. Avoid the roadblocks, go through the village.'

Fungai looked out of the back seat as the driver navigated the narrow, rutted alleys of the shanty village next to the old airport. Small round mud huts hugged what used to be a street. A group of young men huddled together around a fire, a full moon giving them all the light they needed. Emaciated-looking dogs rummaged through garbage heaps, squabbling amongst themselves over the few pickings of remnant rotten food.

'This is Africa,' Beki spoke for the first time since giving directions. 'From the six-star Hilton Hotel to the shanty village next to an airport, owned by a Frenchman. Hungry dogs and angry youth hanging out in the night, hoping for a better day tomorrow. It drives me crazy. Every day.'

The driver hooted as they approached the wire-meshed gate. A sleepy night guard stepped out of what looked like a human-sized dog kennel. The driver dimmed the lights as the guard approached. 'Identify yourself,' he said even as he unlocked a rusty padlock, saluting awkwardly as the car passed by. 'Midnight visitors? You never know these days,' he lamented as the car passed.

Like a car, Beki rolled the small plane out of the hanger, headed to the only runway and then off they went, gunning the Cessna to full speed before lifting off. 'No fuss,' she said on the intercom, the driver turned co-pilot next to her.

'No air traffic control?' Fungai asked.

'Nope! The air is ours, for now at least.'

Flying over the sleepy city, they headed south west, soon reaching the Atlantic coastline, beautifully illuminated by the full moon, their shadow reflected five hundred meters below. They turned south east, hugging the coastline. The lights of the city to their left quickly gave way to the darkness that marked rural Africa. Far below, a shiny snakelike ribbon threaded its way through the darkness, ending into the shiny grey ocean. Fungai looked at his watch, it was approaching 3.00 am.

'We will use a private airstrip just outside the city of Baju, and then from there we find our way to Zimai.' Beki announced through the headset. Fungai liked the 'we' part, but he kept that to himself.

Chapter 7:
President Onim

Fuming, Onim made an effort to stand up. His knee gave in, collapsing back onto the floor. 'You idiots, give me a hand,' enraged, he shouted to his men. Two of his men approached warily—they knew his anger well. They had all encountered his unprovoked battering. 'I will get you, Fungai,' he said to himself as they helped him to his car. 'Back to base, ASAP,' he instructed his driver.

'Base, Charlie here. How are we going with the plans?' Onim enquired, using his military issue radio.

'Charlie, this is Golf Kilo. Everything is as planned, over.'

'It is time, tomorrow will be a new day. My day!' Onim bragged to his men. 'From tomorrow, you live like kings, I promise.'

✧ ✧ ✧

"The President, the Vice President dead." Read the headline of The People's Daily. "It has been confirmed that in a surprise attack, a rogue unit of the Fifth Battalion of the army overwhelmed the President's and Vice President's guards. The unit proceeded to murder President Abawoli and Vice President Ahmadu in their homes. Mr. Onim Sukuta, the Minister for National Security, has condemned the killings, calling it a cowardly act. He has promised he will not rest until those involved are apprehended and punished to the full force of the law. As the third in line, he will be sworn in as Acting President pending Cabinet confirmation."

After he was inaugurated, President Onim suspended Parliament with immediate effect.

'My dear citizens, in this time of mourning,' he announced on the national radio, 'the Parliament will be on recess until all the perpetrators of this heinous crime are eliminated. We live in dangerous times. We must take extra measures to protect our leaders. I, therefore, invoke emergency measures. The government has accepted that I operate by decree.' With this one statement, President Onim took away power from the elected ministers and gave himself absolute power. Complete control.

Phone calls started coming in almost instantly.

'This is President Alhaji Nima. My condolences for the loss of your President and Vice President, and congratulations to you, Mr. President.' President Nima was the notorious dictator of the Peoples Republic of Impula. By the end of the day former ministers, ambassadors and other dignitaries were lining up to congratulate President Onim.

By 6 pm, exhausted but buzzing with excitement, he sat down for his usual end-of-day glass of single malt Irish whisky. Gazing at the drink, he remembered the previous evening with his then-friend Fungai. Immediately, his mood changed, his excitement turned to anger. 'That insolent son of a bitch will know who I am.' He must be the one foretold by the Warkara. I must find him and finish him.

'Juma, come over here,' he called out to his new Aides-de-camp, appointed the moment he declared himself the Supreme Commander of the Armed Forces. 'Fungai and the lady he escaped with, where are you holding them? I want to see them now.'

'Sir ... ah ... Mr. President, I understand that they have not been apprehended yet. Your personal guards are chasing every lead. They evaded the men who were observing them.'

'What did you say? That despite having the whole military operation under me, two civilians, foreigners to this country, have managed to evade your units!? Are you telling me you have failed?' Onim yelled at Juma, needing someone to blame.

'I will get the guys who are responsible for this mess.' Juma responded quickly, realising he was very close to hanging by a rope.

'Get those miserable bastards here, now! I will interview them personally. In the basement cells.' He poured himself another drink, contemplating what he would do with the four useless men. 'Incompetent idiots,' he shouted in anger. 'How do they lose two sitting ducks?'

Ducks ... lakes ... crocodiles, he thought logically. Smiling, his mood changed with the coming spectacle. After a while, Juma was back. 'I have two of them in the basement cells, sir.'

'Let's go,' he said, wasting no time. He had already made up his mind.

Unlike the neat, bright, perfumed living room he had just left, the basement was hot and humid. It had a putrid smell, a mix of urine, excrement and fear. An open sewage ran through a line of cells leading to a large, dimly lit pool. Onim, a handkerchief on his nose, rushed along with quick, long steps, sweating but excited. His two aides followed him, pistols hanging loosely from their belts.

'So, Mo, you lost your prey? Tell me how it happened.' Onim spoke in a cool, almost friendly tone, a smile on his face like he was talking to his son.

The prisoner, sweating and shaking with fear, responded. 'Sir ... Mr. President, please forgive me. He lost him,' the man said pointing at Zakaria, his brother in the other cell.

'I see ... so you're not responsible?'

'Yes, Mr. President. Believe me, if I had been there, we wouldn't have lost them.'

'Have you heard of Judas? The guy who sold his mate Isa. You're worse than him. That there,' he pointed to the other cell, 'is your own brother you're selling out!'

'Do you know why they call me Onim—the Crocodile, Mo, or is it Judas?' Onim paused, looking at the poor sod whose suit pants were now dripping with urine. 'Get him to the pool, then let's see what he says.'

As he was frog-marched, the man started screaming. Pleading with Onim, 'please, sir, forgive me, Mr. President. We were poisoned.'

'Now you are talking, keep marching, soldier. And how were you poisoned?'

The pool had suddenly come alive. Creepy things gliding under the water as the four approached. A snout peeped above the water. Then the thrashing started as the Crocs smelled a potential meal.

'The lady poisoned us,' he screamed as Juma and Fela dragged him closer to the pool.

'And how did the lady poison all of you?'

'I don't know, sir, but I went out after she gave us a bottle of Coke. It knocked us out. All of us.'

Onim was intrigued now. 'All of you, eh? At the same time? Now that is interesting. Fela, make sure the forensic people are onto that car. I want a thorough investigation.' Onim said to one of the aides. 'And where are your other two friends?'

'They said they were going home but we heard later they had deserted and disappeared.'

'I have heard enough,' Onim said, getting bored with the story. 'I think we need some fun, don't you think, Juma? Chop his right hand off and feed it to the Crocs.'

Mo started wailing, a high-pitched scream that seemed to echo in the dark, dank walls of the basement. 'Please, sir, forgive me, please!'

Fela and Juma hesitated, most likely hoping Onim would change his mind.

'Come on, you two, I don't have all day. Can't you see the poor Onims are hungry!'

Mo made a desperate effort to free himself but with his hands handcuffed and the strong arms of Fela, he had no chance.

'Give me that machete. I'll do it myself.' Onim took the sharp machete. 'Pull his arm out.'

Onim brought down the machete with such force it cut through the bones and tendons at the elbow. Mo screamed in agony before collapsing.

'Throw the damn arm to the crocodiles,' he instructed Juma, who had dropped the arm on the floor. The crocodiles, four in number, went into a frenzy—pulling, twisting, thrashing, crazed, wanting more. The crocodiles tried to slide out of the pool, falling and rolling back into the pool thanks to the steep and slippery wall.

'Now that is fun. Do you think we should feed them more?' Onim asked like an excited child.

'Sir ... Mr. President, I think it will pain Mo more to be called a one-armed Judas.' Juma responded diplomatically.

'Yes, you're right, Juma. Get his brother to take him back to his family. Let them see what happens to people who fail me ... and I want Fungai found, dead or alive,' Onim said, remembering why they were here. 'And that woman, what was her name ... Beki, find her, bring her to me. Alive!' Later that night, President Onim seemed to be in a good mood. *Perhaps this is the best time to tell him*, Juma thought. 'Your Excellency.' He approached the President, handing him his glass of Irish whisky. 'I am informed Fungai and the lady were spotted in Baju. Our informant tells me that the lady was buying provisions like they were planning for a long-distance travel by road. That is about all we know for now.'

'Keep looking. I don't care how long it takes. Use whatever resources we have, including my spies and diplomats. I will get that bastard Fungai.' He was almost busting with anger. He had been looking forward to feeding Fungai to the crocodiles, then taking the woman as his.

The more years that passed, the more obsessed with revenge he became. 'Many enemies have tried to get me, I have outwitted them, except Fungai and that bewitching woman Beki.' Onim told Juma as he drowned a twenty-five year single malt Taliska whisky. 'Any news?'

'Actually, I do have news, Mr. President. I have reliable intel that Fungai will be in Zimai next week for a meeting of some sort. I will get all the details.' Juma announced.

'That is very good, very good indeed.' The news made him happy. Like a greyhound, he had something to chase. 'Get General Fela onto it while I get President Nima to provide the logistics. I want that bastard blown into dust.' Remind Fela that failure is not an option.' He shouted in a buoyant voice.

"Bombing in Impula! Dr. Fungai, the renowned Africanist, feared dead." The Impula Standard newspaper headline read the next morning. *Things can only get better now, especially if I can get the woman Beki*, thought Onim.

Chapter 8

For The Greater Good

"A snake that you can see does not bite."
(African proverb)

If it was times of old, Aminata binti Osman el Nijere, or Bekizeli Zendi commonly known as Beki, would have been a princess or even a queen. But as it were, she lived in a high-end neighbourhood of Zimai, the capital city of Impula.

'Breaking news,' the newsreader on the television announced. She was one of the few people who had a TV, a 30-inch tube, placed in a custom-made wall unit. 'The city centre is on high alert. The police, assisted by the Presidential special forces, have bombed the Meridian building in the city centre. We are yet to establish who they were after.'

Beki watched, fascinated, wondering what the operation was about. Black and white images of smoke and dust rose from a building that looked very familiar. Uniformed police in combat gear and army soldiers in their distinct black fatigues surrounded the Meridian building. She watched as an army helicopter circled the building. Police sirens, screams and people running away from the blast created a cacophony of mayhem and confusion.

It reminded Beki of a horror movie she had seen recently but she didn't think twice about it. Events like this had become commonplace. President Nima, following his friend and benefactor President Onim, had made himself supreme leader. He had declared war on opposition leaders, referring to them as terrorists.

Eight months pregnant, she continued with her chores, lumbering along, finding it difficult to do even the simplest of things in her small apartment. From the TV in the seating room, she heard the popular presenter's voice again, this time speaking in a low, conspiratorial tone. 'We can now confirm that all the leaders of the *Antu* movement, an underground organisation calling for a united Africa, are believed to have been killed. The president has taken credit for eliminating what he termed a "dangerous cancer".'

Beki froze in her tracks. Neighbours heard her scream. Her next-door neighbour rushed into her apartment to find her lying on the bedroom floor. Though she had blacked out, she had tears in her eyes, her anguish clear as daylight.

The TV presenter continued with his retinue of bad news. 'Witnesses say that a military helicopter was seen shelling the fifth floor of the building while the President's elite forces ran up the stairs. Our reporters on site confirm there was an exchange of gunfire. A bomb blast, believed to be by the military, set the building on fire. Smoke and dust continue to spew out of the building.'

Beki heard voices as though coming from a tunnel. She thought she was dreaming. *Why am I lying on the floor?* Then she remembered the news on the TV. She opened her eyes to see her neighbour kneeling next to her.

'Are you okay? Do you have any pain? What happened?'

'I'm okay,' she responded and stopped at that. Some things are better not said. She remembered Fungai's words. She knew the news to be accurate. Fungai had confided in her that they had an important meeting today, one that 'would change the course of their struggle,' he had boasted.

'A day may come when you must take care of yourself and our child. You should have plans in case something happens to me.' Fungai had warned her a few months ago.

'Shut up,' she had responded at the time. 'Nothing will happen to you.' Preferring denial to entertaining the possibility of life without him. 'You plan for everything, and everything always works for you,' she had said.

'Nevertheless, hope for the best, plan for the worst,' he had responded.

'You were right ... again!' she commented loudly.

'What did you say? Who is right again,' asked her neighbour.

'I'm sorry, I am a bit confused right now.' She responded evasively.

It was difficult to accept he was gone. *I know you are alive, you bastard, you always plan for all eventualities. You must still be alive. You have to be alive,* she reasoned. She was annoyed with him for putting himself in danger for an ideology so big as to be almost impossible.

She remembered the last hour they had spent together that morning. She recollected how Fungai had fondly fondled her big eight-month-pregnant stomach, how she had cuddled comfortably on his large muscular chest, feeling safe, happy and contented.

She had responded in kind, massaging the hard muscles of his lower abdomen. 'That is nice, very nice,' he had said in his deep, sonorous voice. Her hand had moved lower, finding his manhood, now thick and hard, tenderly stroking it while, all along, whispering how much she loved him. He had stopped her just when she was getting really heated up. 'I love you so much, my queen, you know how to make me happy but I have to go now. I have a big meeting today.'

She understood him perfectly. His mind was on other things. 'Okay, perhaps tonight?'

He had sat up, slid out of bed, and knelt as though praying but instead, he kissed her stomach and whispered, 'young one, I know you can hear me. Know this: Daddy loves you so much. You're going to be a great one, you are a Ramla, like your mother is a queen, you will be a king.' Then, abruptly, he had stood up and left for the bathroom. It was 6 am.

On his way out, he paused in the doorway. He was wearing his immaculately tailored, navy-blue suit, blue tie and shining black shoes. *He looks so smashing*, Beki had thought, wishing he could spend more time with her. 'I love you, queen-bee,' he had said fondly, waving and blowing a kiss as he left. Just like that, he was gone. That image, him standing in the doorway waving and blowing a kiss, *I will cherish forever*, Beki thought.

The neighbour helped her to her feet. Though feeling a bit dizzy, she was fine. She straightened up, full belly and all. *I am strong; I have a plan*, she motivated herself. She knew she had to be strong. No one was to know what had happened to him and she had to start moving quickly.

Fungai's perpetual enemies would be on the move. She knew without a protector; she was a target now. *President Onim knew where to find Fungai. He will know where to find me*, she concluded.

'Thank you very much for coming to my aid, you're a great neighbour. Please excuse me. I think I will go to the hospital for a check-up. Thank you again,' she said, showing the neighbour the door.

Though she had not admitted to Fungai, she had prepared for this very day. She quickly packed her one-night bag, filling it with all her valuables. She had enough cash to last her a few months. All along, she had known that Fungai, as the leader of the underground *Antu* movement, meant danger to both of them.

Leaving her apartment and lugging her two-wheeled travel bag, she walked to the taxi stand just outside the gate. Almost immediately, a taxi pulled up. She quickly entered as the driver put her bag in the boot. At that moment, two dark green Peugeot salon cars entered the gate of the compound, heading to her apartment.

'Please, hurry up, I am starting to have pain,' Beki, invoking a voice full of pain, begged the driver. 'Take me to Shama Private Hospital.' The Driver took off in haste, no doubt thinking she was about to deliver.

'Thank you very much for dropping me off,' she told the diver, passing on a wad of notes. Much more than the fare. She knew he would remember her.

'Thank you, Mrs. Fungai. God bless and be safe.'

How did he know her, she wondered? But then, Fungai was well-known and respected.

She walked into the hospital's front door, then down the corridor to the nearest toilets. Quickly, she put on a doctor's white coat that she had been carrying in her bag, put on fake broad glasses and stepped out of the toilet, walking confidently as though she was part of the establishment. She headed to a back door, 'exit' illuminated above it, then a short distance to a taxi rank just outside the hospital.

'The Old Vard hotel in the city centre, please,' she told the driver. As they drove through the city, Beki noticed the mayhem had subsided. The city centre was back to normal.

No one noticed as a young lady doctor came out of a taxi and entered the Old Vard Hotel. Beki walked across the lobby to the ladies' room, a doctor in a hurry. She came out a tired, disheveled hotel maid rushing home after a heavy shift. Walking a short distance to the bus station, she boarded a small taxi bus heading to Noah's slum, a shanty village on the western outskirts of the city. A tired young woman alighted at a noisy, muddy back street of Noah's slum. She walked and tentatively jumped over open drains, dragging her bag through narrow pathways to a compound fenced off with barbed wire. Entering the compound, she headed to the main door of a white-washed, mud-walled structure that looked like a classroom in a poor neighbourhood. An old woman mopping the floor of the front office looked at her, immediately dropping the mop, surprised.

'What are you doing here, Aminata?' The old woman asked in a hushed tone. 'Sit down and tell me everything.'

'How are you, auntie. It has been some time. I need to lie low for a few months, and I thought a home for homeless women is the best place in my circumstances.' Beki spoke after drinking from the water jug.

'Why can't you go back to your mother, and why now?'

'Mama Maria, have you heard the news, the Meridian bombing?'

The old woman looked at her, and this time, she noticed the anguish in Beki's eyes. 'Oh no!' she responded. 'I never connect the dots. I see news they look for a woman named Beki. I forget you change name.' She responded in her broken english.

'Don't say anything else, auntie, let's leave it at that. Let me just say that they are looking for me. My safety is all I want to think about for now, and there is no safer place than Mama Maria Women's Refuge.' Beki, now Aminata, said with a sad smile.

'You always so clever thinking of everything.' A conspiratorial smile on her face. 'You think I don't know who send all that money in envelope? You have been planning for this eventuality for the better part of a year, haven't you?' Mama Maria spoke in her native Olof tongue.

'Let's just say I am another homeless woman desperately seeking refuge. I may also need a good discrete midwife. You're the best from what I hear, Mama Maria.'

'You give me too much credit.' Mama Maria responded, tears in her eyes, she held her arm and led her to a private office. She went into a chest at the back dark corner of the room, rummaging for something. She dug out a green bag and pulled out a black gown, which she passed to Beki.

Beki took the gown. 'What do you want me to do with this?'

'Wear it, of course.'

Beki removed her old clothes and put on the black burqa gown and headdress.

At that moment, a young woman knocked on the door and entered the room.

'So sorry. I didn't know you had a visitor, Mama Maria,' she said.

'It's okay, please meet Aminata. She will be staying with us for some time. Can you show her to the room at the end of the corridor? She is very tired, so make sure no one disturbs her.'

Beki, now known as Aminata, settled into the life of a refugee woman. Within a month in the confines of the refuge, she gave birth to a baby boy, naming him Fumi, after Fungai's father.

"Death Is No Death..."
(Anonymous)

Every day, without fail, Beki would wake up, walk to the street newspaper vendor and buy the two main papers. *The Zimai Times*, a pro-government paper, covered the President avidly. Sometimes, it had articles on President Onim of Zonga. *The Daily Standard* was more balanced, covering the news of the various militia activities around Africa.

'Why are you so fond of reading the newspapers, Aminata?' one of the young women had enquired.

'You never know,' Beki had responded.

'You know, I heard that the police have been looking for Fungai's girlfriend.' One of the women at the refuge had announced one morning after coming back from the market. 'They are saying that the police went to her apartment. A taxi driver told them that he had taken her to Shama Hospital. Apparently, no one in the hospital saw her. They say she had just vanished.' Beki was worried the girls might connect her appearance with the disappearance of Beki, Fungai's girlfriend.

As she read *The Zimai Times*, an article caught her eye. 'Ms. Bekizeli Zendi, the girlfriend of Fungai, is in grave danger from the terrorists. Anyone with information should contact the police.' The paper had written. She had put it down immediately, picking *The Daily Standard*, hoping for better news. An article on page eight read, 'there is speculation that Ms. Beki Zendi, girlfriend to the Africanist Dr. Fungai, who was killed by police in his uptown office, has fled to London, fearing her life is in danger.'

This is not going to go away soon, Beki thought. *It is only a matter of time before someone recognises me, even though I am always in a burqa. But what can I do?* She wondered, and then she remembered a discussion they had with Fungai. 'You know, dear,' he had told Beki in his usual jovial mood. 'I have seen my end. I know I will not die young. So, when *The Daily Standard* says Fungai is dead, remember the African saying from the West. "Death is no death."' They had been watching The President's Monthly Speech on TV.

As she scanned *The Daily Standard*, she noticed an article with the heading, "Death is no death."

'You Mother fucker ... all along you planned, played everyone, knowing they might come for you.' Beki whispered to herself.

'Why are you cursing, my dear, and look at you smiling! What is it now?' A smile had appeared on Beki's face without her realising. *There was hope, a small possibility that he was still alive,* she thought. He had singled out *The Daily Standard* newspaper. *That is where I start to look for a message from the dead,* she decided.

'The dead are not dead. They leave us for a better place.' For a moment, she stood still. *Did she hear right? Am I going crazy?* She wondered. A priest broadcasting a Sunday mass on the local radio station using the national language continued. He spoke with a distinct accent from the Tano region. He repeated the statement, emphasising and concluding with 'the dead are not dead.' Aminata thought she heard wrong but the signs were too clear. The message, delivered by someone from the Tano people—Fungai's people! Now, that is definitely not a coincidence.

She picked up *The Daily Standard*, perusing for any mention of *dead*, nothing. She was about to put it down when she noticed it in bold on the obituary page: *"The dead are not dead; may we meet again, in a better place, Ramla."*

Ramla, meaning king in the Tano language, was also the name of Fungai's grandfather, a freedom fighter believed to have been murdered by the colonial government while in prison. *Confirmation! You are alive, my dear, and I know where you are.* She felt a warmth spread inside her. She could not resist a smile. Tears of joy ran down her face. *One day, we may meet again,* she thought. *Until then, I have to survive, but how?*

'Who is this Beki girl the police keep on talking about.' One of the women in the refuge asked another young woman, a teenager who had been beaten up and left for dead by her husband.

'Oh! You know the Meridian building bombing? Beki was the boyfriend of Fungai, who people say was the leader of the *Antu* movement that is trying to overthrow the government.' The girl who read the newspapers avidly, like Aminata, answered the other woman.

The older woman looked concerned. 'Poor girl, she is as good as dead. President Nima and his friend Onim are animals. They will eat her alive.'

'They are offering fifty thousand Kwach just for information leading to her arrest. That is a lot of money. I could start a second-hand clothes business with that kind of money.'

'You and your greed, you think they would pay you just like that. You think they would admit they got help from a simple girl like you? You must be dreaming. Anyway, go start cooking now.'

It is only a matter of time before I am identified. Aminata sitting at the next table, knitting a sweater for her son, thought, *I need to make my move, and soon.*

It was midnight, she could not sleep, kept awake by a mind that could not find a way out of her difficult situation. *I cannot put my son, Mama Maria and the women in harm's way. I have to save myself, help Fungai and fight Onim at the same time.* She made up her mind there and then. She had to do the unthinkable. At daybreak, she kissed her son on the cheek. 'I am sorry, son. I have to leave you.' With tears dripping down her face, she left. She was in her apartment before 6.30 am. At 8.00 am, she called *The Daily Standard*, asking to be connected to the Chief Editor.

'This is the Chief Editor, *Daily Standard*. Who am I speaking to?' He asked in a rather humble tone.

'This is Bekizeli Zendi,' using her full name. 'Fiancé to Dr. Fungai.' She heard a deep breath on the other side of the line.

'How do I know you are who you say you are?'

She thought for a moment and took a gamble. 'I am reaching out to you because "*death is no death*,"' hoping the Chief Editor was one of them.

Silence, followed by a big sigh. 'Thank the gods of our people. How can I be of assistance, Ma'am?' Now speaking in a whisper, as though he did not want anyone else to hear.

'I will call the police headquarters. I want you to cover the arrest at my apartment. Make sure President Onim gets to know I was arrested. That is the only way I will survive this.'

'Where have you been, Aminata Binti Osman?'

It was Beki who kept silent this time. She was wondering how he could know this. He must be close to the centre. 'Well, let's just say I was hiding in plain sight. Put the spotlight on me, please. It will all work out fine. I sacrifice for the greater good.' After hanging up, she called the Police HQ.

'Can I speak to the Inspector General of Police please?'

'This is the Police HQ. Who are you? Why do you want to speak to the Boss?'

'Listen carefully you moron, if you don't pass me to the IGP you will be out of a job by the end of the day. Now I won't ask again, connect me to the IGP.' Beki responded in a commanding voice.

'Woman, who do you think you are?'

'I am Bekizeli Zendi, fiancé to Dr. Fungai. Now you pass me to the IGP, or I disappear.'

She heard noises in the background, no doubt the poor corporal was asking his boss what he should do. 'Okay, madam Zendi, I am forwarding your call now.'

'Hello, who is this?' the IGP asked, a hashed voice indicating he knew exactly who it was.

'Am I speaking to the Inspector General of Police?'

'Yes, this is him.'

'I am Bekizeli Zendi. I want to hand myself in. You can pick me up at my apartment,' Beki instructed and then hung up.

Beki looked out of the fourth-floor apartment window as *The Daily Standard* TV van pulled up in front of her block. Soon, the police will be here. She took the lift, stationing herself on the steps leading to her apartment block, waiting for her arrest. *The Daily Standard* cameras pointed at her, already transmitting live news, not more than twenty meters away. *No way are the police going to manhandle me in public,* she thought.

Back at the women's refuge, the women were cleaning and preparing for lunch as the news came through. 'Ms Beki Zendi, fiancé to Dr. Fungai, is giving herself in. We are reliably informed she has called the police headquarters.' The TV cameras focused on Beki, now wearing a navy-blue suit and a prominent head scarf. She looked exceptionally beautiful and distinguished.

'Mama Maria, Mama Maria … come over, quickly. Isn't that Aminata?' The young girl who had just yesterday been talking to Beki asked excitedly.

'You know, girl, sometimes your head is full of imaginations. That is not Aminata. I don't ever want to hear about Aminata again in this home.' But Mama Maria continued watching, worried. *I hope she knows what she is doing,* she prayed, making the sign of the cross.

Police sirens. Beki counted four, perhaps five, a large arrest team for a woman unarmed. Perhaps they think it is a trap, she thought.

'Hands up, woman,' a policeman aiming a rifle at her shouted. The film rolled, *The Daily Standard* TV crew recording everything. 'These bloody media, how did they arrive before us unless she called them first?' The Inspector General of Police lamented as he, a very obese man, struggled out of his saloon car, swagger stick in hand. He noticed Beki. She looked stunningly dignified with her navy-blue suit and elaborate headdress.

'Lower your guns, officers. Can't you see she is unarmed?'

By this time, a small crowd had gathered, having heard the siren, rare in this upper-class neighbourhood. As the Inspector General approached Beki, four policemen by his side, someone started shouting, 'leave Beki alone, she has done nothing, she is innocent.' Others started shouting, 'leave Beki alone, leave Beki alone.' Someone threw a stone at the Inspector General, narrowly missing him. One of the policemen panicked, fired his gun; a man, part of the small crowd that had gathered, fell. Pandemonium followed. Beki maintained her posture, resolute, unafraid, hands up, right-hand palm clumped tightly into a fist, the sign of the black struggle. Defiant. The cameras did not miss this.

The Inspector General rushed to her, pulled her hands down and pushed her in front of his large body, using her as his shield. 'Let's get out of here before another person is shot,' he said to her ear. The four policemen formed a protective ring around them, moving together to the Inspector General's car. The commotion continued, another gunshot, this time it was in the air, the cameras rolled. The world had witnessed the arrest of "The defiant Beki, fiancé to Fungai, who must not be forgotten." *The Daily Standard* had written. *President Onim will see all this, and he will be asking for me, alive and in one piece.* This she knew without a doubt.

'Ms. Beki Zendi has been arrested in Zimai.' Juma told President Onim. 'Apparently, she called the police.'

'And the media, yes?'

'Yes sir, the media arrived before the police.'

'Clever woman. You know, they say patience is a virtue. I want her brought to me immediately. Actually, go there, use my jet. In the meantime, I will talk to President Nima.'

"After a six-month house arrest in President Onim's mansion in Oko, Ms. Beki Zendi, fiancé to Fungai, has agreed, under duress, we must add, to become the wife of the President. It is said that she was the reason President Onim and Dr. Fungai, who were formerly good friends, became enemies. Is this the end of the Fungai-Onim saga, or is there another episode? Only time will tell." *The Daily Standard.*

Beki would remind herself every day. *For the greater good, I sacrifice. To ensure my son is safe so he will grow up to be the leader he was born to be. For that, I will give my life. I will give in to the bastard Onim, but I will be repaid by information to help 'the dream' come. Fungai's dream.* She became a master of duality, an actor extraordinaire, quickly gaining the trust of the President, using her position to goad and mould him into a monster while providing information to *Antu.* People started calling her 'The Madam.' As the Matron of the Help Africa Organisation, or simply 'HA', she championed and funded many humanitarian causes. Her clandestine role within *Antu,* no one knew but Fungai, whose whereabouts were unclear and her father, Osman el Nijere, a Professor at Harvard.

Chapter 9:
Fumi From Noah's Slum

"It's not what you take,
but what you leave behind that defines greatness."
(Edward Gardner)

'Oh man, did you see the Brazil versus Italy game yesterday? Wow! That was a great game. I want to be like Pele, the way he dribbles, oh man... that is what I call good football.' Fumi, ten years old, bare feet, wearing faded track pants with holes at the knees and a dirty singlet, told his three friends. They had been playing football in the muddy fields at the back of the Mama Maria Women's Refuge.

'Fumi! Fumi! Come over, you will miss your lunch,' Mama Maria called out. She had been watching the boys play as she winnowed mung beans. Watching the boys play was a favourite pastime after a hectic morning session.

'Coming Grandma!' Fumi responded. 'See you later, losers,' teasing his two friends as he jumped over the barbed wire that fenced the compound.

'You know, you will hurt yourself if you keep on jumping that fence.' Mama Maria said, fondly hugging Fumi as he passed by on his way to the large kitchen where everyone ate.

One morning, after enjoying a 4v4 game with his friends, Grandma Maria told Fumi. 'You know, my boy, you need to speak English good, the language spoken over the seas. You may have to go there one day. From that morning, Fumi dreamed of going over the seas, somewhere like Liverpool, where his favourite football team was from. 'I would be the happiest person on earth if I could play for that team,' he had told his friends. So, he worked on his English, reading comic books and children's books given to him by a friend of Grandma Maria.

One Saturday morning before he left to meet up with his friends, Mama Maria called him. 'Fumi! Come over here. This lady wants to talk with you.' He had seen the lady come into the office. Mama Maria had closed the door, and the lady had been there for some time. *This is serious*, he thought.

'Fumi, my name is Memi.' The motherly-looking lady introduced herself. Fumi looked at her, wondering what is such a lady, wearing expensive clothes and jewellery, doing here.

'I am told you dream of going overseas, is that right?'

'Yes, ma'am. I want to play football with Liverpool FC.'

'Well, you may be the luckiest boy I know because listen to this …' she paused, 'there is a family that has invited you to go stay with them in the USA.'

'USA? That's where Mohammed Ali, the greatest boxer in the world, comes from?'

'Yes, indeed it is. In the USA, you can become whoever you want to be. They have very good football academies, you know, especially in Boston. That is where the family lives.'

'What is an academy?' Fumi asked, looking at Mama Maria, feeling stupid he did not know that word.

'It is like a football school,' the lady responded.

'You can go to a football school? Wow! I like that.'

'I think we should give Fumi time to think over this. Can you come back next week?' Mama Maria asked Memi.

'Of course, Fumi needs time to consider. Remember, it is up to you, Fumi. If you don't want to go, it's fine.' On her way out, Memi handed a package to Mama Maria. 'There is more information on the family who want to host Fumi. There are also some clothes and some money for anything he might want, whether he is going or not.'

After the lady left, Mama Maria seemed sad as they sat in the front office but Fumi was so excited he couldn't stop talking.

'Grandma, imagine they have schools to teach football ... Academy!' he said, holding his chin in a cheeky pose.

'Yes, yes, I know but think it carefully. You know, you go, I miss you. Maybe never see you again.' Mama Maria spoke in a serious tone.

'Oh ... is that why you look so sad, Grandma? Don't worry, I will come back with lots of money, then you can share it with all my sisters and aunties.' Everyone in the women's refuge referred to each other as sister or auntie, depending on their age.

'I think you take time. You think what you want in life, then you decide. Now you tell no one about this, okay?' She told Fumi as he was about to leave the room.

'It is our secret Grandma. Just you and me.'

Why my boy Fumi, and why now? How they know about him? Mama Maria wondered. *I have not heard from Aminata. I know she organise this,* Mama Maria concluded. *She leaves. Become wife of that horrible President! Shame on her.*

I receive lot of money. I am sure she send the money; she is the boss of Support Africa. That girl is too clever for her own good. Now she want to take my boy away? Mama Maria pondered.

As she contemplated the role Beki played in all this, she remembered the large bag Memi had left behind. An envelope sat on top of the clothes, and a pair of shoes packed tightly in the bag. 'Let me see what in the envelope,' she spoke to herself. The first thing she saw was a photo of a man, a woman and a young girl. 'The Crawford Family,' she read. It was at the bottom of the photo. She looked more closely. Why? That house look familiar. Then she remembered her trip to Boston ten years ago. *Yes, that is house near house of my brother Osman.* She went and grabbed her thick photo album, quickly flicking through the pages, and she found what she was looking for. A picture she had taken from her upstairs window that faced the street. Snowflakes falling on the front lawn of the house across the street. She remembered the day vividly. It had been her first time to see snow. She scrutinised the picture more closely, comparing them. Behind the snowflakes, a grey house with white trim—the same house as in the photo Memi had left. 'It is same house!' She laughed loudly even though she was alone. Fumi living with a family next door to my brother ... his grandfather? *Aiya!* She shouted with excitement.

A week later, the lady came back. 'I have talked to the family that invited you. They told me you could come back anytime if you don't like it there. They even bought a two-way ticket just in case. What do you say, Fumi?'

Fumi posed, pretending to be contemplating. 'Grandma Maria told me that the world is larger than our village and my destiny is written by my ancestors. So, I say, destiny, the world, here I come!'

'Well said, Fumi. I didn't know your grandma is so clever. Okay, say bye to everyone, let them know you will come back one day.'

A voice from somewhere woke him up. 'This is your captain speaking. We will be landing at the Boston Logan International Airport soon. Hope you had a lovely flight. Please fasten your seatbelts ready for landing.'

Before landing, Memi whispered to Fumi. 'Remember, the people here are a bit different, so don't talk to anyone unless they talk to you. Give yourself time, and you will be just fine. Here, this is my number in Zimai if you ever want to talk to me. Okay?'

'Yes, Auntie Memi, thank you very much for everything.'

The airport was massive. It was like a maze with many people moving in all directions. He had never seen so many types of people. 'Wow! This is amazing and scary,' he told Memi, who was one step ahead. Fumi looked out of the taxi they had caught from the airport. The streets were wide and clean. No mud anywhere. Everyone seemed so busy rushing somewhere. He remembered his friends in the muddy field behind his home, his grandma crying as he hugged her goodbye, the smelly sewage that ran onto the narrow streets in Noah's slum. The memories came flooding—he was already missing home. *The world is indeed larger than our village*, he reminded himself.

'Here we are,' pointed the taxi driver.

Huge houses lined the clean street. On one side of the street, an old black man in a suit and a long black coat looked at the taxi as though he had been waiting for its arrival. On the other side of the street, he saw a man, a woman and a young girl almost his age. They were white, just like on the TV. He had never met a white person in his life.

Fumi looked confused. The taxi seemed to have parked on the wrong side of the street. He saw the white man and woman approach. 'Welcome home, Fumi. My name is Ben Crawford,' the white man said as he opened the taxi door. The woman paused and looked at him like she was measuring him up. Then, with outstretched arms, she hugged Fumi, like his grandma had done.

'Come on inside the house, Fumi, it is cold outside. My name is Jennifer but you can call me Jennie.'

Across the street, the African man waved at the family, a big smile on his face. 'Is that the boy you told me about?' He shouted as he crossed the street. 'What did you say his name is?'

'Yes, this is Fumi, come over for a minute, Fumi. Let me introduce you to our neighbour, Professor Osman el Nijere.'

'No, no ... don't confuse the young man, just call me Mr. Osman. Okay?'

'Yes, sir.'

'Gentlemen, the boy is tired, cold, hungry ... let him have a rest. You old men can have a chat with him later.' Jennifer suggested, pulling Fumi and his bag into the house. Fumi screamed in terror as a small, fluffy white dog came rushing towards him.

'Hey Pooch, stop, sit.' the girl who was almost his age shouted at the small dog. 'It's okay. Pooch is harmless, he's excited to meet you like I am.' The girl spoke with a different kind of English, almost impossible to understand.

'How did you get him to stop and sit?'

'Come.' The girl pulled Fumi's arm towards Pooch. 'Let me introduce you to Pooch, the naughty dog. Let him smell your fingers, then he will know you're a friend. Pat his head like this … then he will become your friend. Oh! I am Sandra, by the way, but you can call me Sun, as the sun that brings light to our world.'

'I am Fumi from Africa, Pooch.' He announced to the little dog. The girl burst out laughing as Pooch licked Fumi's fingers, then stood on two legs, trying to get Fumi to pick him up.

'You naughty dog, come over here, I will carry you.' Pooch ignored Sun, following Fumi to the dining room where Mrs. Crawford was brewing tea.

It took Fumi almost six months to feel comfortable in his new environment but only one football training session to get into the under twelves Cambridge Juniors Soccer Academy. After the initial cultural and language barriers, he blossomed, becoming a top scholar and athlete.

'You know, Fumi, I have never met a boy with the soccer skills you have.' His coach at the academy once told him. 'What I like most about your game is your vision and ability to read the game. You seem to know where to be, where and when to pass the ball. If you continue like this, you're certainly going places.'

Fumi knew what the coach meant. He could see things, like 'shadows' around other players that moved just before a player moved. He could predict what they were going to do a fraction of a second before they did. It was like he had a special gift. Fumi, do you see, feel, observe things that other kids don't? Professor Osman had once asked him. He had just looked at the prof and smiled, not wanting to say too much.

'Your instincts are amazing. How do you do that? Every time I try to beat you one-on-one, it seems you know what I am going to do before I do. I don't get it.' One of his teammates had told him.

'I don't know, I just look at you, then my body seems to move even before I think,' he had responded.

In math, he could see patterns that other students could not. In chemistry, he literally saw chemical reactions, like in a slow-motion 3-D movie. But he could not mention this to anyone lest they think he was a freak.

'How is school,' Mr. Crawford once asked Fumi.

'Good, Mr. Crawford, I am enjoying all my subjects,' he responded.

'You know you should stop calling me Mr. Crawford, it sounds strange coming from you. Just call me Ben, for God's sake.'

'Yes, Mr. Crawford,' Fumi responded with a grin. His grandma had told him it was impolite to call elders by their first name. But he could not bring himself to call him dad or uncle, so Mr. Crawford or Sir it would remain.

'Hey Fumi,' Sun shouted. 'There is this girl, she has a crush on you. She can't stop talking about you ... "your brother is so smart, I saw him play football, he is so quick", blah blah blah.' They all burst out laughing as she went up the stairs, followed by Pooch.

$\diamondsuit$

Chapter 10:
Fungai - Follow The Afternoon Sun

*"He who comes from a strong clan
won't lose his cattle to the lion"*
(African proverb)

'He who comes from a strong clan won't lose his cattle to the lion,' Fungai heard his grandfather, as though he was talking from outside the mud hut up on the Ostrich mountains. He looked around, a silhouette, receding into the thick morning highland mist was all he saw. '*Mkulu*,' he shouted, using the polite term for an elder. He ran after him … the rooster crowed, a sharp, high-pitched tune announcing the coming of dawn.

He woke up with a start. Sitting up, he focused on his surroundings, his grandfather, an ever-present shadow in his consciousness.

Where am I? He wondered. Then he remembered as he saw young men lying around the circular hut. He swung his feet off the narrow metal bed, stood up, ready to do his morning stretching just as the rickety door of the hut opened.

'Good morning, John! How was your sleep? I woke up when you started shouting after your grandfather. He must have been a real character,' Morani spoke, a smile on his face. 'Good timing, though, I just managed to get my sister to make us breakfast before she left her hut.'

At that moment, a tall, slender, wide-hipped young woman with a cleanshaven head, long beaded earrings and an elaborately beaded necklace walked into the room. Her bearing was that of a warrior—strong, upright, squared shoulders, self-confident. She carried a pot, smoking hot but she did not seem to feel the heat. Her eyes were averted respectfully.

Fungai felt his body respond as he looked at her lower the pot gracefully to place it atop the three stones marking the fireplace. A warm feeling from his lower abdomen crept downwards, awakening his loins. Their eyes met just for a minute as she took a quick peek at him.

'Here is your breakfast, brother.' She spoke with a soft voice and a smile that would shame the sun with its warmth. She looked at Fungai, this time directly, appraisingly, no doubt sizing him up. For some reason, she reminded him of Beki. At that moment, he wondered how his fiancé was doing. *I will have to find a way to let her know I am not dead. The dead are not dead*, he remembered the old African adage.

'Who is this, older brother?'

'Oh! This is John, he saved my life,' Morani responded as he continued packing stuff into his small goat-skin travel pouch, not bothering to introduce her.

Fungai thought he saw a twinkle in her eyes as she quickly averted her gaze downwards, towards the steaming pot.

'Sidai, my name,' she introduced herself, curtseying politely, eyes downcast. A shy smile appeared on her face as she straightened up to her full height of six foot plus.

'I hope to see you later,' she said as she took a step back, turned and left the room.

'Don't get any ideas, John. She is my favourite sister, and I am not about to allow some stranger to put white clouds in her head.'

'I hear you, brother ... but oh, oh! Her beauty shines like the sun.'

'I know, and keep off. She is about to go to London for her studies, and we don't need her distracted ... for now at least.'

Using a wooden spoon to eat, Fungai filled up a calabash bowl with the thick soup of spiced meat, vegetables and sweet potato. 'This broth tastes fantastic. I feel extremely rejuvenated and energetic. My heart is thumping like a drum. I have never tasted anything quite like this before. What spices did your sister use?'

'You will have to ask her. She might have added roots and herbs meant to give us energy for the coming journey.'

'It is very good and satisfying,' Fungai concluded as he put his bowl on a rack by the wall.

'You better be, we have a long journey ahead ... that is if you are coming with us. You could head back to town, you know?'

'I am tempted to stay here,' Fungai responded with a wink. 'But there is no way I will miss the walk with you guys. To me, it is an adventure of a lifetime. Besides, the police are most likely looking out for the guy who smashed one of their own.'

'What! How do you know he was a policeman?' Morani asked.

'Well, for one, the gun he was carrying is standard police issue, his haircut, his cockiness, no doubt a junior police officer. Certainly not military, given his poor fighting skills.' Fungai responded.

'How do you know all this?'

'We should leave now, don't you think?' Fungai responded, terminating the discussion.

'Well, I get it. Perhaps you will tell me your story one day.'

The Land Rover was waiting for them outside their shack.

'We drive to the foothills of those blue mountain ranges, the forbidden mountains, we call them.' Morani pointed to the hills far to the west. 'After that, we climb and climb for a whole day. Do you think you are up to it, or are you a city boy who can't stand climbing?' Morani teased, a smirk on his uniquely long face.

'We will see,' Fungai countered with a smile on his face. He deftly shouldered his backpack and jumped into the rundown Land Rover.

They hit the road. Soon, the track came to an end, but they continued on what appeared to be a non-existent road. Thorny shrubs scratched the side of the already battered Land Rover. Morani manhandled the weather-beaten vehicle over rocks, pushing through scrub bushes, twisting and turning but always climbing. Finally, they stopped at what seemed to be a wall, a sheer cliff face.

'This is it. The end of the road. From here, we walk and climb,' Morani said with a smile as he turned off the Land Rover, leaving the key under the dusty mat on the floor of the car.

Before he could stretch and adjust the army-style canvas backpack on his shoulders, Morani and the four young men were already on their way. 'Are you coming or what?' Morani shouted at him, now almost thirty paces ahead.

Walking at a brisk pace, they followed a footpath at the base of a cliff. The young warriors, full of energy, way ahead. They seemed to be having a good time, talking in hushed tones and, once in a while, screaming and laughing with excitement. There was no question about what they were talking about.

They weaved their way through thickets of bush and tall trees. Fungai saw many types of monkeys. The baboons gawking at them, then yowling, before taking off in troops. The playful, inquisitive vervets seemed not at all surprised by human presence. Up high on a Ficus tree full of fruit, Fungai saw a shy colobus spying on them, then quietly disappear in the thick foliage of the tree.

'Come on, John, we don't have time for sightseeing. This is not a biology class excursion,' Morani shouted jokingly from upfront. Quite obviously, Morani and his young brothers were preoccupied with getting to their destination, not bloody monkeys.

And so, they continued for half a day, weaving their way through thick bush, creeping through crevices saddled with moist green and grey moss, always climbing higher and higher. Fungai's leg muscles were screaming, tired of walking for hours on end, yet Morani and his unit of four kept on. Moving at a constant pace, showing no sign of tiredness, as though fueled by the bush itself.

'How are you going, John? Are you still excited about the excursion?'

'Stop enjoying me, brother. You know I will disappoint you and your bunch of amateurs. I have just started warming up.' His hamstring, calf even his glutes were screaming—on fire. He was not about to say this to the young warriors.

As they approached an open wooded area, he saw the young men sitting under a small tree, talking excitedly as they gulped what seemed to be wild fruits.

'I think you need a break. I know I need it.' Morani said as he sat down a short distance from the young men.

'Mwanza! Are you going to share with us, or are you going to horde everything?' One of the young men brought a handful of fruit.

'What are these fruits? Fungai asked.

'This is the Marula fruit, ready and ripe, almost fermented. It gives you strength while making you a bit giddy. That is why you see these chaps chattering excitedly. Only a few of us know this location otherwise, we would find nothing here if others knew about it. So, eat up but not too much, or we will have to carry you.'

The fruit was sweet yet somewhat sour. It had soft and juicy flesh, just what Fungai needed. The young men stood up and started collecting more fruit, packing it in their goat-hide pouches.

'Our sisters will be happy with this.' Fungai heard Mwanza telling his friends. 'The perfumes and oils they will get from this, and all to impress us ... nice, eh!'

'Yes, you heard right, John, we call the Marula tree the wonder tree. A favourite fruit we use to make wonderful home brew, oils that are said to keep the skin of a woman young, intoxicating perfumes and, listen to this, it is a medicine for all types of ailments such as skin, stomach, even the illness of the head. Everyone loves it, even the elephants and monkeys love it,' Morani explained to Fungai.

'Enough talking. You see, the sun is starting to make shadows. We need four hours to reach our destination, let's get going,' Morani coerced his young warriors.

At that moment, there was a crackle, like that of a VHF radio. Morani dug into his shoulder carry bag and out came a small Sanyo transistor radio. It could have been bought from any small electronic shop in downtown Zimai. He turned on a dial, a voice ... his sister loud and clear.

'Brother, as you had feared, someone is following you. The madman who came to the village early in the year, we saw him leave after you. Your boys followed him, reporting back that he is following you. They say he carries a gun and several knives.'

Fungai was amazed, not by the news, but by the radio. How did they manage to transform a simple transistor radio into a very high-frequency radio able to communicate over several miles in very mountainous terrain? Only military-grade comms devices could do that, yet here we are. While wondering about the radio, he was also considering the news they had received. Someone was following them, and it seemed this had been planning for some time.

'Thanks, sis, you have confirmed my concern. I will let you know what happens.'

With the boost of energy from the Marula fruit, they picked up pace, walking in single file, always climbing, the shadows now to their left and back, heading north and west, towards the border. The boys never stopped their chatter, no doubt goading each other in a tongue that sounded familiar, yet Fungai did not understand a word.

They were now passing through a narrow tunnel-like path with high cliff walls on either side. Morani, only a few steps ahead, made a howling sound like that of a jackal. It was magnified and echoed by the rock tunnel they were confined in. As though they did not hear, the four young men kept walking silently and more slowly, allowing them to catch up. Morani gave a signal, lifting his chin and turning his head to the right, the young men immediately understanding his message.

They continued walking as though nothing was afoot, following the narrow path that all of a sudden made a sharp right turn. Twenty paces after making the turn, Fungai looked over his shoulders. The two warriors behind him had vanished. Morani put his finger on his lips, a sign for silence. After another fifty paces, Fungai saw the two young men at the front disappear into a crevice, the afternoon shadows screening their presence.

'Kneel, then lie down as though you are sick,' Morani whispered. 'And let's see what's following our tail.'

Fungai went onto his knees, one hand on his stomach, the other on the ground, supporting himself as though in agonising pain. He was facing towards where they had come from. Morani faced forward, pretending to be taking care of his friend. The four young men waited, hidden in the shadows within the rock cliff face. They did not have to wait long.

He had been trailing them for the whole day, keeping his distance, making sure they did not get wind of him. He thought he had done a good job thus far. There was only one track to follow, which made his work easy. His instructions were clear, 'all we need to know is the village, hidden somewhere to the north and west of the border town. For that, we will make your life comfortable for the rest of your life. Land, cattle and money await you.' The man they called the Boss had told him. As he took a bend on his trail, he saw them not more than fifty paces ahead. The new guy was on his knees. It seemed like he was in pain while the other, the one they call Morani, was consoling him. He hesitated just for a moment before quickly ducking into the shadows. He hoped they had not seen him.

The one he knew as Morani, the leader of the small band, took hold of the elbow of the stranger, still on his knees, pulling him up and supporting him as they continued walking. He breathed a sigh of relief ... he had not been spotted. They walked slowly, a step at a time. He followed, making sure he was always in the shadow. Then, he felt a presence behind him. He turned. Two of the young warriors stood shoulder to shoulder facing him, their short swords and clubs at the ready, not five steps away, blocking his escape. He knew then he had been outwitted, cornered. The only option was to fight for his life.

The two warriors hidden in a crevice saw the stout, middle-aged man walk past them only three meters away. One peeped cautiously before they stepped out into the narrow path, shoulder to shoulder. The man turned. They knew he had a gun; they were prepared. As one, they jumped the man, swinging their clubs high and bringing them down, hard and fast. The man jumped backwards, trying to pull his gun from its holster, but the young men were too quick. He blocked a club with his left forearm; he heard the crack of his bone. Screaming in pain, he turned around to run, but Morani was waiting for him. The tall man who had been sick a few moments ago had also taken a fighting stance, like a martial arts expert, fists closed, ready for a fight. He felt a sharp pain in his neck before he lost consciousness.

The man slumped to his knees, then fell flat on his stomach.

'Search this bastard.' Morani commanded his warriors. 'Check for guns, knives and anything that may identify him.' Mwanza, the second in command, it seemed, frisked the man quickly.

'Jesus, this guy is armed to the teeth.' Mwanza shouted as he came up with two guns besides the rifle still hanging on his shoulder, two large knives, a pen knife and a knife hidden in each of his boots. He had no papers or identification.

'Not surprising,' Morani said. He does not want to be identified.

After a short while, the man groaned before opening his eyes. As he focused on Morani, he groaned even more, his shoulders slumped, he looked beaten.

'Who are you, and why are you following us?' Morani asked.

'I am nobody, and I am not following you. I was just walking in the bush, just like you. We just happened to be following the same path.'

Morani could see this was going to be difficult. The man looked like a mercenary, and he was not going to give out information easily.

'Look, we don't have time. Let me deal with this mercenary. I know how to make men talk.' Fungai asked Morani, avoiding using his name.

'Go ahead, be my guest, just don't kill him before we get the information.'

'Give me the small knife,' Fungai asked the warrior holding the man's stash.

'Now, remember we're in the bush. You're a madman who left the village and went into the bush. I will cut your foot at the ankle; you will not be able to move. You will be dinner for the hyenas tonight. That is if you don't tell us what we want to know.' Fungai spoke to the man softly as though talking to a friend but his eyes belayed total seriousness.

The man looked at him with scorn. 'You think you can scare me? I will not tell you anything.'

'Well, at least we know you know something now, which means you were sent by someone … last chance, man.'

'Fuck you, whoever you are.'

'So be it. Hold him down, boys.' The four warriors went on their knees, pinning the man down. With one smooth movement, Fungai pushed the knife through the soft tissues between the Achilles tendon and the fibular bone. Blood spilled on the sandy ground. The man screamed in pain. Fungai twisted the knife, the sharp end facing the Achilles tendon.

'Who sent you?' Fungai asked again, in his calm voice, as though he was talking to a naughty child.

'They will kill me and my family if I say anything.'

'They may kill you, but not today. On the other hand, I will cut your legs right now and leave you here. The hyenas will eat you while you're alive! Tonight. Which do you prefer?'

'I will take my chances with the hyenas.' The man responded.

'As you wish,' Fungai said as he swiftly sliced the Achilles. The man howled in pain, and then started crying. He started talking, spilling everything—and that is when Fungai realised where he was going.

'We have heard enough, let's get going,' Morani said abruptly.

'Please don't leave me here. Take me with you … I can give you more information,' the man pleaded as the group started to move.

Morani looked at Fungai as though asking, what should we do?

'Give me the gun.' Fungai took the gun and knelt next to the man.

'What else can you tell us?' Fungai asked the man. The man looked at him, lachrymose, begging for mercy.

When he realised there was nothing more the man could tell them, Fungai made his decision. He leaned closer to the man's ear. 'May your ancestors welcome you with smiles.' He pulled the trigger, punching the man's chest twice. The man slumped backwards, dead.

'A hard, determined yet merciful man, the hallmark of a great leader. Who are you, man?' Morani asked, looking at Fungai, now with renewed respect. He turned and started walking.

'We're almost there. We have made good time. I didn't think you would keep pace with us but I see you have done this before … perhaps in the military?' Morani asked, a mischievous smile on his long face.

'I will tell you one day … perhaps.' Fungai's mind was working overtime. From the dead man's story, the place they were headed to was an enigma. The elders of the community were prepared to kill to keep it a secret. *Why?* Yet they were allowing him, Fungai, a stranger, to go to their hidden village. *Why?*

Fungai heard a humming sound at a distance. The sound seemed to become louder with each step they made. A rainbow floated above the river they had been following for some time, like a neon light marking a waterfall. Water cascaded from high up the escarpment, generating a fine mist against the waning sun, like a light behind a curtain. The effect was almost magical. He checked his watch, a gift from Beki. It was 4.26 pm in the afternoon.

Thick mist shrouded everything. It was difficult to make out the young warriors a few paces ahead. Step by step, Fungai followed their chatter, making sure he did not slip on the slippery moss-covered pebbles and rocks that led to the waterfall and rock pool.

They approached an open area that somehow was not shrouded by the mist. It had the feel of a camping site that overlooked the stream. Mwanza was already lighting a fire. The other three young warriors were nowhere to be seen.

'They are out fishing for our dinner. We should be able to enjoy our local bounty of freshwater eel, catfish and hopefully tilapia. How does that sound for an African bush menu? You know, I reckon you have earned a small rest.' Morani reasoned.

'Thank you, Morani. Fish for dinner, just great!' Fungai responded as he set his backpack down and lay down face up. High up in the sky, an African eagle glided effortlessly. As he followed its flight, his mind cleared, he felt calm and peaceful, a state he had not experienced for a long time. He dozed off.

'Wake up, John,' Fungai heard a voice, as though a part of the dream he was having. He felt the movement that had interrupted his dream. Instantly, he was fully awake, alert, ready for action. He heard the falls humming, the cool, moist breeze, then he remembered where he was. The sweet aroma of roasting fish floated in the air. He remembered the dream—a fish caught in a bamboo trap, screaming to be let free.

'Food is ready! Mwanza's restaurant featuring grilled tilapia, eel, and bush yam.' The young man announced jovially.

✦

Chapter 11:
Fungai - The Hidden Village
The Ancients' Cave

Stomach full and sitting amongst friends in one of the most beautiful parts of Africa, and no enemies … for now, Fungai was at peace at last. He was just about to stretch out and start enjoying the late afternoon sun when Morani, sitting next to him, stood up abruptly, his backpack in his hands.

'Your day is not yet over, bro, get your gear. I need to show you something before it's too dark.' Morani whispered.

'Thanks for ruining my peace of mind.'

Before leaving, Morani approached Mwanza. 'We will go first, follow procedure. Stay overnight and break camp at first light. As usual, pretend to move out but hide out of sight until mid-morning. Make sure we are not followed. You know what to do should someone be following us.'

'Why the procedure,' Fungai asked Morani.

'You will see.' Morani responded as he started walking up the river towards the waterfall. Fungai followed two paces behind. They skirted the pool, walking behind the water mass. Like a curtain, the sheet of water cascaded from the overhanging rocks, hitting the pool with such force it splashed everywhere, creating a mist so thick that Fungai could not see Morani a few meters ahead of him.

'We're now approaching the cave of the Ancients, John. Follow my voice and talk to me so I know I have not lost you.' Fungai followed, tentative at first, then more sure-footed. The floor was covered with slippery pebbles, rocks and moss.

'We're here,' Morani whispered as though talking to himself. Fungai saw him standing at attention, face slightly tilted upwards towards the ceiling of the cave. *What's he looking at?* Fungai was wondering as he approached.

'Look up towards that shiny stone, high in the ceiling, do you see it?'

'Yes, I see the shiny stone. It looks like a gemstone but how does it shine through this mist?'

Morani lifted his hand, waving to the bright gemstone. Fungai heard a hissing sound. A light breeze brushed across his neck. Instinctively, he turned and saw a crack, and then a crevice. It had appeared as though by magic, splitting the solid rock wall in front of them. *Was he imagining this, or was it real?* In awe, he wondered as he watched.

'Let's move,' Morani instructed, walking through the narrow opening. Fungai, full of questions and trepidation, followed tentatively, wondering what he would find on the other side of this seemingly magical door. He didn't have to wait long. What had been a dark space was suddenly washed with such brilliant light that he raised his right hand instinctively to shield his eyes. As his eyes adjusted to the brightness, he noticed the light was being emitted by a mesmerising array of what looked like a myriad of gems. The light had a blue hue, making it seem like a perfect replication of a bright, clear, sunny day at noon.

He realised they were in a rough-hewn rock tunnel. The bright gems lining the walls and ceiling seemed to be part of the rock. There must have been thousands of them.

'What are they, these bright gems?' Fungai asked Morani in amazement.

'You look like you've seen heaven. Everything will be explained. For now, your first lesson starts. Your question should be, where are we?'

The air in the tunnel, dry but fresh, was completely different from the dank air of the cave entrance they had just left.

'First, know that you're a very privileged man to have been allowed into this place. In fact, you're the only person I know of to be allowed without undergoing the Seven Stairs initiation ceremony. Only ordained leaders and warriors who have gone through the initiation can come in here.'

'So why am I allowed and by who?'

'I don't know. Apparently, our Chief knows you more than I do.'

'And how does he know who I am? Who are you people? I thought you were cattle keepers with limited education and technology?'

Morani did not respond. He looked at Fungai and winked, as though saying, we are happy to be considered ignorant herders. He started walking along the brightly lit corridor. They came into a large round hall just as brightly lit. The roof, high and dome-shaped, like a large mosque. It was clear the hall was hewn from sheer rock.

How could this be? This is in the bush, in the middle of nowhere, yet here we are, in a space so breathtaking it reminds me of the magnificent Masjid Al Haram Mosque in Mecca that I visited last year. Fungai, in awe, thought to himself.

He looked from the ceiling to the walls. His eyes were attracted by strange patterns and markings. As he scrutinised them more keenly, he realised it was nothing like he had seen before. He focused on what was obviously ancient art and writings. There was the full-sized figure of a tall, skinny, human-like creature, with a narrow face and a prominent, elongated forehead, like an upside-down bowl, large round eyes, a sharp nose, a small mouth and a narrow V-shaped chin. Next to this humanoid figure was an airborne craft hovering over a dark lake. He noticed huge elephants, almost double the size of modern-day elephants, with massive ivory tusks pulling what looked like large trailers piled with rocks. Other weird-looking creatures and inanimate figurines filled the walls of the large dome-shaped theatre.

At one end of the hall, writings in an unfamiliar script run in lines from top to bottom. The script reminded him of ancient Egyptian, Amharic and Arabic characters he had studied in his ancient civilisations class. There were also what looked like numbers and formulae laid out neatly in rows, columns and circles. Some looked like vector geometry and architectural depictions of a pyramid. The drawings and scripts were so well preserved they looked like they were done only yesterday.

Fungai looked at Morani, who had been hovering around him, waiting patiently.

'What in the world is this?' He asked.

'Ancient scripts and drawings in a cave brother. What else? We had better get going. The Chief is waiting for you. Why are you so important to him? I wonder. But it is not my place to ask questions.'

Fungai sensed a negative vibe, as though Morani was jealous or felt threatened.

'Morani, your Chief, how does he know I am here?' Fungai asked again.

Morani produced the two-way Sanyo radio. 'You see this here,' pointing to what looked like a tiny lens. 'It is like a camera that transmits images and voices, same as a TV.' He explained. 'The Chief saw glimpses of the fight in the bar, right? Then he wanted to see you. At the village, while you were eating, I switched on the image camera and took your picture, which I later sent to him. He immediately gave instructions to take care of you.'

'"Bring him to me," he said. "Protect him at all cost. Die if necessary, so that he can meet the Elders." That is how important you are to him and, therefore, to me. The question for me is, who are you? Why is the Chief, my father, so keen to meet you? And was it a coincidence that you saved me and joined us?'

These questions triggered the memory of his grandfather, Ramla ra Fumi. Something he had told him about his ancestors who were from 'where the sun goes down.' *Was it a coincidence or a subconscious urge to go west to seek the place from where my ancestors came from? Or was it the compass written in my DNA like a matriarch elephant that led me westwards towards the border and to this particular pastoral tribe?* Fungai kept these thoughts to himself.

'When we have time, I will tell you my story but as you said, we better get going,' Fungai responded, slapping Morani's shoulder fondly like they were real brothers. He looked at his watch, indicating he was ready to move.

At a brisk pace, Morani set off, Fungai following. They exited the Dome of the Ancients through another secret door directly opposite to the one they had used to enter, into another tunnel similar to the one they had used earlier. The level floor of the tunnel gave way to stairs, well used by the look of it, heading up straight like an arrow. They ascended. Following Morani, now breathing heavily, Fungai started counting one, two … ninety-nine, one hundred. He had picked the habit of counting stairs and steps in the military, where everything was done in numbers.

The hundredth step landed on a circular amphitheatre big enough to accommodate a small group. Well-used marble seats ran the length of the wall, forming two semi-circles, broken to the right and the left by steps that ascended further up.

Fungai walked slowly around the room. Like the Dome of the Ancients, though much smaller, the wall was covered with the same ancient motifs. He was again mesmerised by the artistic perfection and intricacy of the futuristic machines, in contrast to the ancient landscapes and animal life.

'Just amazing,' he heard himself saying.

'Yes, it's amazing. And to know this was done by my ancestors makes me very proud,' Morani, now by his side, commented. 'We keep on moving. We have another three hundred stairs to go.'

They took the steps on the right side of the room. By the time they reached the fourth landing, Fungai was heaving, his chest burning from the exertion, sweat covering his face.

'We're almost there,' Morani encouraged him, himself breathing heavily, hands on hips. 'Let's have a drink before we move on.' He walked towards an earthen pot near the exit of the room, scooping water with a calabash cup and dowsing it over his sweaty head before taking a long drink. He passed the calabash scoop to Fungai, who did the same.

'That makes me feel much better,' Fungai said, breathing deeply the fresh air coming from the exit. He looked out through the exit, making out the night sky at the end of the tunnel.

'The elders are waiting for us, or should I say for you? I suggest you put on your best behaviour, though I can tell you're a gentleman. Talk only when permitted, and do not raise your voice for any reason. You do not want to attract an early death.' Morani warned, smiling but serious.

They walked in silence towards the skylight, the tunnel opened into a wide cave-like opening, ending in a platform with a protective balustrade. Holding on to the rough-hewn protection, Fungai looked across the landscape. It was magnificent. In the distance, he saw the deep blue waters of a crater lake. Houses hugged the steep slopes of the hill below them to his right and left.

Two young men dressed in warrior attire approached them. They came to attention.

'Welcome, older brother,' one of them said, shaking Morani's hand, then Fungai's.

'The Chief and the Council of Elders await you. My mother, no other, has prepared a feast for you.' The young man said, looking at Fungai while bowing his head in respect.

'His mother, my mother, is the Chief Wife, head among many and the mother of our tribe.' Morani explained, looking at Fungai's quizzical eyes. 'With her own hands, she makes a meal for you? A very rare and privileged occasion. She has fifty women who could have done that but she chose to do it herself! You have to be someone important.'

He did not wait for the answer as he walked to the right, across the boardwalk, suspended on the cliff face towards what seemed to be the largest hut. Warriors armed with spears, machetes and mallets stood at attention in front of the large grass-thatched house.

'Welcome, sir, the elders are waiting for you.' One of the guards, with a revolver on his hip belt, announced.

Tentatively, almost in awe, Morani walked through the door. Fungai followed closely. The hall was surprisingly bright, the walls and the rafters lined with glowing stones similar to the ones in the Dome of the Ancients buried deep under the earth. A large bench-like table made of rough-hewn hardwood ran the length of the circular hall. The Chief and the Chief Wife sat at the far end of the table. Other elders, men and women, sat on either side of the table.

As they walked in, the room went silent. Morani approached the Chief, head bowed, respectively—subservient. Fungai assumed the same posture.

'Come, come, my son, sit next to your mother.'

As Fungai approached, the Chief stood up and the other Elders did the same. The Chief stood there, staring as though he had seen a ghost. Then he approached Fungai, grabbing his shoulders with surprisingly strong arms and hugged him.

'Welcome, son,' he whispered to his ears. 'We have waited for you for a long time. We heard the news and we thought you were killed but here you are.' He released him from his strong grip.

Fungai, confusion in his eyes, was wondering, *who are you people?*

'I see your confusion. It's okay. I am Baba Mkulu, the Chief. Please rest your legs, eat and drink, then we talk.'

Before Fungai could sit, the woman, the mother of the tribe, tall and strong looking not more than a year older than fifty, stood up and approached him. She held his shoulders, looking deep into his eyes. She reminded him of someone, but he was not quite sure who.

'You, my son, are your father's son,' she whispered. More loudly, her voice clear and commanding with a hint of defiance, she announced. 'My son is back, safe and healthy as a bull. Isn't he?' She appraised him with proud eyes, a huge grin on her face. In close proximity, her face was not unfamiliar to him. Fungai wondered, *have I met you before?*

Fungai was, to say the least, confused. *How could this be,* he wondered? *I'm of a different tribe, from possibly a different country, yet this woman refers to me as my son.*

Around the table, the elders stood up one by one, bowing, saluting. 'We welcome you, Fungai, son of Fumi.' He looked across to Morani, sitting next to his mother, head down, bowing in respect. Fungai, overwhelmed by the respect, wondered, *why?* Such respect is accorded only to the most esteemed Elders. He was only leader of *Antu,* a rather small clandestine organisation known only to a few—and now on the run from his enemy Onim the Crocodile.

'My son, I can see you are confused. Sit down. You have had a long journey. Everything will be revealed in time but first, we eat. When is the last time you ate your own mother's food? The woman asked.

After eating, the Chief enquired, 'how was your trip, Morani?'

Morani stood up, speaking in a loud and clear voice, he narrated their journey back from the cattle he had sold on behalf of the tribe, the attack in the bar, the capture of the assassin and their journey through the caves. 'Here, Father, this is the money from the cattle sale. The accounts are also there.' He passed the goat-skin bag to his father, the Chief.

The Chief, Baba Mkulu, as he was fondly referred to, read the accounts quickly. 'You did well, my son. Your skills in negotiating have rewarded us with a good price for our cattle. We will all have enough money to see us through the coming dry season.' The chief announced for everyone to hear before he proceeded to call names and distribute the money to all the elders in the room.

'Go home and sleep well, tomorrow, we meet to continue our discussion.' The Elders filed out, bowing to the Chief as they left, clearly not unhappy with their spoils.

The great hall was now empty, the Elders of the Tano having left except for the Chief, the Chief Wife, Fungai and Morani. Morani looked at his father as though asking for permission to stay. The Chief looked at his wife first, confirming it was okay.

The woman, who looked very familiar, cleared her throat, indicating she wanted to be heard. Fungai settled back in his seat, expecting a revelation. Baba Mkulu nodded towards a clay jag hugging the wall.

'Again, welcome my son. I did not introduce myself properly. The Elders call me Theki. Everyone else simply calls me Mama, but my real name is Thekisele bi Fumi.'

'What?!' Lightheaded, mouth agape, Fungai felt groggy like he was going to faint. He leaned forward, holding onto the rough table. He took a deep breath to clear his head, now swimming with questions.

'You are who? The wife of Fumi?' He heard himself asking.

Theki stood up and wrapped her arms around Fungai's broad shoulders.

'For a long time, I have looked forward to this moment but now I am lost for words. It's been such a long time!'

Fungai could feel her heart thumping, her breath heavy as she held on to him for a long time, choking with emotions, tears dripping down her face. She started sniffing as though she had a running nose.

'Look at me, son, who do you see?'

Fungai looked at her. He saw himself. He looked at her again, then, it was his time to hug her. He held her tightly, his chest heaving heavily, he started crying, he could not help it.

'I have missed you so ... so much, Mother!'

'And that young man that you saved in the bar is your half-brother. More, you will know in due course.' Mama Theki told Fungai. 'Don't stay too late, tomorrow you start a new phase of your life.' She left the three men with their honey wine.

Elders of The Tano Tribe

"When spiders unite, they can tie down a lion"
(African saying)

The three sat quietly for some time, each lost in their own world. Fungai felt elated, satiated somehow, now that he knew his mother. It was a climactic feeling. His emotions ran high and it felt good ... exceptionally good. He looked over to Morani, noticing, for the first time, his likeness to him. Tall and broad-shouldered, large round eyes, a long sharp nose, a high forehead, angular jaws, a V-shaped chin and his skin, dark as charcoal.

Morani looked up and smiled. 'I knew there was something familiar about you, but I couldn't catch it.' He said, standing up and approaching Fungai. 'You look like someone I have seen in the mirror, only uglier!' he said jokingly as he hugged Fungai.

'Sit down, boys. I want to tell you the story of your life, Fungai, the son of Fumi.' The Chief started his story. 'You were born in this village on the day of the eruption. Now ... that was a day to remember—the day our lives changed.' He continued, speaking in awe.

'The earth, as though responding to the screams of your mother giving birth, rocked under our very feet, vibrating like a bowstring after release. Flamingoes, marabou birds, crows, swifts, weaver birds, ibis and other birds big and small took to the skies. They were all flying against the wind, heading east. Elephants, wildebeest, buffaloes and even duiker, rarely seen in the open, took to the hills. All it seemed, heading for the caves. Everyone was looking up, wondering what was happening. Your father, Fumi, was the first to realise what was happening. Speaking loudly for everyone to hear, he spoke:

'"The gods are speaking. It is written in the books of the Ancients that the earth will open up and it will breathe fire and smoke. It is written the birds will fly to the east, and the animals of the plains and the forests will run for cover into the caves. Look up, look to the plains.'" he pointed to the skies and the plains. "The prophecy has come to be: as the animals of the wild seek shelter in the caves of our ancestors, so must we. Everyone, gather nothing other than food. Head to the belly of the earth, to the Dome of the Ancients. All our healers, gather your herbs, concoctions and your magic tools—we will need them in the days to come. Warriors, sound the drums and run the message. We must save our people."'

Chief Mkulu sipped on his drink as he continued with the story, now animated like a small child. 'The sky was filled with the chirping, screeching, twitting, whistling and the other sounds of birds. On the plains, the elephants trumpeted, jackals howled and lions roared. The monkeys shrieked and screeched, jumping from tree to tree, heading ... strangely to the Ancients' caves.

'On the far side of the caldera, far to the west, the earth burst open, growling like the king of the lions, spewing the very devil out of the depths of the earth. Ash and rocks rained on the land all around. Hot flowing lava shot from the centre of the ancient lake, hissing like a snake, spewing vapour and red-hot magma that bust into the sky, then back into the lake. The devil himself could not have been crueler. At that moment, you, Fumi, decided it was your time to come out of your mother's womb on the fourth landing of the Ancients' stairs as your mother and her midwives tried to escape the curse of the eruption.

'Our tribe lost everything. All our herds, except a few goats, were lost. Our neighbouring tribes faired much worse. When the eruptions stopped, the black rain came. We had nothing to eat, not even wild vegetables, grain or fruit. There was no game to hunt, not even birds of the sky. The few animals that had fled to the caves, we could not hunt as it was forbidden by our ancestors. As the Ancients had done in years past, the tribe had to break up into smaller groups and head in different directions until the land healed and it was time to come back.

'But before that, the Paramount Chief of the tribe, the great Mbogo Mkulu, called for a meeting of the Elders and warriors, all assembled in the great Dome of the Ancients.

'"It is at such times, desperate times, that you, our warriors, the best of the best, need to serve the people," The Chief spoke. "Fumi, the tip of the spear, you will lead your men. Follow the great river, as it flows south, you will find Mayi Bula, the deep blue waters where fish, birds and wildlife abound. The Paramount Chief, your father's brother, owes us two thousand heads of cattle. Don't ask for it. He will not give it willingly. Just take it but don't kill any innocents. While doing your deed, let it be known that it is I, Mbogo Mkulu, who takes back our rightful inheritance, what is owed to our tribe. Let it be known that necessity forces us to do so. After this is done and the cattle are safely out of his territory, go back to your uncle alone and explain our circumstances and beg for his forgiveness. He might spare you, but most likely, he will kill you. Do so to prevent future bloodshed between our people."

'I was the righthand man of your father,' Baba Mkulu continued with the story. 'And so, we left. For many days, we trotted, resting little and surviving on wild animals until we found what the local people called Mayi Bula. The deep waters were surrounded by rolling hills and valleys. The golden-coloured grass was as high as our hips and ripe with seed. The beautiful plains were filled with cattle and wild animals. We realised we were in the land of our people when we heard their tongue, similar to ours. And as requested by our Paramount Chief, we took by force what was ours. Many warriors perished in the inevitable skirmishes. Before the

Chief, your uncle could master a proper force, we were many days gone, north and west, towards our homeland. When we could hear our language spoken no more, we knew we were out of your uncle's lands.

'"It is time I went back and soothe the Paramount Chief," your father, my captain, told us. "You're now the tip of the spear," he said, pointing at me. "Go back and inform our people and let it be known I will do as ordered. If I don't come back, please take care of my newborn son and young wife."

'He turned back, almost to certain death, as we continued back to our people. We have never heard of him since. By his sacrifice, our tribe regained its herds, survived and thrived. We owe that to your father. Children sing of the great warrior Fumi, the son of Ramla, who saved our tribe from starvation and death.' Baba Mkulu yawned expansively and stood up. 'And now, it's time to go and rest.'

Sidai: Paradise

In an instant, he was wide awake and alert—a lesson from his military days. He felt a presence even before he opened his eyes, then the scent that brought the memory of his fiancé Beki. A soft hand brushed his bearded face. He could not resist a small smile and a deep heave of contentment. Then, without warning, a knife was on his neck, pressed lightly against his jugular. He tensed, thinking of his next move.

'Easy soldier or you're dead.'

The memory of his Sergeant in the special forces training camp came to mind. 'Never lower your guard, especially where a woman is involved.'

'You men are all the same. A bit of perfume, a brush of a woman's fingers and you lower your guard? Soldier, you fail—miserably.'

Fungai felt the knife on his carotid vein. With all his strength, he pushed back.

Having anticipated this move, the woman tightened her grip on Fungai's throat and at the same time pushed her knee hard on his back; Her knife drew blood. *Fifty-fifty chance I can disarm her before she plugs the knife into my neck,* Fungai thought to himself. He decided there was no need to risk that. Cussing, he tapped, accepting defeat ... this once. Sidai loosened her grip, slowly pulling the knife away.

Fungai turned to be met by a big smile. Sidai looked like an angel with a knife ready for slaughter. 'Thanks for making my day,' he lamented, still annoyed with himself. 'You should wake me up every morning and I will be a very happy man.' He said more to hide his embarrassment than to compliment. Inwardly, he was still cursing. 'That is the last time you will catch me unaware.'

'Uh ... we will see,' Sidai responded with a smug smile on her face. 'Come on now, my brother awaits you.'

'Why didn't he wake me up himself?'

'I begged him. I wanted to see what you look like when you're asleep and at peace and when scared,' she said, a smile on her face.

As he stepped out of the grass-thatched hut onto a timber deck and into the bright mid-morning sun, a panoramic view, majestic and primordial, confronted him. It made him feel like he was in the heavens, flying high, looking down on God's creation. His senses were overwhelmed by the sheer beauty of the landscape. Far to the west, he made out bluish-green hills that marked the western rim of the caldera. Far below him, he saw the shimmering light, glazed dark-blue waters of the sacred lake, a mist already rising as the waters warmed up. A flock of flamingoes silently gliding and landing on the shallow shore crowned the picturesque scenery.

'This is just ... wow.' Fungai could not think of a better expression.

'Yep, this is my home, my paradise.' Sidai, standing by his side, her arm lightly brushing against his, responded. Fungai looked at her, then back at the beautiful vista in front of him.

'If Morani is my half-brother and he is your brother, then you must be my half-sister. Yes?'

'Wrong. I have no blood relationship with you, so ...' Bi Sidai responded, looking at him with a wicked smile. 'You see,' she started to explain. 'Morani is my half-brother, same father, different Mothers, got it? Anyway, it is time for breakfast, then you men will have your day. See you later.' She said with a smile as she trotted off, swinging her hips unashamedly.

'What a girl!' Fungai exclaimed when she was out of earshot.

'I heard that.' Fungai turned around to see Morani with a huge smile on his face. 'Don't let her get to you. Someone else loves her. A younger, much more ... should I say, handsomer fella. Mother has made a huge meal for us. After breakfast, I will show you around.' They walked towards a large hut under a huge drooping fig tree.

'Good morning, my boys. Today is my happiest day so far—my two boys together enjoying my meal! What a wonderful moment, sit and eat.'

Theki looked on as her two sons ate, slapping their lips, noisily sipping soup and finally liking their fingers, full, contented. A huge basin-like rattan platter lined with banana leaves that had been piled high with roasted sweet potatoes, yams and boiled meat sat on the rough bench table, now empty, same as the clay mugs just a few moments filled with thick meat broth.

'That was the most delicious breakfast I have eaten for some time, Mother. I have missed that,' Morani complimented.

'Thank you for the breakfast, Mother. I agree it was amazing but what is even more amazing is to be with you and this young man.' Fungai added, lightly punching his new-found brother on the shoulder.

'We have to get going. I have been instructed by Father to educate my brother,' Morani said as he stood up.

The two brothers leisurely walked around the village, using platforms made of roughly hewed wooden planks that linked one home to the other. Once in a while, Morani would stop and introduce Fungai to a villager. 'This is John, our visitor,' he would simply say. They came across women, baskets full of vegetables and fruits balancing atop their heads. Yet others, like dancers, walked straight backed, effortlessly balancing earthen pots full of liquids precariously on their heads. Fungai was impressed by a young woman who, in addition to a pot on her head, had a toddler secured with a flowery-coloured calico cloth on her back. The women would politely stand aside as the two passed. 'Have a fruitful day,' they would say politely.

'Spearhead, Spearhead, do you read me?'

Morani quickly grabbed his radio. 'Lion 2, I read you?'

'We have a situation. Two young men, fighting over a woman, Sector 3, near the training ground.'

'I am close by. Will be there shortly. In the meantime, try and calm the situation. Over and out.'

'Come, let's see what's happening.' Morani dashed and almost collided with a woman who had suddenly come out of her house. Fungai followed suit, keeping pace with Morani. They could hear shouts and screams now. Shortly, they came to an open space the size of a kraal, where an animated group of men, women and children were jeering, gesturing and generally creating a ruckus.

Fungai: Protect The Weak
"He who is destined for power does not have to fight for it."
(African proverb)

'Stop him, please stop him, he will kill my brother,' a woman shouted. The group stood still, transfixed, looking at a man wielding a machete.

'I will kill you today! You dog. You will learn not to chase my woman.' An enraged man shouted, standing over a young man with blood all over his body. The man raised his machete and brought it down hard, aiming at the other young man's neck. Women and children screamed in fear, while men heaved, awaiting a bloody contact.

'Stop.' Morani shouted, but the man was so enraged he did not hear him. The machete came down. The young man rolled to the side just in time. It struck the ground, cutting deep into the soft soil, missing the neck of the young man by a few fingers. The man raised the machete, readying himself for another downward strike, eyes red, crazy with anger and hate. Fungai had anticipated this and was already in motion. He picked a medium-sized stone as the man was about to bring the machete swinging downwards again. Twenty meters, he estimated. He threw the stone with all his strength, aiming at the crazed man's head. As though in slow motion, Fungai followed the stone's path as he saw the man bring down the machete. The stone missed ... the poor young man, flat on his back, lifted his hands and twisted his body, protecting his head and neck. Fungai saw the machete coming down, cutting deep into the young man's shoulder. He heard the crunch of bones as the machete cut through the shoulder blade. The young man screamed in pain.

Fungai sprang into action, moving like a leopard, quick and nimble. In an instant, he was next to the man who was about to strike again.

'Hey, you coward, look at me,' Fungai shouted, a harsh tone bellying his power. The enraged man turned, machete raised in mid-air and faced Fungai.

'Who the hell are you,' he screamed, red-eyed, with rage.

Fungai goaded him even more. 'You donkey turd, come on, let's see you fight a real man.'

The man momentarily forgot the young man lying on the ground. He rushed, machete raised, jumping high and screaming, the machete came down, aimed at Fungai's head. 'I will teach you a lesson, you son of a dog.' He screamed, ready to kill.

Silence followed ... everyone's eyes were glued to the scene, even Morani was paralysed.

Fungai stood motionless, the man was upon him, rushing as he brought his machete down, assured of a kill strike. At the very last moment, Fungai pivoted right on his heel, the movement quick and sleek like a ballet dancer. The machete flashed downwards right in front of his face. He put out his right foot, tripping the assailant, who lost his balance and hit the dust flat on his face.

'Be as quick as a leopard, give the opponent zero chance to recover.' Fungai remembered his military training. He pounced on the assailant, a hungry leopard, onto his prey. Pushing his knee hard on his lower back, both his hands went for the neck choke—a vice, clamping, squeezing hard enough to choke but not to break the neck. The man's face puffed out, eyes rolled, his body went limp, Fungai loosened his grip. He placed two fingers on the carotid vein, feeling the man's pulse, it was slow but steady. 'He will live.' He spoke out loud for all to hear.

Everyone was silent, spellbound, no doubt wondering what had just happened?'

Morani was the first to move. He approached Fungai, patting his back. 'You are a nutcase. That, my brother, was extremely stupid and very brave.' The audience started clapping.

'You saved my son.' A woman shouted, followed by more shouts of congratulations from the gathering.

'This is John. Don't mess with him, or you will be like our friend down here. Brother, welcome to Tano village, where men fight and die for a woman.' Morani said jokingly. 'Everyone, thank John for his bravery. If not for him, this stupid young man would be dead, pointing to the bloodied young man. 'And we would have to execute this piece of cow dung here.'

'Clap ... clap ... clap!' everyone applauded Fungai in unison. Three claps, saying thank you, welcome and hello, at the same time. Young men came around him, shaking Fungai's hand, admiring his courage. Sidai was the only woman to approach him, a smile on her face. She held his arm as though saying, *this is my man*. Other women, young and old alike, spied him with shy, downcast eyes and suggestive smiles on their faces while others stared at him in adoration.

'Again, you save someone,' Sidai whispered in his ears, almost hugging him in the process. 'You continue to build favour with our people but you also call the attention of evil beings.' Fungai understood perfectly what she meant. He had been in politics long enough to know achievements come with envy, malice and danger.

'Morani, the Paramount Chief wants you and your friend to the *Ikulu* immediately.' An old woman, a walking stick in one hand, spoke to Morani.

'What has happened, Mama Mkulu?'

'I have no idea but you have to hurry now.'

'The *Ikulu* … the Elders Hall this early? It must be a serious matter. We better move.'

Sidai let go of his hand reluctantly. They hurried along the raised boardwalk under the thick tropical foliage. The blue volcanic lake, way down to the right, glistered with the morning light. As they approached the *Ikulu*, they saw a small gathering of on-lookers whispering with excitement.

'What is going on?' He heard Morani, a step ahead of him, ask.

'We will find out soon,' Fungai responded.

The small gathering near the entrance of the *Ikulu* gave way as the two approached. The hall was dark, the only illumination the embers of a smouldering log. Fungai could barely make out the figures seated around the fire at the centre of the hall. He made out the Chief, hunched over the fire, a heavy blanket cloaked around his shoulders. Morani, still one step ahead of him, stopped, putting out a hand, telling Fungai to stop—not to approach the elders.

'Approach Fungai, the son of Fumi.' The Paramount Chief announced with his deep voice. *Why the formality*, Fungai wondered?

He saw five old men crouched around the fireplace, their posture and faces serious and contemplative. A loan figure was standing at attention behind the Paramount Chief of the Tano Tribe. *That stance is familiar*, Fungai thought. Then he saw the face of a man now clearly illuminated by the ambers. 'What the hell …' he heard himself whisper.

His trusted lieutenant, the man who had given him the warning of danger, in what seemed like a lifetime ago, now stood not five strides away. *How did he even know of this village or that I would be here?*

'Yesterday you met the heads of the five clans,' Chief Mkulu announced as a matter of fact in his baritone voice. 'Obviously, you know Masika, your trusted friend and lieutenant. From your reaction, I gather you did not know he is a member of the Tano tribe, eh!' The Chief said this with a sly smile. 'It also happens he is your blood cousin and a senior commander of our warriors. An equal to Morani.'

Fungai's amazement was obvious as he gaped at Masika, wondering... *for all this time, we have been working together, and you never mentioned anything. What other secrets don't I know?*

'Masika travelled overnight to bring a message for you. My son, speak out now, tell us what is so urgent that you have to risk your life and travel at night.'

Fungai looked at his former lieutenant, considering how little he knew of himself. He had lived with this man for years, treating him as his head of security, confidant but never as a tribesman. He had recruited him personally on a recommendation from one of Grandfather Ramla's friends, who had vouched for him, saying that he knew Masika well as a boy and as a warrior. They had attended a secret military training together, always at his side. Looking back now, it was becoming clear that these people, the Elders of the Tano tribe, had been with him all along.

Fungai heard Masika heave deeply, he cleared his throat and stammered '... ehe ... ehe ...' struggling to bring out his words.

'They are on their way here.' He finally announced without preamble. 'Presidents Nima and Onim believe you might have joined your tribe. He thinks the disappearance of his two intelligence officers is linked to The Organisation. He has unleashed a platoon of his elite soldiers to raid the tribes and get information about your whereabouts by whatever means necessary ... and that is why I am here, boss.' He finished and stood, chest out, at attention as though awaiting orders.

'Well, thank you for bringing this information to us, Masika.' Chief Mkulu responded as he looked up to Morani, then to Masika.

'Whatever is necessary, we will do. In the meantime, secure our people, our villages, our cattle. Send the old, children and women to our pastoral kin in the forests. It is time to teach the two idiots we're the venerated Tano people.

'Fungai, you discuss strategy with Morani and his generals, then come back to this gathering, we have other things for you.' Orders stated sharp and clear, that was Chief Mkulu's style. No room for misunderstanding and certainly not for discussion.

Later and as instructed, Fungai re-entered the *Ikulu*, bowing low to the Paramount Chief.

'Am back, Mkulu. We're more than ready for what is to come.'

The Chief bowed and clapped twice, acknowledging Fungai but also showing respect only reserved for senior members of the Tano tribe. 'Your duties are elsewhere.' The Chief said as he handed Fungai a large horn filled with honey wine.

Fungai was inclined to decline the offer, after all, it was barely noon but he remembered the Chief does not do something like that without a reason.

'Please have a drink, you are about to go on the journey of your life.'

The wine was light, sweet and bubbly, more like champagne that he had tasted in many of the African Union's meetings.

'Your journey will prepare you to be the leader of our people.'

'But you need me here to fight with you against the tyranny of Onim, Nima and their armies. I need to take revenge for my fallen comrades.'

After a thoughtful moment, the chief said, 'Remember this, "patience can cook a stone,"' quoting an old African proverb.

Fungai felt groggy. The Chief rushed to him before he collapsed.

He dreamed of a stone on fire, cracking, then melting red into hot liquid.

Chapter 12:
Secretes of The Ancients' Ira: White As Snow

An albino or a ghost? Am I going crazy? Fungai wondered. He scrutinised the youngish-looking figure before him. She was as white as snow, with a hint of pink pronouncing her cheeks. Curly Afro hair, white as the snow on the snow-peaked Ostrich mountains that he knew so well, capped her head. Her long face was marked by a high forehead and a rather long, narrow nose that contrasted with her thick pink lips. Her long eyelashes framed her big eyes. A narrow but prominent V-shaped chin sat proudly on a long neck that seemed to sprout out of surprisingly broad shoulders.

What an amazing face, is she even human? Fungai wondered. A long, thin but masculine left arm held a fighting stick in a relaxed yet ready way. He knew the stance—that of a warrior.

Fungai was not quite sure where he was or how he had arrived there. The last thing he remembered was drinking wine and smoking some kind of cigar with the Elders as they discussed the next move for their tribe. Now, he was sitting in an automated wheelchair in a cubicle that looked like an elevator. Standing before him was an albino woman who, moments earlier, had seemed like a ghost.

'Where am I?'

The woman came closer. Fungai could now make out the deep pink iris of her eyes. They seemed ageless and full of wisdom. Her intense gaze made Fungai uncomfortable. Tiny spider web-like lines around her eyes contradicted her youthful frame—large shoulders, ample bust, narrow waist, wide hips and strong legs, all covered by a fine, loosely fitting, see-through cotton gown that went as far as her thighs.

'I see thirst in your eyes. I feel the desire in your loins. I sense your hunger for knowledge—in that order. from what I hear, you are not very different from your father and his father before him. But you have something else. I can feel it, yet I cannot see it.'

Fungai collapsed back into the wheelchair, having made an effort to stand up. His legs not able to support him. He felt drowsy and unbalanced, like someone who had too much to drink.

'My name is Ira, or the snow in our tongue. I will be your guardian and companion.'

'What? Why do I need a guardian and what do you mean by companion?'

'Didn't the Elders inform you of your task?' Ira asked, a hint of irritation in her voice. 'You will go on a journey deep into the earth. You will become *The One*.' Those were the last words he heard from Baba Mkulu before he blacked out.

'Your journey starts now.' Without warning, Ira sat astride Fungai's thighs. She placed her head against his chest, an endearing embrace as though she were his lover. Fungai was confused. She looked up at him, her lips moving in sync with his heartbeat. In a strange and alien language, she started murmuring incantations in a sing-song lullaby. He went into a trance. He could hear, see, feel and think but he could not move—completely immobilised but awake and alert.

He felt her warm fingers on his temple. A sensation like nothing he had experienced before spread throughout his body. Like a worm, a warm stream crept from her fingers, digging deep into his head. Bright, distant stars exploded in his vision, followed by an amazingly peaceful feeling. Sublime ... heavenly ...

His mind opened up, magnifying his vision a thousand-fold. Focusing on her face, he saw the fine lines of her skin, like rivulets filled with sand and pebbles. Her fingers, the conduits of this new experience, kept on moving, massaging, stimulating even more senses. He felt like responding, saying something, but he could not move a muscle—he was paralysed.

Fungai felt her body still glued to his stiff body. For what seemed like an eternity, she looked deep into his eyes. Her eyes pulled him in; he was helpless to her gaze. Abruptly, she pulled back, breaking the connection in one swift motion.

'An enigma you are. I can feel you, yet you have a dimension that is beyond me. The blood of the Ancients must flow strong in you. You are one of only a few.'

What the hell are you talking about? Fungai wanted to ask but he seemed unable to talk.

'Let's move on,' Ira said as she started pushing the wheelchair. She moved quickly and with ease, through narrow tunnels, turning left and right. After several turns, Fungai lost his sense of direction. Ira's presence was overpowering. Her strong jasmine fragrance and warm, minty breath did not help. He realised his mind was drifting in the wrong direction.

I need a distraction. 'Focus on the small details,' he remembered his covert training with the military intelligence unit. The cobblestone floor, perfect rectangles arranged in a pyramid pattern, repeated over and over again along the corridors they were moving on. The cobblestones are well worn out, a sign of years of use. The wall and roof are bare natural rock, with numerous organic-looking fluorescent lights, like fireflies that light up as we pass, turning into dull grey after we pass. 'Magical,' he heard himself say, his voice sounding strange even to himself.

'Yes indeed.' Ira responded.

Another right turn, Ira stopped abruptly. 'We're here,' her voice, unlike before, was soft, soothing and enchanting, adding to the magical aura of the place.

'Like many generations of your ancestors, you will be given knowledge that few have.' The door opened, having somehow sensed their approach, leading them into a large room. A cot with tubes and cables, like a hospital bed, occupied the far side of the room. To the left, cushions were laid out over a beautiful red and blue rug, lined part of the wall. A traditional gourd sat on a low ebony-topped table.

Fungai noticed a small ingress to the right. On closer scrutiny, he realised it was the bathroom. Exercise equipment, hanging or placed on shelves, lined the wall to his right. Ropes, hand combat kits, sticks, spears, shields and swords were neatly arranged. A whole section was dedicated to guns, ammunition and accessories. *What is this place?* He wondered.

Ira helped him onto the hospital-style cot.

'Lie down and try to relax. All will be explained,' Ira said as she stood at attention next to the cot.

Before Fungai could stretch himself, the door hissed, like it was being operated by some hydraulic pump, then opened.

What the hell!? A creature, like from another world, wheeled into the room. Fungai remembered the figures he had seen in the Dome of the Ancients. *This cannot be real*, he thought.

'Mind your thoughts. I can read your mind as you read a book. I hear your thoughts as you hear your transistor radio. I can read your future twenty years from now. Not today, though! And yes, I am absolutely real.' The figure spoke slowly as if to make sure Fungai understood him. His voice, low and scruffy, left a powerful impression on Fungai. 'You can call me the Ancient. My blood dates back before the time of humans. We are of what you would call of ancient origin.'

Fungai looked at the Ancient more closely, noticing the high pointed forehead, long and narrow chin, eyes close together above a hooked nose that was too long for the face. His ears, starting as a narrow tube, flared out like the bell of a trumpet. They seemed to be an addition rather than part of his long, thin face. A few strands of white hair were sparsely scattered on the sides of his bald, ash-black oblong head. All said, and after the initial shock, the Ancient's overall appearance was not unfriendly or scary. In fact, it looked rather familiar. In contrast to the narrow head, the Ancient's shoulders were broad and squared, like those of a warrior in his prime.

As the Ancient approached, Fungai felt the urge to stand, as he would when a senior officer approached. He just managed to sit up.

'Relax, Fungai, I will explain,' the Ancient spoke, placing a hand on Fungai's shoulders. 'I am of ancient blood, most of my kind are gone. Bits of my blood run through a few humans. But it is getting weaker over time.

Fungai had heard of the Ancients' myth, but he had believed it was just another bedtime story.

'Since your birth, twenty-nine seasons ago, we have watched and, to some extent, nurtured you. Your grandfather did a great job in your early years and your teacher and the nurse helped us take care of you while you were in school. Do you remember them?'

Fungai could almost hear the cogs in his brain going back. He remembered the mission school, the priest who used to call him Francis telling him the Fox, his grandfather, had been arrested by the colonial administrator. He remembered the kind nurse taking care of him when he fainted after hearing the news.

All this had been planned, orchestrated? This was almost impossible to believe, he thought to himself.

'Yes, I have played a small part in shaping you, clearing your path. But you have proved to be worthy in every way. You have not disappointed us. You have exceeded our expectations. To a large extent, you have been a master of your own device.'

A master of your own device? Where did I hear that? He wondered.

'No, you have not heard that anywhere, I just made it up. But you will hear it in lyrics in the future.'

Fungai did not like the way this ... strange looking ancient humanoid ... could read his mind.

'Mind your thoughts,' the Ancient spoke with something close to a smile on his face. 'Ira here was born at the same time, in fact, the same minute you were born in one of the Tano villages. We have trained her to have telepathic powers, among other things. She has felt you, comforted you and transmitted ideas to you. Consider her as our medium, reaching out to you whenever you are in need, in danger, or just feeling down. She helped you anticipate the future. This skill you have used well to survive.'

'Today, you start the next phase of your journey. All the knowledge that she has, she will pass to you. All the abilities she possesses, you will have. She will be your guide and partner. Whatever you need, she will provide. Now, if you will allow me,' the Ancient approached and, like Ira, placed his head against Fungai's chest, listening to his heartbeat. He started chanting incantations, like a catholic priest reciting prayers in Latin, in a tongue that Fungai assumed to be the language of the Ancients. Unlike Ira's sweet smell of jasmine flower and marula fruit, he had an earthy smell like a fusion of herbs and soil.

'Yes, I know, I smell like a bowl of soup mixed with manure,' he said, cracking a hearty laugh. 'And yes, I don't smell or look as beautiful as Ira.'

Unbelievable, Fungai thought. *He is reading my thoughts, even before I finish thinking.*

'I thought you said you would not read my thoughts.' Fungai commented, now a bit relaxed.

'Oops! I couldn't resist. My ability to read your mind is a power you could possess if you were able to use your full brain power. You humans have failed to exploit your full potential. Do you know you only use ten per cent of your intellectual abilities? Come, son, we start your lesson now.'

The Ancient placed his fingertips on Fungai's temples. At first, the fingers felt cold and lifeless, then a warmth like nothing he had experienced before permeated throughout his body. He could feel every nerve, every muscle warming up. He relaxed; his hands slipped to his side. His eyelids closed. He was asleep, yet alert. Then—the dream ...

Fungai: Arrival Of The Ancients

In the dream, it seemed like Fungai was a cast in a movie set. He was one of many, not the actor though. He was just there on the set, like an extra, observing, seeing, feeling, even smelling, completely immersed.

In one scene, they were in some form of craft that was moving through space with stars all around them. Some of the stars were only specks at a distance, while others were fireballs passing them at an amazing speed. 'Focus on that blue star,' a soothing voice guided him. A blue speck way out in the distance seemed to be growing and glowing brighter. As they approached it, its shape became clearer. It reminded him of a mushroom.

The scene changed. They were now floating above what seemed like a blue liquid. The craft reduced speed then skimmed the surface of the blue liquid.

'At last, we have arrived at our destination, our new home.' A familiar voice announced. It felt like they had been travelling in space for some time. 'We made it ... arrived. Joyous shouts from other passengers erupted around him.

'Others like us have been here before. We know where we're going.' The same familiar voice announced, like a captain of a passenger plane.

We glided into the bluish liquid before coming to a stop. He scanned around the craft. He saw creatures swimming. As he looked above from where they had come from, he saw others flying. Way out in the distance, he saw land creatures that he identified as dinosaurs.

The dream changed—a different scene and perspective. He was standing on the precipice of a rock, looking down into the shimmering waters of a familiar lake. Blue waters in the dead centre of a crater. A flying craft shaped like a mushroom fleetingly skimmed the dark blue waters. Its colour seemed to change as it moved, reflecting the hues of the dark water from blue to aqua green to shiny metallic greys. 'It is as beautiful as it is scary,' he said to himself. A stem-like structure protruding from the underbelly of the mushroom-like vehicle belched a bluish-grey substance. It created a huge water fountain as it caressed the water's surface before it slowly descended and then disappeared into the deep waters. He heard no sound but he sensed air moving around him, vibrations that tickled his skin and penetrated deep into his brain. He was confused. It was like his body was not his—like someone else had taken control of it. He had never experienced anything like that before. It was bewildering and frightening.

He noticed he was not alone. Others like him, young and old, observed the object in amazement. Some started to run, hiding in their round mud huts. Others stayed put, mesmerised by the object even though they were scared. The cattle and wildlife ran off helter-skelter, also confused.

'Wake up Fungai, wake up … wake up!' He heard a voice, a faint echo coming, then fading away.

He woke up.

A bit groggy and confused by the dream that seemed so real that he could feel the tickling vibrations, see the craft so clearly hovering over the deep waters before disappearing into what he now realised was *Mai Siri*, the sacred secret lake.

Fungai noticed the young woman, white as freshly fallen snow. Her pink eyes close to his, clear and full of compassion, beaming a message to his brain—a message of love and caring.

Fungai, fully awake now, realised he had been moved onto a bed in a different room. A display of multi-coloured, organic-like gems lit up the room with light as bright as a sunny day at noon.

'Where am I?'

'This will be your, or rather our, room for the duration of your training,' Ira responded, a huge smile on her face. The large gap between her front teeth making her seem kind.

'What just happened?' Fungai asked, seemingly confused.

'What did you see in your dream?' Ira asked.

'Well, there was this spaceship that disappeared into the lake, I think the Mai Siri.'

'You just had your first lesson on the arrival of the Ancients. What you saw happened over ten thousand years ago, long before Julius Caesar and Jesus. The Ancients have been here since. Only a handful of *The True*, as they call themselves, survive today but their blood runs in you, me and a thousand or so souls scattered around the world. Only those with a high level of their blood can experience what you just went through, and even then, only one or two in a generation. I am not one of them. You are *One*. Now we eat, then you rest. You have a long night ahead of you.'

Ira clapped twice. The door opened, three girls entered, placing three trays of food on the low table on the side of the wall. The first tray was a steaming hot stew. It contained different sea creatures, some had hard shells, others had long tentacles, some looked like insects. The stew filled the room with an unfamiliar but exquisite aroma. A second tray was piled with different types of bread and the third tray had two bowls of what looked like a white pudding. The food was accompanied by a gourd of wine—or so Fungai hoped. His stomach grumbled noticeably. The girls laughed, exchanging conspiratorial glances with Ira. The girls, not more than sixteen, were the same as Ira—albinos, yet all had different features. One looked almost like the Ancient Fungai had seen earlier, another was more like himself in features, except for the very pale skin colour. They all looked extremely athletic. They walked like trained warriors, light on their feet, strong but measured steps, body upright.

'Sit, enjoy the food.' Ira said pointing to the cushion on the floor next to the small table. Though apprehensive of the insect-looking things, he ate with gusto, clearing the stew and several slices of bread. The food, strange as it was, was excellent.

'The food is weird but unbelievably good,' Fungai commented as he finished his serving of the white pudding.

'Have some wine.' Ira filled a cup with a bluish-pinkish liquid that bubbled like champagne as it was poured, passing it to Fungai before filling her own cup. The strong aroma from the wine was nothing like he had smelled before, even though he had lived in several countries and experienced many wines.

He sipped the wine, amazingly light on his tongue, like a mix of air and liquid, yet velvety smooth, neither sweet nor bitter. It had no musky after-taste like most alcoholic drinks do. Utterly amazing.

Fungai licked his lips with appreciation. 'This is like nothing I have tasted. I can only describe it as ... out of this world,' he declared, looking at Ira now, posting a sweet smile.

'The formula is of ancient origin and you are correct, it is literally from out of this world. The Ancients say it used to be the wine of the people in their other world.'

Ira clapped her hands again. The girls filed into the room, cleared the table and immediately left.

'It's midnight now up there in your world, you must be tired,' Ira said as she stood up and approached Fungai. She presented her arm, helping him up with a firm grip and a strong pull.

'I like strong women.' Fungai remarked as they stood close to each other.

'Careful what you wish for. If you charm a snake you may get bitten, so you better have an antidote for its poison,' Ira responded with a sly smile. 'You rest. Tomorrow will be a busy day for you.' Ira sighed loudly as though regretting that she had to go. She released his hand, walked backwards two steps, curtsied politely, turned and left the room.

Fungai stayed awake for a long time, reliving the day, remembering every detail. His mind was full of questions. Feeling good, he closed his eyes. 'Good wine requires patience,' he remembered a saying from his late Grandfather Ramla as he fell into a deep slumber.

Fungai could not breathe. Hard and sudden, he twisted his body but strong arms choked his throat, strong legs around his waist, pinning him down. This was the nightmare of warriors, to get caught napping. He was getting out of breath.

I have to do something quickly. 'Brain beats brute strength,' he remembered his Captain's motto. He feigned submission, pretending to have blacked out. He felt the attacker's grip loosen. Immediately, he kicked his legs hard, upwards, recoiling like an acrobat doing a back flip. The attacker was unprepared for the sudden and powerful move. They landed on the hard stone floor. A high-pitched scream of a woman, magnified by the acoustics, reverberated beyond the room.

The attacker was no longer strangling him. He took long, deep breaths to clear his mind but he was still confused. Looking around, he saw Ira on the floor, blood streaming from the back of her head. He noticed the Ancient, standing not three paces away, a smirk on his face.

The Ancient clapped his hands, clap, clap, clap, appreciating Fungai's fighting skills. 'You're indeed the son of Fumi.' The Ancient declared boisterously in the language of the Tano people.

'Have you ever heard of the phrase, "sleep with one eye open?" Lesson one, you must never be caught unawares again!' With finality, the Ancient uttered with a commanding voice. 'We believe a strong body is as important as a good mind. You will be in the hands of Ira, the tip of our warriors' spear, a combat master and the best there is.' And then, the training started. True to the Ancient's words, Ira was better than good. She was truly a master.

'Men think strength is the greatest weapon. I say men are morons,' Ira goaded Fungai. 'I see you think the same, so like most men, you're a moron unless, of course, you can beat me.' She brought down her fighting stick hard, aiming for Fungai's head.

He had not anticipated her speed. Before he could react, he was already on the floor, not only bleeding from his nose but also with a dislocated shoulder and without his stick, which she had snatched as it fell. The pain in his shoulder was excruciating but worse, the shame was humiliating. Hiding the pain and shame, Fungai picked himself up, one knee, then the other, now angry that he let his guard down … again! He straightened up and tried to square his shoulders. Pain shot through his dislocated shoulder but, like a warrior, he showed no sign of discomfort.

Smiling, raised eyebrows, Ira asked, 'you're sure you want to continue?'

'Yes, let's get on with it.'

'No. Come over,' she instructed.

She inspected his shoulder carefully, tenderly touching the bruise, feeling the muscles. Suddenly and without warning, she pulled and twisted his upper arm. Fungai screamed in pain even as he heard a popping sound. The pain subsided. He rotated his shoulder slowly, it seemed fine.

'You're evil and good,' Fungai told her.

'Ready? This time don't be a moron, use your mind, let your eyes guide you,' she said touching her eyes and head. 'You must think like a fox, watch like a cat, uncoil like a cobra and bite like a hyena. Speed, my friend, is *your* friend.'

Now up and alert, Fungai jumped high, coming down with a spin kick. Ira moved, only slightly, at lightning speed. She shifted her weight to one foot, pirouetted and flipped backwards. Airborne, she smashed his chest with both legs before landing, one hand on the floor. Fungai, in shock, fell backwards, barely managing to soften his fall with his arms, his chest exploding with pain. For a moment, he couldn't breathe. He wondered, *will I ever beat this woman warrior?*

'Good effort, but obviously not good enough.' Ira said as she tapped his back, offered a hand and pulled him up.

'Worry not, my friend, you will get there,' she said, as though reading his mind.

Somehow, by the end of the three hours of training, though bruised, bloodied and dog-tired, he could defend himself. He had learned more hand-to-hand combat in that short time than he had in his entire military career.

'This is only the start. I expect you to challenge me as an equal ... in six moons.'

'What? Am going to be here for six moons?'

'Have you got somewhere else to go? The last time I heard your friend, President Onim the Crocodile, was after you. And you have all that science, astrology, astronomy, philosophy and whatever else those old Ancients do out there to learn.'

'You have a point there.' Fungai accepted the logic but he still couldn't understand why he was here in the first place.

'But why me? Why not Binti Sidai or any one of the other warriors?'

Ira looked at him for a long time. 'You, my friend, are the chosen one—*The One*,' she emphasised.

'Now enough of that, we need food.' She clapped her hands three times and on cue, as though they had been waiting outside the door, the girls walked in with three trays of food.

'There is yet another lesson I am supposed to give you,' Ira said as they finished their meal. 'This one, you will enjoy. Shower first, then back to class.'

The lesson was better than good. It was combat but of a different kind. Soft whilst rough, fantastic, emotional, climactic, draining and satisfying at the same time. Ira, sleeping in his arms, snored loudly, visibly happy. Her face angel-like, her body soft and remarkably relaxed.

What a woman! Physically tough as nails. In combat, dangerous, unyielding and unforgiving, yet in bed, soft and sensual, like a flower petal. Emotionally, they seem to have connected at a level he had not experienced with any other woman, including Beki, who he loved very much. As he was drowsing off, the warning of the Ancient invaded his mind. 'Sleep with one eye open.' Before falling into a deep, dreamless slumber.

The next day, as usual, Fungai heard the footsteps of the Ancient—now familiar. Unlike other days, the Ancient did not enter the room.

'Follow me, Fungai,' the Ancient instructed, a frown on his face. The Ancient turned and started walking along the corridors. Fungai followed, keeping pace, a step behind.

'Your people say, "Listen to the wisdom of the ancestors, become wise." Our kind cannot move in your world freely. If we did, we would be seen as aliens and therefore threatening. We would be treated as enemies. Why? You ask. Because humans fear difference, and as you know, fear breeds hatred. That is the nature of weak minds. Yet, on rare occasions, we go out there, hooded and all, to recalibrate our compasses and to update our knowledge of the *homo sapiens.* We have witnessed the worst and the best of your nature. Over the years, we have seen wars, genocides, hunger, diseases, slavery and other extreme suffering.'

The Ancient stopped, turned and stared at Fungai with his squinty, wet-looking eyes. 'But we have also observed the growth of science, innovations and technology—that, my son, is where we must focus your energy,' the Ancient surmised. He waved his hand chest high as though swatting a fly. An opening appeared, like a trap door, hidden within the ancient wall of the corridor with tiny glowing lights.

They walked into what seemed like another world, a mystic yet futuristic world. Small rooms dug into the walls were lined up like Egyptian burial chambers. Each was occupied by a small team, clearly immersed in their work. In one chamber, Fungai noticed sophisticated-looking gear with dials and screens that seemed to glow with an organic backlight. In another, a group of Ancients observed real-size 3D images of other Aliens who seemed to be going about their business, oblivious, in a different world.

'Those are images of our Ancestors captured thousands of lightyears ago and only now being received by our team. It is an effort to piece together the knowledge of our past ancestors.'

'Is your world still in existence?' Fungai enquired.

'That is precisely the question we're trying to answer. Every day we receive images but it is like chasing history. All the information is many lightyears past. We are yet to catch up with their time. Our technology does not allow real-time communication.'

They continued moving along, seeing the Ancients involved in experiments in astronomy, science, technology and even math. Moving on, they entered a large, dome-shaped, semi-circular theatre, which looked like a huge greenhouse. Part of it was filled with alien vegetables, grains and fruit trees meticulously cultivated in neat rows. Fungai saw shrubbery, vines and trees he had never seen before. The plants were a mix of numerous vibrant colours. An organic kaleidoscope of the rainbow, unlike anything he had seen. It was entrancing, a sensory, almost spiritual delight. Beautifully coloured birds and butterflies of all sizes and shapes fluttered among the greens, reds, yellows, purples, blues, violets and indigoes of the vegetation. A colony of small wasp-like insects humming in unison dangled from one of the trees. They came across pens enclosing alien-looking domesticated animals. Fungai looked up, expecting to see a blue sky, but all he saw was the high roof of the large dome. A skylight pierced the dome, creating a hallowing light that covered every part of the huge garden.

'We have seventy-nine of these gardens, with thousands of curated plants from other ancient worlds. This space is dedicated to organisms from our planet. If need be, we can feed the population of the people of the Tano tribe for years. We have done so in the past but that history is for another lesson.

'You have seen with your own eyes, not through dreaming, a bit of our work and our world. Remember, this is as real as President Onim blasting your office not a week ago. You will learn more but for now, you take a break and get to discover other things with your soulmate, Ira.' He concluded.

My soulmate? Is that what Ira is? Fungai wondered.

Fungai had lost track of the days and weeks spent in the belly of the volcanic mountain. His routine was as regular as clockwork. Ira woke him up. They had breakfast before she disappeared. He took a quick shower before the Ancient appeared for what Ira termed a 'dreaming session with the Ancient.'

In one of such 'dreaming' sessions, models of chemical elements, differently colored and of different sizes floated in the air, they came together forming complex chemicals. Sometimes they separated, in slow motion and sometimes they explode, producing noise, fire, heat, pressure, electric shock, high frequency buzzing, all forms of energy in the process.

He learned charts of different elements, their energy levels and sources. He saw magnetism and anti-magnetism at work, fusion and diffusion. In the background a voice explained every chemical element and reaction with unforgettable clarity. What was most amazing was, he remembered every lesson—days later.

When not in the 'dreaming' state, the Ancient took him around, exploring the underground environments. 'That one is a transactinide,' he heard the voice of the Ancient. 'This group here are reactive elements.' The old Ancient pointed to a strand of a shiny rock outcrop as they walked through one of the caves. 'Be careful with these,' he continued, 'they have a power that can bend your mind, make you see visions and do things you can't imagine. This formation here creates ultra-low radio waves that can penetrate kilometres of other rocks and also generate radioactive sonic waves. The rocks are highly catalytic and will explode with the right trigger.' All the time in a monotone, the Ancient explained, imparting knowledge like no other teacher had done.

The dreaming sessions gave him knowledge of the universe, stars and planets, some unknown to mankind. Most scary, though, was the knowledge that there were other lifeforms living with us, yet not visible or discernible to us—but affected by human action.

'From now on, you will feel them and sometimes see them. Learn to read their form, nature and movement and you will see and understand things well ahead of others. This will not only allow you to combat Ira, your friend, as an equal but it will give you predictive powers that others will think is magic or prophetic.'

In another dreaming session, he saw what was and what will be. He visualised masses of data of all kinds. He came to understand in great detail how the global systems worked. How politics, human and geopolitical relations, money and influence worked.

'You humans are obsessed with power. It turns out, though, that power is like poison. The fear of losing power drives people to do evil things rather than using it for good.' The Ancient explained to Fungai. 'See for yourself.'

As though observing through a peephole, he saw powerful men and women making life-and-death decisions from way before the pharaohs of ancient Egypt and kings of Mesopotamia. Like watching a movie, he observed Hitler ordering armies to do unspeakable evils to the Jews to cement his power with his Germanic clan. He saw Jews in Israel do the exact same thing to Palestinians. He watched as Idi Amin of Uganda slaughtered whole villages just to prove that he was powerful. Then, the movie turned to the future. He saw leaders in what was considered progressive democratic nations promising democracy, peace, order and freedom while they planned to usurp more power, domination and war. They talked of legacy but destroyed what was.

'It is the nature of humans to destroy,' the Ancient observed in a sad tone. 'You will also help destroy in order to create. That is what humans understand, that is the way it shall be.'

As the Ancient said this, his life flashed before him like a movie being fast-forwarded. He saw his final moment, his final instructions—keep the dream alive. Following this revelation, he saw his son becoming a great leader of his people.

'You have seen your history, your people have been the victims of domination, subjugation and slavery. They have borne the brunt of human greed and calamities from drought, hunger and disease resulting from the actions of others. Your purpose in life will be to give your people a chance to defend and protect themselves from the atrocities of others.'

By the end of each lesson, Fungai was exhausted but always buoyed by the knowledge and wisdom he gained. He would be looking forward to the physical lessons with Ira and now with other warriors of the Ancients.

'You ... you ... I see you have gained our knowledge, haven't you?' Ira, smiling, commented after a training session. 'You can see now. You can truly see, can't you?'

True to the Ancient's teaching, he was able to feel other life forms. He was able to see his opponent's movement well before it happened. He felt them, the unseen lifeforms, what Ira called the *Pepo*, meaning shadows or winds in the Tano tongue. They warned him, he listened, sensed them and moved with them.

He evaded, blocked and countered so well that not a single blow touched him. He was able to twist and turn faster and jump higher than Ira. It was as though the *Pepo* conducted and assisted him. Other warriors became wary of him. They soon started treating him with deep respect, reverence almost. They bowed to him as they did to the Elders of the Ancients.

'The One ... you truly are.' Ira told him after a hectic session. Wrapping her arms around him in a loving embrace.

'I don't know what you're talking about but I am happy that you're happy,' Fungai responded. Accepting her accolades.

For many days the training continued, giving Fungai unbelievable knowledge of science, technology, history and philosophy. His mind and body were in a prime state, his ability to predict, see and feel the *Pepo* made him a formidable human specimen for a future he was just starting to discern.

'Knowledge is important but even more so is how you use it. The question is, do you use it for good or for evil?' the Ancient contemplated in one of their training sessions. He was speaking as though reflecting to himself, an old man lost in his thoughts. 'The Elders' Council of the Ancients wishes to talk to you. Follow me.'

Fungai: It's Time

They moved through the corridors, Fungai following the Ancient as trained, a step behind and slightly to the left, in silence. Ira did the same but to the right. Through the lush vegetation of the subterranean arboretum, Fungai reflected on how meagre his knowledge had been before meeting the Ancients. He considered how much he had learned and yet, there was more.

'We now approach the House of the Elders,' the Ancient warned. 'Remember, you are here to listen and learn.' Guards, fully geared with laser guns, stood guard in front of a huge ebony door. They raised their left arms in salute to the Ancient. One looked at Fungai as though he was an alien, nevertheless, he bowed low to him.

As one of them opened the door, they entered a huge room filled with light from the dome-shaped roof. A giant ancient form sat at the head of a huge oblong table. On closer scrutiny, Fungai realised the Ancient was a female, the only one he had encountered thus far. Her thick lips, lighter than the rest of her face, opened up into a huge smile. Strangely, the smile and her light grey eyes made him relax.

'Son of Fumi, please have a seat.' She welcomed him, pointing to a seat next to her. 'Did you know your grandfather's name, Ramla, means the prophet or seer in the ancient language? Most of us knew him as we now know you: a great warrior. We owe a lot to him.

'My blood runs through you. For a thousand generations, we have lived with the Tano people. At one point, we were dominant. We ruled over many local tribes, then came the era of the plagues and our numbers dwindled ... more like decimated. A few of us survived, a bit more of the mixed Ancient and Tano blood survived. You, Fungai son of Fumi, come from one of these lines.

'You have the gifts from both races and like your grandfather, you have learned to exploit these gifts. You are now able to see and feel things before they happen. I am told you not only visualise but can manipulate the shadow forms, what your people call *pepo* or ghosts. Son of Fumi, use these gifts wisely.' The leader of the Ancients cautioned.

'Remember, this is a gift. Many have come seeking the knowledge of the Ancients, and some even died in their quest for it. Lore talks of white men coming from the north, asking of the lost clan of the Ancients. The lore says they drank water from the forbidden springs. They all went mad and killed each other. Their leader called himself Livingston. You may have read about him.' She spoke with a rough but calm voice, a smile on her narrow, long face.

'Now, unlike your warrior father, you will use your knowledge to give your people and your young nations hope—a dream. You already know what I am talking about, don't you?'

Strangely, Fungai knew exactly what the Ancient at the head of the table was talking about. He had dreamed of this the night before.

'It is time to start your journey. You will be *The* One among a small group of wise men and women scattered around the world. People of science and inventions, makers of things, healers, people who deal with money and politics. You will have connections that go to the top, including with intelligence organisations in many countries. Use our resources and knowledge wisely. Build your dream. Now go in peace.' She concluded with a wave of her long arm.

'Thank you, Nana Mkulu,' he responded, using the respected term for a great grandmother. Bowing low, he clapped three times, a sign of acknowledgement and respect, before leaving the Elders' Hall. And his journey began. It would lead him to the USA, Europe, China and ultimately Australia, where he would set up his base.

Chapter 13:
Fumi - Sydney

**"It's not what you take, but what
you leave behind that defines greatness."**
(Edward Gardner)

Fumi saw Professor Osman el Nijere mowing the lawn in front of his house. The Prof waved him over. 'Come over, son. How was your day? How would you like an African dish for dinner? Come by tomorrow. I promise you will enjoy it.'

After dinner, Professor Osman el Nijere cleared his voice. In a low, measured professorial tone, he spoke to Fumi. 'A wise man once said, "It's not what you take but what you leave behind that defines greatness." When you are my age, old and approaching the end, what do you want to be remembered as? A great football player or a great thinker and leader of his people?'

Fumi had not anticipated being questioned about his future. But he had been excited that he would be entering university in the fall. He stood up from the low sofa, went to the fridge and got a Coke, allowing himself a moment to reflect on the question.

'Well,' he started. 'Soccer has been my dream from when I was a small boy playing in the muddy field behind Mama Maria's refuge. My friends tell me I am a great player. "You should definitely give it a go," they say. But you, sir, have told me I am destined for great things as a leader to my people. At this point, I am not sure of my next move.'

'Son, when you are lost and you need to get your bearings, look back from where you have come.' The professor spoke in a low monotone as though talking to himself. 'For now, I would advise you to take a break, go back to Africa and catch up with your Mama Maria. Maybe that will help you find your purpose. You know, your destiny is written in the books of your ancestors.'

Where have I heard that? Fumi wondered. *Yes! From Grandma Maria,* he remembered. *Is it a coincidence that the Professor uses the same phrase she once did and, at the same time, asks me to go and visit her?* This thought lingered in Fumi's mind long into the night.

'How was your dinner with the Prof yesterday?' Ben asked as they sat down for breakfast, as was customary in the Crawford home.

'It was great. He made a beef stew with peanut sauce, served with plantain. I swear it tasted exactly like Grandma Maria's stew. But the meat was more tender. An expensive cut for sure.'

'Good to hear you enjoyed your meal. What did you talk about?'

'My future, finding my purpose in life, going back to my roots, visiting Grandma Maria in Zimai to help me make up my mind before going to university.'

'I think that's a great idea. Jennifer can organise travel for you.'

'It's okay, Mr. Crawford. I will do that myself and don't worry about the ticket, I have enough saved from allowances and tutoring. You have already given me so much.'

'As you wish son but remember, we're here for you.'

And so, Fumi left for Zimai. He had a great time meeting his old friends, but most importantly, he saw Noah's village with new eyes. The poverty, the daily struggles of men and women to feed their families, something he had taken for granted. It reminded him of the Professor's quote, '... it is what you leave behind that defines greatness,' he made up his mind before heading back to Massachusetts.

After taking a quick shower and changing from his travelling clothes, he went to the house across the street. 'Hello Prof, I am back,' he announced himself.

'Yes, I can see that. How was your trip? Did you give that letter to Mama Maria?'

'Yes, I did, she was overjoyed to see me, then ecstatic when she received your letter. You must have gifted her a lot of money because she couldn't stop asking about you. It was weird. She wanted to know everything. How does he look like? Is he healthy? What does he like eating? She couldn't stop asking questions about you.' Fumi said as he passed a letter from Mama Maria. 'She told me to deliver this to you immediately I arrived.'

The Prof accepted the letter, his eyes averted, something clearly on his mind. 'And how was she?' He enquired.

'She has grown older but in good health. Now she has a big place with many women and girls, so she does not have to work too hard.'

'And how is Zimai?' The Prof went on.

'It is poor. People are struggling to make ends meet and the old President Nima has become delusional and dangerous,' Fumi summarised. 'Thanks for suggesting I visit Zimai, it did help me see things differently. To separate a population from poverty, one has to influence governments and people, and that requires power. And as you know, information and money can be very powerful. So, finance and IT is what I will study, and a bit of soccer on the side.' Fumi said and then strolled to the fridge and poured himself a glass of orange juice.

A big smile spread across the Professor's old face, followed by a haughty laugh that reverberated within the large living room. 'Son, I couldn't have made a better move myself. One eye on what is, another one on what can be … I dare say that is wise—very clever indeed,' the Prof said loudly in between his affable laugh. He went over to Fumi and gave him a huge hug.

'By the way, I got a letter of offer from your economics school. I also got a sports scholarship. I am taking both offers, playing college soccer while I focus on IT and finance,' Fumi told the Professor.

'This calls for a celebration.' He went over to his wine cabinet and pulled out an 18-year-old Balvenie whisky. 'For eight years, this bottle has been in the cabinet waiting for this very occasion. I bought it the day you arrived. You remember the day?'

Four years later, just before his graduation, the Prof, now retired, invited Fumi to his home. 'I have some friends who would like to meet you,' he told him on the phone.

As he entered, he heard voices at the back of the house. The Prof, a woman and a man, stood on the balcony, looking out at the Charles River some distance away, chatting. They turned around as he slid the back door to the balcony. Their casual wear, jeans and t-shirts, pronounced their fit bodies. As a soccer player, Fumi was fit, but these two looked extremely fit. *They have to be in contact sports or perhaps the military!* Fumi wondered as he approached them and shook their hands. Firm grips, course palms—gym, weights ... definitely sports people. *Their stance, legs firmly grounded, spread out, chest a bit out ... I wager my bet, military or some other such agency,* Fumi concluded.

'How are you, son, meet my friends, they want to make you an offer.' Fungai noticed that the Prof did not introduce them by name. 'Meet Mr. Fumi Crawford, my neighbour and former student.'

Fumi got himself a beer from a small fridge at the end of the balcony.

'Fumi,' the woman started. 'I will be direct and to the point. We are here to offer you a job. My former Professor has spoken highly of you but we have also been watching you. I am told your IT and finance skills are exemplary, as are your soccer skills. We are looking for an analyst to join our small government intelligence team.'

So, I was right, Fumi thought.

'The pay is lousy, to tell you the truth,' the man interjected. 'But you will be working with some of the best analysts this country has.' In concert, the woman picked up from the man. 'You look like someone who likes being fit. I can assure you our training will keep you in tip-top shape. Besides, you will learn a lot of other skills.'

These guys know how to get what they want, Fumi was thinking, *but at least they are honest.*

Later that evening, after the two had left, Prof sat Fumi down. 'You have a long journey ahead of you,' he started. 'To be a leader, you will face many challenges and even danger. You will need to understand how the world works, especially the who and how. This agency will provide you with all that, think of it as a training ground. Work with them for a couple of years, learn as much as possible and then see what comes up after that. In the meantime, I have my own proposition to make to you.'

The Prof explained his concept. Fumi loved it, so they set out to work.

And so, it came to be, as his destiny had been written. As a government analyst, he learned secrets that only a few knew. He developed skills that made him a formidable man. On the side, he worked with the Prof, secretly developing and patenting a finance platform that was way beyond anything in the market.

'There is a private client who is interested in buying our program for his exclusive use. He is willing to pay way beyond what we could get if we put it out in the market.' The Prof informed Fumi one evening after testing the program for bugs for maybe the fiftieth time.

'What are we talking about in numbers, Professor?

'Let's just say it is more than enough for a lifetime. You will be so rich you will be able to remove President Nima if you so desire.'

'Well ... now you're talking Prof!'

The Futures Group

'Hi Dr. Crawford, what do you know about The Futures Group?' Fumi asked Ben at the family Sunday dinner.

'Why do you ask?'

'I got an unsolicited offer to attend an interview with them in Sydney, of all places, all costs paid.'

'Wow!' Sandra shouted. 'It seems like you're going places, bro. Can I come with you?' She asked, a grin on her face.

'You should talk to Prof Osman. He might have a connection with The Futures Group,' Ben responded in a way that suggested he knew more than he wanted to share.

After dinner, Fumi went across to Prof's house. The Professor seemed very excited.

'Fumi, my son, how are you? Anything exciting happening to you?'

'Sir, that's precisely why I need your advice. Do you know anything about The Futures Group—TFG?'

'Well, funny you should ask, the Chairman was my colleague at the university. Brilliant chap, I must say. I must also disclose that I have worked for The Futures Group before.'

'So, you had something to do with this?' Fumi asked, a grin on his face.

'Well, I admit I have talked with their chairman about you. They are also the company that wants to buy our computer program. You see the connection?'

'Prof, you shouldn't have done that. I know you mean well but perhaps you could have consulted me first?' Fumi said with a smile.

'Why don't you go to Sydney, then make up your mind after that?'

As he made travel arrangements, he could not resist the feeling that there was a bigger game at play and the Professor was in the thick of it.

Arriving in Sydney, he met the Chairman of the Board of The Futures Group. He had expected it would be a white man. Instead, it was a very big black man, not unlike himself, wearing a Nike tracksuit and loafers as though he was going boating. He occupied a huge office overlooking Sydney harbour. For a moment, Fumi was confused, he had thought he was meeting the CEO, Mr. O'Rilley.

'Hello Fumi, welcome to Sydney.' The old man, who looked somewhat familiar, spoke with a huge smile on his face. He seemed extremely excited, like he had just reconnected with an old friend he had not seen for a long time. Fumi wondered, *what's the fuss about?*

'I hope you had a good flight.'

'Yes sir, first class. Thanks to your company, I couldn't ask for more.'

'Don't mention it. Only the best for my boy. By the way, everyone calls me Mr. Fungai.'

Mr. Fungai came around the huge desk and took time to look Fumi over like he was appraising him, which made Fumi feel very uncomfortable. Then, without warning, he gave him a vigorous hug, like a father would to a son.

'Have a seat, son,' Mr. Fungai spoke with a strong African accent that had a tinge of an American drawl. 'Mr. O'Rilley, my acting CEO, could not meet with you. Instead, you meet this ugly old African. But then again, you're lucky to meet the Chairman of TFG,' Mr. Fungai said with a wink.

Again, Fumi could not hide his surprise.

'Yes, Fumi, it is I, an African, who is the Chairman. And you, an African, though much younger and much more handsome, will be the CEO. That is, if you decide to take the job.'

Fumi could not believe this. He felt dizzy. His research of the TFG had yielded little information except that it was a privately owned multi-billion-dollar company with operations and assets across the world. To be the CEO of such a company was a very big deal.

'Miss Melissa, the lady who picked you up from the airport, will take care of your logistics. Tomorrow, she will bring you over to my house for a Friday night barbecue. I can explain TFG operations then. Melissa! Please come over and meet this lovely Harvard lad,' Mr. Fungai shouted across the room to the young lady. 'Take a day off tomorrow and show him around?'

'Thank you, sir. I would love to see Sydney.' Fumi said.

'Okay, it is settled then. See you tomorrow evening,' Mr. Fungai concluded, a huge smile on his face.

'What a character,' Fumi commented as they took the lift to the basement. In a new BMW, she drove leisurely, allowing him to appreciate the views of the beach, the waves and the blue waters. He lowered the window, the fresh spring breeze was refreshing after the long flight. They turned onto Campbell Parade, then up a hill to an apartment block perched high on a rocky outcrop that overlooked the Bondi beach on one side and the Bondi golf course on the other. They took a private lift to a penthouse on the 15th floor.

'180 degrees views of the famous Bondi beach, the sea, a golf course? Fantastic! How much rent do you pay for this?' Fumi remembered his small, dingy bachelor's studio in Boston.

'We don't pay rent Mr. Fumi. We own the whole block.'

That is when he realised he was now in the premier league of business.

'I know you're knackered from the long flight. I will leave you now but be ready at, say, six, the best time of the day to take a walk along the beach and perhaps order a packet of fish and chips? You will enjoy it, I assure you.'

'Thanks, Melissa. A walk and fish and chips sounds lovely,' he managed to respond before crashing on the sofa. Out of habit, he switched on the TV, flicking through the channels, searching for nothing in particular. All the talk was about some 'Melbourne Cup,' a sort of horse race in Melbourne that apparently stops the whole country. Still pondering on what kind of a horse race would stop a country, he dozed off into a deep slumber.

✦

Chapter 14:
Fungai - The Chief Is dead

"When roots decay, they spread death to the branches."
(African proverb)

Fungai stepped into his underground office, which looked more like a command centre. He reminisced on the day of the bombing thirty years ago. It was so clear in his mind, like it was yesterday. He had come a long way but felt dark shadows were gathering. They became clearer with every new day: darker, more menacing *pepo*. Ghosts that would not leave him at peace. He knew his days were coming to an end, such was the curse of a seer.

He placed his old Apple laptop on the small table next to the wall on the left. As was his custom, he surveyed the huge room, his command centre. On the right wall, like soldiers on attention. Seven large computer screens lined the wall. A large glass-topped computer pad dominated the semicircular desk. A keyboard, headphones and what looked like a gaming console completed the high-tech appearance of the room. The old MacBook laptop seemed out of place. Bookshelves lined the left wall while a small kitchenette hugged the wall across the box-like elevator. To the far side of the large room was what looked more like a workshop and electronics lab. All manner of tools, meters, wires, computer components, an assortment of drones, cameras, lenses, computer boards and other high-tech paraphernalia clogged a large workbench. On the side of the bench were cabinets and shelves that held even more equipment and materials. One held what looked like a geologic collection of rocks, gems and soil samples. A beautiful mural depicting an African eagle perched on an acacia tree against the backdrop of an African sunset dominated the back wall of this large room.

This room never ceased to make him feel safe. It was as though he was insulated, in command and nothing could touch him. He walked to the computer desk and waved at the central screen. It came to life. The large clear glass pad on the table immediately displayed a built-in keyboard. He tapped his password as he put on his headphones. A large family room appeared on the screen. He heard the voice of the woman he had once loved so much, many years ago. The mother of his boy.

Fungai picked up the gist of the talk. Beki was explaining how to prepare a vegetable salad dressing to a young woman in her Olof language. Though she was on the other side of the world, hearing her voice always warmed his heart. He missed her but he knew and accepted such was his fate. 'A life without your son and love, giving in to the man you loathe the most in the world, that is a sacrifice few can make. I love and respect you, Beki.' Fungai spoke softly to himself.

'Hey Beki, I am having visitors in half an hour,' came a booming voice in heavily accented English. 'Tell the cook to prepare food and drinks for four, we will be in the men's house. Make sure we are not disturbed.'

Fungai waved at the computer screen to his right. A house plan appeared. He touched the screen to see the figure of the person he loathed the most in the world, President Onim, the crocodile, his nemesis. Onim's face had changed. In place of the handsome young face, with neat, crew-cut hair and a well-groomed beard, was a wrinkled face blighted with dark blotches on bloated cheeks and forehead. A scanty grey goatee contrasted with his completely bald head. His eyes that sat deep in his face were blood-shot, glassy, looking like those of a fish gone bad. They told a story of an insomniac, someone tormented by nightmares and evil thinking. It was obvious he drank too much and did not sleep very well.

He kept on sniffing, like someone who had a cold. He wiped his red blood-shot eyes, wet at the corners, with a frayed handkerchief. He was breathing heavily, clearly out of breath, a sign of a very sick man. He looked directly at the camera, stood up, picked up some papers and turned, leaving through the main door.

Fungai touched 'camera 3' on the computer screen. Three men sitting on lounge chairs stood up as their President entered the room. 'Gentlemen, sit down,' Onim commanded.

'Thank you, Mr. President,' they responded as they sat.

'Well, what is the meeting about?' Onim asked.

A man who was clearly their leader cleared his voice. 'We have found him, Mr. President. It appears you were always right, he never died in the fire from the bomb blast. He is in Sydney, Australia. We have confirmed his identity and location.'

'What!? Are you sure, Juma?'

'Yes, Mr. President, here is his photo.' Juma passed a black and white photo.

Fungai zoomed into the photo. It was him, alright. The photo was taken through his sitting room window. *Clever guys,* he thought. They must have used a microdrone. *I wonder how they disabled my drone and digital camera scrambling device.*

'Bloody hell. It's the bastard, alright. Look at him, the smug look on his face, looking polished and gentlemanly,' Onim said, boiling with anger, venom in his voice. 'You have mocked me all my life, you mother fucker. You escaped from my grip, you died on me only to reappear, alive, in Australia? This is the last time you will outfox me, you son of a dog.' Onim ranted for a while longer, not able to sit, he moved around the room like a lion in a cage.

'I have survived many assassination attempts, some by local enemies, others by foreign governments. I thought I had eliminated everyone in that pathetic organisation *Antu,* who considered themselves more African than me, planning to have one government in Africa? What a joke. Like a cat, Fungai survived, like a fox, he outsmarted me, it is his time to go for good.'

Fungai watched on the screen as Onim continued on. A lunatic with a mission.

'Never mind,' Onim said, consoling himself. 'I am more powerful now. I have more resources. I have the element of surprise, I will get you, old friend. This time, you are not escaping my wrath.' It was as though Onim was talking to him in person.

'The Croc is fired up ... oh! I have foreseen this day, and I am prepared.' Fungai spoke to himself as he vigorously rubbed his hands against each other, taking joy from the angst of his enemy.

Jose Tsango: Complicit

"The scars in my heart are not from my enemies."
(African Proverb)

At 11.30 pm on a warm Saturday night, Mr. Fungai headed to his study, leaving Taska, his border collie, asleep on the couch in the living room. He had made all the preparations and done everything he needed to do. 'I am ready to go,' he murmured to himself.

At that very moment, on the other side of the world, President Onim was reviewing his plans to finish Mr. Fungai, his old friend, his most worthy adversary. 'This time, there will be no fuck-ups, okay?' He shouted to Juma through his cell phone.

From his daily surveillance of President Onim's home and local intelligence from Africa, Fungai already knew all of their plans, when they would come, how many and how they intended to terminate his life. He had seen his killers, he knew their names, families and where they lived.

Juma and Fela, the best among President Onim's security personnel, had set up a base at Crows Nest, a North Sydney suburb along the Princess Highway. They had done their homework, scouted out Mr. Fungai's residence and set up 24-hour surveillance. After three days of staking out the residence, they had established that Mr. Fungai's security team occupied the house adjacent to Mr. Fungai's. Juma had sent photos of the two security personnel to the President's intelligence unit in Zonga. He had received a two-page dossier.

"Matadi, former special forces and intelligence officer, Zonga. Found guilty and jailed for life on charges of sedition with intent to overthrow the government. Capsized in a boat en route to Kwamunge Maximum Security Jail, presumed dead. Relatives unknown," President Onim read. A photo of a younger-looking Matadi in combat attire was attached to the one-pager. "Mr. Jose Tsango: born in Baju, studied in Paris. IT and cybersecurity specialist. He was head of the National Intelligence Service in Baju. Left to pursue a Master's degree in IT security in Australia. Now an Australian citizen. He regularly sends money to his family, Mother, wife and three teenage children in Baju."

As part of their surveillance, Juma and his mate had followed Fungai and Matadi, observing how they talked to each other, their body language, congratulating each other whenever one had a good golf shot. He had seen them lunching after playing, concluding they were not just employer-employee, they were good friends. Besides, as his intel report had indicated, 'no known family.'

Juma made his decision. 'Matadi would be a difficult nut to crack. He is too close to Mr. Fungai. Jose Tsango, is an easier target, he's our man,' he told Fela. He remembered an African saying, 'Use honey to catch the honey badger.' He knew how they would get Jose.

Jose sat at the bar counter of the popular Patonga Beach Hotel, enjoying a cold beer while chewing the complementary peanuts. The peanuts, for some reason, reminded him of his grandmother, a peanut farmer. He felt a light breeze from the sea, he looked out, squinting from the reflection of grey-blue water. A catamaran was pulling into the jetty. A couple stepped off, joyfully laughing as they shook hands with the skipper. He sipped his beer. *I like Australian beer, especially this Carlton draught, frothy, creamy, mildly bitter with a dash of sweetness. It is delightful,* Jose was thinking, oblivious to the African man approaching him.

Juma had been in the pub for twenty-five minutes. He had observed Jose come in and head to his favourite spot. He knew today was Jose's night off. He was also aware Jose would drink two beers, always two beers, before leaving for a night out. They had placed a tracker under the seat of his motorbike. They had followed him for three weeks.

What a predictable character, Juma thought.

Juma approached Jose casually, giving him time to see him, to appraise him.

'How are you, sir? May I join you? My name is Juma,' offering his hand. He knew no African man would refuse another's handshake.

'Sure,' Jose responded as they shook hands. He did not offer his name but he did offer Juma a beer, as is the custom in most of Africa. Juma took a long swing of the Corona, clearly enjoying it.

'I very much like Australian beer, you know. Our beer back home tastes like diluted vinegar. By the way, I am from Zonga and where are you from? You speak like someone from a French-speaking country. Dembo, perhaps?' Juma asked.

Jose stood up abruptly, signaled the bartender and paid the exact amount on the bill. He looked directly at Juma with what many would consider intimidating and, with a deep and firm voice, as though telling him don't bother me again, said, 'thanks, enjoy the beer, Mr. Juma.'

He walked out of the bar, lit a cigarette and took in his surroundings, looking out for anything out of place. Cars lined the road right and left. Nothing unusual but he still felt unease.

A slight breeze was blowing from the sea, making it a very pleasant autumn night. *I wish my wife was here. It would have been a lovely evening to have a drink outdoors before retiring to bed,* he thought to himself as he strolled to his motorbike, taking in the clean evening air. 'It is a dog's life to be a security man,' he lamented aloud as he thought about his wife and children. 'A man has to do what he has to do,' he whispered to himself. 'Still, it would have been lovely to be with her tonight, eh!'

He put on his helmet, swung his leg over the bike's seat, inserted the key, turned it on ... Nothing. Mildly alarmed, he tried cranking the bike again. Nothing again. *Now, this is strange,* he thought.

He was about to crank it a third time when he heard Juma's voice. 'Hey, what seems to be the problem?' No one took note, just two African guys having a chat outside a pub.

'My bike won't start but it is no problem at all. I will deal with it. Don't worry about me,' Jose replied.

At that moment, a newish dark grey Holden Commodore parked behind the motorbike. An oldish-looking African man with broad shoulders and an athletic gait approached them as though coming to say hello.

'This is my ride. Are you sure there is nothing I can do to help,' Juma asked again, sounding concerned.

'Put your hands on the handle,' the new guy said with a rough voice. He was now a couple of meters away. He had one hand inside the pocket of a black leather jacket. It was clear he had a gun. Jose knew he had been set up, caught napping, waylaid.

'My gun has silencer, shoot, I will.' The goon said in his rough voice.

'What my friend here is trying to say is, if you make any silly moves or call attention, he will not hesitate to shoot you. All we want is to talk to you. We have a proposition, Jose, or should I call you Tsango wa Zando?' Juma said this in an extremely calm voice, the voice of a man in full control, a well-trained military officer.

He was convincing. Jose knew the goon wouldn't hesitate to kill him. He would be dead within minutes if he tried to fight these two guys.

Juma held his right shoulder while the other guy held his left arm at the elbow. They led him to the dark grey Commodore. Anyone watching would have thought they were friends assisting a rather tipsy mate to the car.

As he stepped into the car, the other guy drove off slowly, as was common in the sleepy village of Patonga.

In a casual voice, Juma started talking. 'Now, you must be wondering why we want to talk to you. I will get straight to the point. You will help us assassinate Dr. Fungai. Why would I do that? You ask. Because we will kill your wife and your three children if you don't.' He said this as a matter of fact, as though killing women and children in a far-off country was the most normal thing for a person to do. From the way he said it, it was abundantly clear it would not be the first time he had eliminated a family. *This was no bluff. In his line of work, this is the way things are done. Use the family as a weakness, as leverage, Jose* was thinking.

'But we are reasonable people,' Juma continued. 'We don't expect you to help us for nothing. One hundred thousand US dollars has already been deposited into your wife's account in Baju.'

'This is large enough to take care of your family, yet not so much as to raise suspicion, don't you agree?' The other guy continued to drive, windows open, driving away from the beach and up the hill towards Pearl Beach. The thug drove with his right hand dangling out, pretending to be enjoying a lovely autumn evening, while all along, alert as a cat just about to pounce on a mouse.

'Hey, look here,' Juma said. He was sharing the backseat with Jose, a gun in one hand. He passed a smartphone to Jose. Jose noticed the 100,000 dollars deposited ten minutes ago into the bank account he shared with his wife.

These guys are good. Now I am in whether I like it or not, Jose thought.

'Who do you work for?' Jose asked.

'That is none of your concern,' Juma responded. 'The important thing is to know that your wife is safe and your kids' education is taken care of. Yes!? Now, I will ask only once: will you participate in the assassination of your boss, Dr. Fungai? Yes, or no?'

'How do I know my family will be safe after the act?' Jose could not bring himself to say after killing Mr. Fungai.

'You don't. If you do what we want, then your family will live, for now. If you disclose this operation to anyone now or in the future, we will kill your family.' Juma responded.

'What do you want from me?'

'All we want is for you to disable Mr. Fungai's security system and provide access to his side door, simple!' Juma responded.

'And how do I disable a security surveillance system that has multiple layers of protection?'

'Just be ready to move when we ask you to, okay? By the way, inform your wife that your boss paid your settlement money for injuries caused by the car crash you had last year. Instruct her to tell no one, including her mother or children. You better be convincing. We don't want people asking questions.' Juma explained.

What options do I have, my family or Mr. Fungai? I have to do what they want, Jose reasoned.

They drove him back to his bike. The nameless guy following behind, he raised the seat, fiddled with some wires, lowered the seat back, then walked back to the car and drove off.

'Bloody bastards,' Jose swore, angry at himself.

Obviously, they have been following me for some time and I did not notice! I let my guard down. Now, I am being punished for it. Shit, shit, shit!

The next day, at ten in the morning, he got a call from Juma. Jose was kind of surprised to hear Juma's voice again. He had almost convinced himself that they would not follow through.

'You have an SMS with a hyperlink. You're an IT guy. You know what to do. We move tonight.' Juma said firmly. The phone disconnected before Jose could respond.

As he accessed the SMS and read the instructions, he wondered aloud, 'How did they even get my number?' Jose was now more than ever before convinced these guys were the real deal. They must be President Onim's mob.

Fungai: My Journey Is Over

At 10.00 pm, Jose casually walked to the front of the house and lit a cigarette as instructed. Across the street, a guy wearing dark overalls stepped out of a Ford utility truck and lit a cigarette. Leaning against the old-looking Ford, just another tradie enjoying his evening smoke. Jose came to terms with the fact that he had reached the point of no return, everything was now in plan. The act had started. *There is nothing I can do*, he reasoned with himself, looking at his watch as he went back into the house to wait for the assigned time.

At 11.30 pm, Jose excused himself. 'I will do the rounds, boss,' he told Matadi. They had been watching a gripping game of football. Manchester United was already one down against Chelsea after only ten minutes. Jose knew Matadi was not going to leave his seat until the game was over. He got up and headed for the backdoor and to the main gate, peering quickly to confirm the Ford was still in the same spot.

Hurrying back into the house, Jose headed to the security command room. From the living room, he could hear the TV, the game was still on. He tapped his phone, pressed the 'Applications Manager' button and activated 'Bloodhound', a program he had been instructed to download from the assassin who called himself Fela. His computer screen flickered. An instant later, the security screens went dead. Jose checked the cameras.

Matadi continued to watch the Man United verse Chelsea game.

Jose exited the house through the back door. He noticed that the telltale miniature firefly-like lights of the micro-drones Mr.

Fungai used to secure the compound were nowhere to be seen. The bloodhound had sniffed them and snuffed them out.

What a program! He thought in wonderment. *How did the bloodhound manage to bring down a security system worth over a million dollars?* He had been sceptical that Juma could bring down their security system. Now, he was more than convinced they would do what they had said.

Jose rechecked the magazine clip of his Walther PPK 22 pistol and stuck it under his belt at the small of his back. He knew he couldn't trust Juma and his mate. *What would prevent them eliminating me after they finished off Mr. Fungai? After all, I would be a loose end, a liability,* he figured. *I will not be complacent again. As they say, 'plan for the worst, hope for the best'* he reasoned.

Hanging on his shoulder was his Nike gym bag. In it, a travel kit that included an Australian, Zongan, and French passports. His flip computer, an extra smartphone, a change of underwear and an extra Walther PPK pistol. He used the side gate that led to Mr. Fungai's compound and headed to the garage door on the side of the huge home. The security lights did not come on like they normally would. Presenting his thumb on the security pad and entering a seven-digit security code, he opened the garage door and swiftly entered. He left it unlocked as he walked into the living room.

Taska, the border collie, leapt out of the sofa, wagging her tail, expecting a treat. He put out his hand full of her favourite treat—a string of biltong. Taska sniffed the treat and hesitated. He patted her back, then scratched the back of her head. She sniffed the treat again, took one and started chewing, though tentatively. After a few minutes, Taska looked up at him with sad eyes that seemed to be asking, *why am I feeling funny?* Jose picked up the dog tenderly, placing her back on the sofa. She whined briefly, spasmed, breathed heavily before giving a final twitch. Jose felt sad to see Taska die, he loved her but he had no choice.

At that moment, Juma and Fela entered through the open garage door. Juma signalled Jose to proceed to Mr. Fungai's office. Tiptoeing, Jose went down the stairs, knocked politely, calling out, 'Mr. Fungai, are you okay?'

'Come in, Jose,' Fungai responded but it was Juma who entered first, pushing Jose roughly to the side, a gun in hand, ready to fire off.

'Put your hands on the table and don't make any sudden moves, Dr. Fungai.' Juma commanded.

Mr. Fungai looked at Juma, seeming unsurprised, a slight smile on his face like he was enjoying the situation. Fela approached Mr. Fungai and punched him hard on the jaw, knocking him from his seat. Mr. Fungai struggled to stand up, managing to kneel. Roughly, Fela pulled Mr. Fungai up and back into his chair and tied his hands behind his back.

'Onim's dogs have arrived, at last! You took your time. I have been expecting this moment for a long time. Jose, you should have asked for more money. I would have thought you valued me more than the hundred thousand dollars these thugs offered. You know they could have paid you a million dollars? After all, President Onim is the richest man in Africa. Oh! I bet they did not tell you who they work for! And you, Fela, I see you are still an angry child.'

Juma and Fela looked at each other surprised. *How did he know we were coming?* Juma wondered.

'Jose, get out of here and let me deal with the real men.' He scratched his ear lobe, a sign that Jose knew well. *You are in danger.*

'Stay where you are, or I will blow your brains,' Juma responded. Jose stayed put.

'Juma, how is your mother, Habiba?' Juma looked at the old man. 'How the hell do you know my name and that of my mother?'

'Of course, I know you. It is my job to know my enemy. You are the first son of Habiba, yes? The second wife of Mr. Galgalo, who was a close friend of mine, by the way. May Allah rest his soul in eternal peace. Does she still make that lovely goat curry? If you see her again, tell her *the dream lives* on!' Fungai goaded Juma.

Juma looked at Mr. Fungai with new respect. President Onim did not even know his father's name, let alone his mother, yet he had worked for him for bloody thirty years, doing all his dirty work.

Mr. Fungai had tapped into Juma's emotions. Juma forced himself to focus on the job at hand. 'I will pass your greeting to mother. I will also tell her you died a clean death. I am sorry I have to do this.'

'I know your orders are to finish me but is it possible to grant an old man a last wish?' Fungai asked Juma, who had just pulled out his gun, ready to fire. 'I ask for only one favour, to die a warrior's death on my feet, fighting a worthwhile adversary. What do you say, me, an old man about to die, fight hand to hand against this young fella, Fela.'

'What? This old sack of bones thinks he can challenge me in combat?' Fela retorted, angry that the old man the age of his father could even contemplate to fight him. He looked at Juma questioningly as though asking, are you going to allow this?

Juma knew Fela was good. He had been a Zonga boxing champion but he had also heard of Fungai's fighting skills. It was rumoured that he was a top-level taekwondo master. This will be interesting, he decided. 'We are going to kill him anyways,' he said, 'why not have a bit of fun first.'

Juma approached Fungai cautiously. 'I will untie your hands, be ready.'

'Though I respect Dr. Fungai, show no mercy,' he instructed Fela.

'Stand up, old idiot. Let's see what you have.'

Fungai stood up, heaving heavily, a worn-out old man. *Deception is part of the fight*, he remembered his trainer Ira.

'Come on, old man, give me your best shot,' Fela coerced Fungai with a bully's voice.

Fungai stood at ease, eyes closed, breathing lightly as though in meditation. This old man is buying time, Fela decided, before taking three steps and taking a swing, knowing he would knock out the old man with one blow. Eyes still closed, Fungai shifted his weight to his right foot, pulling his head back just in time. The hook barely glazed his forehead. He swiftly shifted his weight to the left foot and pushed Fela forward with both his hands. Off balance, Fela sprawled forward awkwardly. His head hit the desk made of ebony. A gash appeared on his forehead, blood flowing freely, spreading across his face. He turned around, furious, a wounded buffalo. He looked at Fungai through the blood, now flowing over his right eye.

'You fucking old man, I will pound you to death,' Fela shouted, psyching himself up.

Fungai saw respect and a bit of fear on Fela's face. He had also changed his stance to a classical boxing posture. Fela approached again, this time moving like a boxer, alert, light on his feet. He threw a combination of punches, a double jab, a left followed by a right leading hook to finish. Fungai's training in the depths of the sacred mountains came back. He saw Fela's shadows even before he moved. He shifted weight to the right and left, weaved and ducked, avoiding all the punches. He threw a three-fingered knuckle hook to the lower abdomen, slightly to the right. The shot connected with right kidney. Fela gasped loudly, then bent forward, holding his stomach, the grimace on his face a sign of the excruciating pain he was experiencing. To his credit, Fela straightened up, though still holding the area around his kidney with his left hand. Fungai saw him shift his weight before the kicks. A snap-kick aimed at the knee, another one aimed at the chest, a round kick to finish. Again, Fungai saw all this in time, moving a step back, shifting his upper body to the left and then ducking. He straightened and sent another three-finger-knuckle punch to the face. This time, it connected with the left eye. He heard a popping sound. Fela screamed in pain, both his hands on his face, trying to keep his eye in place.

'You mother fucker, I will finish you,' he shouted, agony in his voice.

Blinded by anger, pain and the soldier spirit that he was known for, Fela refused to give in. He dived head first, arms outstretched for a rugby-type tackle. Fungai felt the anger in the younger man's voice, his dark spirits strong and dangerous. Time to finish this, he decided. As Fela was about to connect, he moved back one step, side-stepped to the left and, like a harmer, brought his left-fisted arm down. The fist connected with Fela's neck. Again,

Fela sprawled forward, barely managing to break the fall with outstretched arms. He tried to push up but his body refused to obey. The blow just below his occipital bone seemed to have affected his mobility. He went back to the floor in a heap.

Juma could not believe what he had just witnessed. A true master indeed. It seemed as though Fungai was a split second faster every time Fela made a move. And the blows, swift, accurate and deadly, had gradually crippled Fela, one of the best he had known. He realised Fela was finished. 'Enough,' he shouted, pulling his gun and firing twice.

Fungai saw the bullets, like in slow motion. He shifted slightly to his left. He felt them penetrate his right upper chest. The pain was excruciating but he knew he would not die immediately. As he went down, he saw Jose move, pull out a gun and fire.

Unobserved, Jose had pulled out his pistol. He pumped two quick shots into Juma, then aimed the gun at Fela, who had just managed to stand up. 'Don't even think about it, Mister or I will blow your brains. Go get Mr. Fungai's wallet and phone. Hurry up, you pig.' He released two quick shots at his feet. Fela moved like a drunk man, still feeling the effects of each blow he had received from Fungai as he searched Mr. Fungai's pockets.

'He has nothing ...' Fela did not finish the sentence. Jose pumped a shot straight into the middle of his head, a red dot marking the perfect hit. Dripping blood, Fela's knees folded before he slumped forward face first.

Jose rummaged through the drawers, conscious that he had little time. They were empty, no computer, phone, diaries, papers or even pens. It reminded him of a desk he had bought from Freedom Furniture. New, clean, with nothing.

He looked at Mr. Fungai, now lying on the floor. He was looking at him, a smile on his face. Fungai winked.

'You're alive?' Jose whispered as though talking to himself.

'Come here, Jose,' he heard Fungai call.

Jose knelt. He put his ears close to Mr. Fungai, listening to the raspy whisper from his dying boss. He nodded to indicate he understood.

'Go in peace, son,' Fungai finished.

Through the kitchen, Jose exited the house, quickly walking down to the private jetty. He fired up the engine and sped off in Mr. Fungai's boat. His watch read 12.25 AM.

How did Mr. Fungai know they were coming? How did he even know their names? Had he removed all the evidence, knowing they would eliminate him? Why did he give them a chance to kill him if he knew they were coming? Who would accept death so calmly? Many questions with no answers, he thought as he rode the boat the short distance to the Jetty across the Patonga camping site. Earlier, he had left a cheap car he had bought that morning in the parking lot, hoping he would have a chance to use it for his escape.

At 12.30 am, the Manchester United verse Chelsea game ended. Matadi switched off the TV, immediately realising something was wrong. The room was uncharacteristically quiet. Instinctively, he turned and looked at the security screens—trouble. The monitors had never gone blank before. Never. They were meant

to be on 24/7. They even had a backup power bank just in case the power went off. He fished his two-way radio.

'Bravo two come in. Bravo two, do you read me?' No response, as though confirming his worst nightmare. Two days ago, Mr. Fungai, in a rather casual way, had mentioned that Onim would soon make another attempt to assassinate him. Matadi had thought this unlikely. Now, he feared the worst. The old man might be right—again.

The only one thing that mattered now was the safety of his boss. He took off at a run, grabbing an additional pistol from the side table. He was in Mr. Fungai's compound in less than a minute. Entering the house through the kitchen, he quickly scanned the living room. He picked up a cigarette odour in the air and noticed that Taska did not jump off the couch as was usual. Quickly, he headed down the stairs and charged into Mr. Fungai's office.

Two bodies, one in the middle of the office and another near Mr. Fungai's desk. Without hesitation, Matadi rushed to Mr. Fungai, lying on the floor next to his desk. He felt his pulse, still there but very faint. Mr. Fungai, struggling, opened his eyes and looked at his trusted man.

'My journey is over,' he said. 'Do not mourn for me, I was ready for this moment. Jose is on our side. Warn Fumi. He's now your boss. Let him know everything. Look after him.' Fungai, now almost inaudible, gave his last instructions as his eyes closed, a smile on his face.

Sirens announcing the arrival of the police jolted Matadi into action. He gave one quick, final salute to his boss. 'May the gods of your ancestors welcome you on the other side.' He prayed, using the words of his people. He felt sad leaving his boss behind, but he had to obey his last order. He had to reach Fumi.

Chapter 15:
The Dead Speak

It had been 12.50 am when Fumi, about to fall asleep, heard his hologram smartphone ring. Matadi, Fungai's security man, was on the line.

'Mr. Fungai has been murdered.' Matadi said without any preamble or niceties. 'The police are here now. I suggest you stay away until tomorrow.' Then, he quickly explained his understanding of what happened. Even before Matadi had finished speaking, Fumi was already out of bed. *How could this be?* He wondered to himself. He couldn't believe Mr. Fungai, the man he considered indispensable, was dead. In the two years he had worked for The Futures Group, Mr. Fungai had treated him as his own son. He had guided him as a corporate head and provided him with some of the most insightful strategies, views, visions and dreams of any other person, including Professor Osman. Their Friday evening barbecues had become a tradition. It was during these evenings that Mr. Fungai would tell him stories of Africa. In a dreamy, reflective way, he would make a case for a stronger African people.

He couldn't go back to sleep or stay still. Pacing around the apartment, one question kept playing in his mind. *Why? Why would anyone want to murder Mr. Fungai?* After more than two hours pacing around, he made a decision. 'I will get to the bottom of this at any cost,' he spoke to himself.

He had a cup of coffee and toast, kissed Melissa, his girlfriend, goodbye before heading to Patonga. Melissa knew he had to go but she couldn't go with him even though she wanted to. She also mourned for Mr. Fungai, one of the kindest, most intelligent men she had met. If she was going to be of any use to Fumi, she had to start searching for answers. Her first task was to inform her uncle Chan.

As the lift went down from his fifteenth-floor penthouse apartment, the emotions and pain that had kept him awake the whole night resurfaced. Over the last two years they had been working together, he had formed a strong bond with *the old man* who was more like the father he never had.

Fumi crossed the Hawkesbury River, driving north towards Gosford. He had driven across this bridge hundreds of times. His mood lifted a bit as he looked over the railings into the wide expanse of the water, glancing at yachts lining the estuary and small leisure boats hidden away in tiny alcoves along the wide river. The death of Mr. Fungai made him appreciate the little pleasures of life, like the beauty of the wide river, meandering towards the sea, bathed in the early morning light. These warm fuzzy feelings were quickly replaced with a sense of loss and anguish. He knew he could not rest until he had answers. That was his nature.

Fumi accelerated up the hill, keeping pace with other vehicles on the four-lane highway. He looped backwards, heading south through the small town of Kariong towards Woy-Woy. As he had done many times in the past, he pondered the reason for the double name. Taking a right turn just before Pearl Beach, he headed further south and then west, through the National Park to his destination, Mr. Fungai's home.

'Police have established that a man in his eighties, of African origin, was shot dead in his home in Patonga on the Central Coast.' He switched off the radio, not wishing to be reminded of this horrible deed.

'Morning, sir.' Matadi came over as Fumi stepped out of the car. 'Here, have a look at this article,' passing over the newspaper.

"Mr. Fungai spent most of his time in his beach house in the small village of Patonga. Not many people knew him. His neighbours referred to him as *the African gentleman*, a label he accepted with equanimity. Though not common knowledge, he was the Chairman of a large corporation with a global reach. He preferred not to call attention to himself," the article read.

Later that morning, a woman who sounded young and polite called Fumi. 'My name is Elysia Broughton, from the Department of Foreign Affairs, Africa desk. I got your contact from Dr. Fungai's Lawyer, Dr. Mulumba Putumayo. The Department would like to have a chat with you. Would you be available tomorrow? Our Minister would like to meet with you at 10 am. We would also like to meet you at our Canberra office around noon if that is okay with you.'

'Sure, yes.' Fumi had replied, sounding confused. *Why would an Australian Minister and a diplomat be interested in Mr. Fungai's death?* He wondered. He needed to know as much as possible, and maybe this meeting would add to his knowledge of Mr. Fungai.

'I will send you the details.'

‹ ‹ ‹

'My condolences, Mr. Crawford, for the loss of your chairman, Dr. Fungai.' The Foreign Affairs Minister had consoled Fumi in her Canberra office, within the Parliament building. 'It would be fair for you to wonder why I would be interested in Dr. Fungai. But he was more than he appeared to be. I think you already know that. I personally learned a lot from him in our various discussions. Again, I am very sorry for your loss. Let us meet again soon.' The Minister concluded with a firm handshake.

Immediately after he left the Minister's office, Elysia called. 'I have sent our address to you. It is walking distance from Parliament House.' Fumi was not surprised that she knew he had finished the meeting with the Minister.

A power-suited Ms. Broughton took Fumi to a plain-looking meeting room. 'Call me Elysia, Mr. Crawford.' The young woman introduced herself, offering a hand. Though her gaze was direct, a half-smile on her said, I am your friend.

'Would you like a glass of water?'

'Yes, please.'

As she was pouring the water, two black-suited men came into the room. They introduced themselves.

'I am Pedro and this is Connor.' No handshake, no surnames, just Pedro and Connor.

'Fumi,' he introduced himself. First name only as they had done. He noticed they had visitor passes like himself.

Elysia started 'the chat'. Fumi realised immediately that the 'chat' was an interrogation. He understood the game well. He wondered how much they knew about him.

'Our condolences for your loss, Mr. Crawford.'

'Please call me Fumi,' he insisted. *Let's play the game*, he decided.

'First, *I* want you to know this is not an interrogation,' Elysia stated. 'Dr. Fungai was a respected African elder living in Australia. You can imagine questions will be asked, the department would like to be prepared should the media ask us to comment. You are free to, shall we say, not respond and by the way, this is *off the record.*'

The emphasis on *I* and *off the record* was not lost on Fumi, neither were the stern faces of Pedro and Connor.

'Who was Dr. Fungai to you?' Pedro asked abruptly.

Fumi had decided he didn't like the duo very much. Nevertheless, he needed to play their game. He was starting to get into the groove, besides, he was well-trained in the art of interrogation.

'I am the CEO of The Futures Group, of which Dr. Fungai was the Chairman. I am sure you know this. You may also know I am an American citizen. My relationship with him, besides the business one, was that of a mentor.'

Clearly, this was not enough for Pedro and Connor.

'Is that all?' Connor asked after twenty minutes of 'chatting'.

'Do you think I should know more?' Fumi asked Pedro, looking directly into his eyes. Pedro's face was like an open book as he looked sheepishly to the side.

Fumi stood up abruptly. 'I have to head off now, as you know, I am a busy man.' He terminated the 'chat' in a way that purposely offset Pedro and Connor. Caught off guard, Pedro reacted as a policeman would. 'Sit down, Mr. Fumi,' he said with a commanding tone.

'Thank you, Mr. Crawford, again, our condolences. We have taken enough of your time,' Elysia interjected, correcting and reprimanding Pedro while apologising to Fumi at the same time. A true mark of a good diplomat, Fumi noted. She looked Fumi in the eye as she said, 'can I get back to you if there is anything else?'

'Sure, Elysia.' Divide and rule, he figured.

'Good day, Pedro, Connor. Should you need more information, please contact Dr. Putumayo, Dr. Fungai's lawyer.' This only seemed to infuriate the two even more.

As he left for his next meeting, Fumi felt that he could trust Elysia. From his experience working with an intel agency and as a businessman, he had learned to mistrust people until they proved they were trustworthy. So why did he feel he could trust a stranger? Was it her emphasis on 'I' as though saying I am not with them? Or was it her endearing look?

After the 'chat', Fumi instructed the taxi driver to head for the Zongan embassy, where he was to meet the Ambassador, also the Head of the delegation for African Ambassadors in Australia.

'It is a pleasure to meet with you, Mr. Crawford. Let me show you around our compound,' the Ambassador said as he stood up from his large hardwood desk. Fumi noticed the two security personnel watching them intently. When they were alone, the Ambassador continued, 'I have known Dr. Fungai for some time now. We share a common vision, though I can't say this openly. You understand? A storm is brewing, you need to take care, okay?' They finished the tour of the gardens in silence. The two security men stood at attention as the Ambassador bid Fumi farewell. 'My condolences again. The General was a great man. Please have a pleasant trip back to Sydney.'

As they drove to the Canberra airport, Fumi thought back on the meeting with the Ambassador. *'Mister?' 'The General?' Since when did the Ambassador of one of the biggest nations in Africa call me Mister? Why did he refer to Mr. Fungai as 'The General?'*

As he drove past the Australian Defense Force Academy, Fungai wondered, *why did the Feds expect I knew more? Why did the Zongan Ambassador let out information that he knew I did not have?* Fumi realised he knew almost nothing of the story of the man referred to as *The General*, the man who had treated him as his son. He needed to do his homework, starting with Matadi and Melissa.

As Matadi drove him from the airport back to Patonga, Fumi's mind started wandering. He remembered that it was only last Friday that Mr. Fungai had invited him for dinner, as he frequently did. After dinner, Mr. Fungai had talked about his grandfather Ramla, the son of Fumi.

'Do you know your name Fumi means the King? Mr. Fungai had asked Fumi.

'No, I didn't know that,' he had responded. The question had triggered a series of thoughts. He had wondered, was it a coincidence that Fungai's great-grandfather was named Fumi? He had concluded Fumi, like Kwame, was a common African name. Mr. Fungai had gone on about how, while grazing their cattle, his grandfather had told him about his days as a soldier with the Royal African Rifles during the Great War. He had reminisced on how his grandfather had taught him how to hunt and to think.

'My grandfather taught me that animals are like humans,' Fungai had said. 'They have senses, they love their young, they feel pain just like we do. You hunt them like you would a man, if they see, smell or hear you, dinner is gone. You have to outsmart them, think faster, anticipate their movement and use the element of surprise.'

'One day, my grandfather sat me down at our favourite spot overlooking the glade where our cattle grazed. Grandfather, sounding grave and serious, had said … "trying times are coming to you. As a leader, you will be tested and you will face great enemies. If you're able to think ahead, anticipate things and be prepared, like when hunting, you will not only survive, but you will thrive. Know this," Mkulu continued, "Bad leaders find reasons to magnify differences in order to divide people and justify a fight. But great leaders find ways to inspire their people to unite."

'You know, Grandfather could see things way ahead of time. He once told me, "my son, you, like I, will travel to foreign lands and accumulate much wealth, but unlike me, you will not come back home alive. Your journey will end in a far country." I miss that old man, sitting on a rock, high in the Ostrich Mountains, chewing sugar cane, watching our cattle graze … that was a great life,' Mr. Fungai had said yearningly.

Sitting in the backseat next to Melissa, Fumi felt guilty that he had not been more attentive. He had considered the stories as the rumblings of an old man. His mind was not at rest, there was something else the old man had done or said that evening. 'Yes, that's it,' he said, speaking to himself. *Later that night, Mr. Fungai had sent me a message just before I went to bed. What was it about?* He fished out his smartphone.

!Ramla.ra.Fumu 😊 —
the king who could read the future.

What was this about? Fumi wondered. He did not believe in superstitions but the timing of the stories and the message was rather uncanny. It was as though the old man was preparing him, giving him a final message.

Matadi made a turn and continued driving on the deserted road, leaving Pearl Beach behind, now on the final stretch to Patonga. Fumi was still deep in his thoughts, remembering, trying to piece together a coherent picture of the last week before he made his next move.

He remembered his meeting with Dr. Mulumba Putumayo, Mr. Fungai's lawyer, close friend and confidant.

'You need to be careful who you speak to and what you say.' Dr. Putumayo had warned him. In a rather circuitous way, he had implied there was more at play than Fumi knew. Fumi remembered getting annoyed with Dr. Putumayo, who had been all calm and business-like, as though Mr. Fungai's death was not unexpected. *Had Mr. Fungai discussed his death with the lawyer?* Fumi wondered as Matadi slowed down the car as they went down the hill towards Patonga beach.

'Mr. Fumi, you are the sole inheritor of Dr. Fungai's estate, which, unfortunately, means you're responsible for sorting out his complicated assets and responsibilities. It will not be a small job,' Dr. Putumayo had said. 'Obviously, you're aware of Dr. Fungai's personal assets in TFG. What you might not know is he also had another very private business, only known to a small group of men and women. He mentioned that you, Fumi, will have to figure that out.'

'Geez, this is going to be a huge responsibility,' he had responded to Dr. Putumayo.

As they entered Mr. Fungai's home, Fumi was awestruck by the beauty of the place. From the sitting room window, he saw the blue waters of the Patonga Creek glistering in the late afternoon light. Fungai's boat, tied up on the small private jetty, danced with the ruffling waters. He remembered the first time Mr. Fungai had taken him out fishing with the boat, he had been scared yet excited. It would have been a lovely day to go fishing, he thought, but his fishing partner was gone. He noticed the smaller boat, a dingy really, used for quick trips up and down the creek, was missing.

'What happened to the smaller boat, Matadi?'

'It's a sad story, boss. Jose sold out the old man, shot the two bastards and then used the boat to escape. I have not been able to locate him. The boat is now being held by the police as evidence.'

'There must have been a reason why he sold out but that is a problem for another day,' Fumi said. He was thinking of his next move. The answers must be in Mr. Fungai's office, *that's where I must start*, he decided.

Fumi: The Antique Table

After an espresso, with a bottle of water in hand, Fumi went to Mr. Fungai's office, hoping to find out who he really was. He approached the old wooden round table that Mr. Fungai so valued, observing the details that so far had eluded him. The Chinese calligraphy in red covered the edge of the table, contrasting with the Star of David carved into the wood, dominating the centre of the table. Three large Mac computer screens sat on a long bench. A large Samsung TV hung on the wall to the left and a smaller security screen next to it.

Mr. Fungai was a very organized man. He would frequently comment that 'a clean desk reflects a clear mind,' but on this occasion, the office was a mess. Papers, pens, clips and other assorted stationery stuff were strewn everywhere, thanks to the homicide police.

Without thinking, Fumi started cleaning up, picking papers from the floor and the table and stacking them into a pile all along, wondering, *what really happened here? Who murdered Mr. Fungai and why?*

According to Inspector Paul Osborne, the police had not made much progress. The official line was that it was a burglary gone wrong but Fumi was not fooled. The two Federal Intelligence agents, Pedro and Connor, had implied otherwise. He was inclined to agree with them.

I am a suspect and I expected no less, Fumi thought. They had interviewed Mr. Fungai's Lawyer, Dr. Putumayo, who had confirmed to them that he was the sole beneficiary of Dr. Fungai's estate, which was substantial. This made him a primary suspect. He had motive.

Unlike Pedro and his colleague, Inspector Osborne had been courteous when interviewing Fumi, setting out to establish motive, relationship and friends. Fumi had repeatedly told him that, as far as he knew, Mr. Fungai did not have any relatives in Australia. He had explained that in African tradition, young people refer to old men as father, uncle or grandfather, and conversely, older people refer to the young as son or grandson. 'Such is my relationship with Dr. Fungai, who sometimes used the term son to refer to me. But I am not.' He had told the Inspector.

'Who were the two suspects found dead at the scene of crime?' Fumi had asked.

'We're not sure sir.' The Inspector had responded, his eyes averted, as though hiding something. Fumi felt the Inspector knew more than he was willing to share. This had made him even more determined to establish the truth.

Fumi could not help but feel the murder was orchestrated. It certainly was not a simple burglary as the police suggested, and obviously, it was not family-related. After all, he was the only 'family' to Mr. Fungai.

As he continued tidying, Fumi remembered the last conversation he had with Mr. Fungai. He wondered whether he had been sending him a message. In retrospect, the conversation had been a bit too prophetic. Mr. Fungai had rumbled on about his grandfather, whose name was Ramla, son of Fumi. Was it a coincidence? He sat down, leaning back on the old leather office chair that Mr. Fungai had been so proud of. He remembered the phone message, his last communication. At the time, he had thought ... 'the old man had too much to drink' but Mr. Fungai never got drunk. This jolted him into action.

For a second time, he dug into his jeans pocket and took out his smartphone.

!Ramla.ra.Fumi 😊 *- the King who could read the future.*

'Why did he italicise this particular phrase? And why did he use full stop (.) instead of spacing? And why the exclamation at the start and a smiley at the end?' Fumi said aloud to himself, he could not remember any other time Mr. Fungai had used such a phrase in the two years they had worked together.

'Exclamation mark, Ramla period ra period Fumi smiley', he verbalised, hoping for some illumination.

The phrase kept coming back to his mind as he continued to tidy the office, looking for clues. After about an hour, Fumi could think of nothing else. He decided to have a coffee break and brood over the phrase, *!Ramla.ra.Fumi*😊, 'the King who could read the future'.

'Fumi... King: the ability to read and conjure the future ... that is what my name means? Fumi remembered the statement, *'The past forms the foundation for our future; it is written.'* Again, a prophetic quote from his past. Was he sending him a message? Did he know his life was coming to an end?

These questions motivated Fumi to reread the neat pile of papers he had stacked on the big old table with elaborate Chinese calligraphy. He went carefully through all the metal cabinets that had been forced open by the police. Files were neatly labelled and arranged by date and subject. Files on tax, investments, bank statements, estate, old-style letters but nothing out of the ordinary. The police had perused through the files and it seemed they had not taken anything. Fumi called Inspector Paul Osborne and confirmed that the police had indeed not taken any papers.

'Did you find an old Apple computer?'

'No, we are still following up on some leads to try and recover any stolen items,' Inspector Osborne had said.

'What other items?' Fumi enquired.

'Well, we did not see any wallet, cash, phone or a watch on the victim, neither did we find any briefcases in the house. Our view is the thieves must have taken these items and the computer.'

Fumi could not help but think, 'that is odd'. If they stole the computer and the rest of the items, why did they not take away the computer screens, the TV or the expensive vases that lined the large living rooms? They must have been looking for something specific but decided to take the phone and the old Apple computer anyway.

Fumi remembered Fungai's sophisticated security surveillance system. It must have recorded the murder. *Come to think of it, I have never seen any surveillance equipment. I don't even know where the cameras are located*, Fumi reflected.

Mr. Fungai had been very secretive about the security system. Fumi remembered asking him once how the system worked, given he was an ICT expert.

'For now, you don't need to know. You are smart, you will figure it out should you ever need to,' Mr. Fungai had responded. In other words, keep out of my business. This is not the kind of statement or rebuff you forget easily.

The thought gave him a new mission, a direction, like a greyhound chasing a toy rabbit around a racecourse. *I have a target, but where do I start?* He wondered.

He began searching with renewed vigour and keener eyes. His vision roamed the ceiling, thinking, *where would I place a hidden camera?* He knew Mr. Fungai always went for high-tech gadgets. He would certainly not use cable connections to the surveillance monitor. No … certainly wireless. Fumi felt behind the surveillance monitor. No wires like he had expected, except the power cable. He subconsciously switched on the monitor, as one does when faced with limited options.

A message appeared on the screen—no signal. *The screen must receive a signal from somewhere! There must be some sort of recording equipment,* he reasoned. In retrospect, he realised he had never seen any equipment other than the old Apple laptop and the large screens. He had gone through the drawers and he was sure there were no electronic devices in the room.

'Argh!' he shouted in frustration, swirling around on the old leather chair, looking for signs. The antique round table with Chinese calligraphy and the Star of David attracted his attention again. He stood up and stretched before heading to the round table. He surveyed it, the intricate red-coloured Chinese calligraphy around its edge, the six-pointed star—two pyramids pointing in opposing directions dominating the centre of the small table. *What is the significance of these motifs?* He wondered. *Or is it just another collector's item?* His eyes were captivated by the star, which seemed to pull him in, notwithstanding the intricate Chinese patterns. He leaned forward and touched the six-point star, instinctively tracing the golden lines with his index finger, first the upside-down pyramid, then the upright one.

As he did this, he thought he noticed something, he scrutinised it more carefully. Yes, indeed, there was a slight discolouration at the centre of the star. A slight wearing-off of an otherwise shiny lacquer polish—which means ...

He sat down on an antique wooden chair that must have been older than he was, contemplating this new finding. After a moment, he decided, what the heck ... he pressed his index finger on the spot. He thought he heard something, like a squeak. Then he felt a tiny tremor which seemed to emanate from under his feet. Without warning, the old seat started to descend as though sinking through the floor. He held tight onto the armrest, though there was no chance of falling off. Soon, he found himself ensconced in a rather tiny lift, luminously lighted, that was swiftly descending to some underground place.

In a few seconds, the clever contraption came to a smooth stop and a door slid open in front of him. What he saw beyond the lift was mind-boggling: a huge, well-lighted space that looked like a combination of a high-tech lab and a garage.

Promptly, he got out of the lift. 'Wow ...' is all he could say. The state-of-the-art screens, not unlike those he had used while working for the intelligence agency in Boston, occupied a whole section of the wall to the right. Right at the end of the room, a large glass box hanging from the ceiling held what looked like a medium-sized three-level chandelier with a series of thin tube-like multicoloured neon lights. The tubes pulsed following a synchronised pattern, like a choir singing in canon. 'What the hell!' Fumi shouted to himself. Only once had he seen a quantum computer in the highly guarded and restricted experimental lab of The Agency. Even then, he had been sceptical of the use of quantum computing.

What else is in this place? He wondered as he looked around the large space. At the other side of the large room, an extensive engineering workbench was stacked with all manner of gadgets, tools, wires, screws, welding rods, clips, glues and the like. Complementing this was a row of shelves and drawers with even more stuff. He noticed the mini-drones, security cameras, a telescope and a microscope neatly arranged on the shelves. With all the cool stuff, Fumi did not notice the loan glass cabinet, brightly lit, nestled between the other shelves. 'What a cool lab! Who are you, Mr. Fungai? You pretend to be semi-retired and yet you have a lab with the next generation computing power and an engineering workshop that would be right there in Silicon Valley. Semi-retired? My foot!' Fumi shouted like an excited kid.

He turned around to have another look at the space. In his excitement at discovering the huge room, he had failed to notice a tiny desk at the left corner of the room. 'What is that?' speaking to himself as he approached the desk. His face lit up as he noticed the weathered MacBook Pro laptop on the desk. *Now we're in business,* he thought to himself. Mr. Fungai had once told Fumi, 'like my old Oxford suits, this hardy old Mac is good enough for me.' He realised then that the Mac was the key to all the questions that needed answering.

Next to the Mac was a white envelope prominently placed as though Mr. Fungai did not want Fumi to miss it. A letter opener, curved out of ebony with a miniature Maasai warrior as its handle lay next to the letter. Once again, Fumi was amazed at how meticulous the old man was. *A letter opener, of all things? What is its significance?* Fumi wondered as he knew Mr. Fungai did nothing without a reason.

Fumi: The Dead Message

Almost in reverence, Fumi opened the envelope using the Maasai letter opener. He knew whatever was in there was going to be major. In the envelope was a letter folded neatly and Fungai's ring made of three simple silver strands twined together like a miniature rope. The third item was Mr. Fungai's old analogue watch with Roman numerals. For the first time, Fumi noticed it had a small separate meter-like dial with strange symbols that reminded him of the Amharic books that one of his Ethiopian friends used to read.

The letter had a single paragraph:

My son, my journey is over, from the highlands of the Ostrich Mountains, I sprung. I have now reached my delta. I now enter the ocean to be one with the many, gone before me. Your time is now. 'Start' from the beginning, cherish what is in front of you. My watch and ring are now yours, honour me by wearing them. Follow my footsteps to my 'end'.

Fumi, sitting on top of the small desk, pondered on the meaning of the paragraph. He got his pen and underlined, 'start' from the beginning, cherish what is in front of where you stand, and follow my footsteps to my 'end'.

Was this statement an old man's way of guiding him into the future? Or was it literal, a manual to figure out the next steps?

Quite obviously, Mr. Fungai knew his time was over. Otherwise, he would not have left the note, the ring and the watch. In which case, he would guide him to establish his murderer and, therefore, his enemy and how he, Fumi, should proceed. This statement was both a manual and a guide for the way forward.

'Start from the beginning'... He had zero clue what that meant.

'Cherish what is in front of where you stand.' He stood up and looked down at the desk as though there was some hidden writing. All he saw was the old laptop, the ebony letter opener, the watch and the ring.

Where I stand? 'I stand next to and above a small desk. The only item I see is an old computer ... that's it, the computer marks the 'start'. He opened the old MacBook and hit the 'start' or power button. The computer promptly booted and requested a password.

'Just great!' Fumi cursed. 'How the fuck am I supposed to know the password?' *Cool down, settle down,* Fumi told himself.

If Mr. Fungai wanted me to open the computer, then he would have given me a clue, Fumi thought. As he continued gaping at the tabletop, which was what was 'in front' of him, he visualised a captain riding an old ship whose radar had dropped off in rough seas. At that point, his gaze fell on the ebony letter opener, which, in his dreamy thoughts, resembled an oar to use to paddle to land. *It is quite pretty for an oar,* he thought. Picking it up, he looked at it more carefully, admiring the intricate details of the Maasai warrior figure, that is when he noticed tiny inscriptions on the stem of the letter opener. They were so tiny he had to put on his glasses. To his utter surprise, he read:

!Ramla.ra.Fumu😊.

'What the heck! Old man. Aren't you a genius? Just awesome,' he shouted, not bothering whether someone could hear him from this secret underground lab.

'Nothing is safe stored out of sight, remotely or in the clouds.' Mr. Fungai had once mentioned to Fumi. He had thought it quaint then, now he understood. He had physically disconnected the Mac from all external links, making sure it could not be hacked. An encryption software developed by his IT company, The Futures Technologies Ltd, made sure it was as isolated as a computer could be, only accessible physically by someone with the right password, entered manually via an old-style keyboard.

No connection to mobile phones, audio-visual channels, bluetooth, GPS, remote-green connections, or other advanced tech. This is old tech it is efficient and fit for purpose.

He adjusted the hinged flap of the laptop, the old keyboard, restricted to the 26-letter alphabet, ten numerals and a few other function keys.

!Ramla.ra.Fumu😊, the King who could read the future, the old man had written.

Fumi typed *!Ramla.ra.Fumi!* No response, he read the line again, noticing the smile emoji character. He tried *!Ramla.ra.Fumu*😊 and to his utter glee, the old Mac came to life. 'What a genius of a man,' he mused.

Mr. Fungai appeared on the screen, resplendent with an African regalia, smiling yet serious. He started speaking with his usual calm, deep voice, like a practised TV orator.

'Well, my son, yes! Don't look at me as though I am crazy. You are indeed my son, named after my grandfather but we will come back to that shortly. I am sure you have seen the small kitchen at the end of the room. Go make a sandwich, it's going to be a long story this time.'

Fumi was in shock. Feeling dizzy, he sat down and looked at the face of an old man on the grainy screen of the computer, the man who claimed to be his father. Mixed emotions coursed through him: surprise from the message, happy that Fungai, of all men, was his biological father and annoyed that he had not told him earlier. He felt like screaming and laughing at the same time. Instead, he took a deep breath, then he paused the recording. Mr. Fungai's face froze on the screen, serious with a hint of a smile. A mischievous look that showed no fear or apprehension. The face of a man in command of whatever was about to happen to him.

'You knew they were coming for you? Didn't you, old man?' Fumi said loudly, knowing no one would hear him. Scrutinising the face more carefully, Fumi noticed a ducker blotch like a tiny map—a birthmark just below Mr. Fungai's left eye. He had the exact mark on his face. He looked at the eyes, looking back at him. This confirmed it. *Indeed, you're my father,* Fumi concluded as he walked towards the small kitchenette at the end of the large room.

Fumi could not contain his excitement as he foraged through the fridge, quickly making a cheese, lettuce and mayo sandwich. Deciding there was no time to make coffee, Fumi grabbed the bottle of full cream milk and headed back to the desk. As he munched on his sandwich, he tapped on the computer pad, Mr. Fungai's face reappeared.

The familiar voice of the old man who claimed to be his father was calming, almost cathartic like the old Central African rumba rhythms Professor Osman had introduced him to. After a long, hectic week, he needed to hear more of the voice. Besides, there was so much to learn if he had to be prepared for what was to come.

Fungai: Lessons From My Grandfather
Knowledge makes dreams come true

'I will start from the beginning. This way, you know where you come from and perhaps take on from where I have left,' Mr. Fungai continued, like a professor, introducing a subject for the first time. *This old man could have made an excellent TV presenter*, Fumi thought. He reminded him of the movie star and narrator, Mr. Morgan Freeman.

And the story began.

'My grandfather, Ramla, was the last in a long line of the great tribal leaders, or *Athamaki* in our native tongue. With the establishment of a foreign colonial government, the tribal chiefs lost most of their overt powers. However, the colonial administrators showered them with ceremonial recognition, allowing them to organise and officiate over cultural ceremonies while denying them any authority over land and other resources. They rewarded good behaviour with allowances and an assurance of status.

'Most evenings, as the sun went down, my grandfather, the Chief, would ask me to light up a bonfire. A few of the village men, mostly elders, would trickle in, sit around the fireplace and *romon*, or chew the tongue. Meanwhile, horns of wine made of sugarcane juice and honey fermented for a week in clay pots half-filled with dried sausage tree fruit, would be passed from hand to hand.

'In a light-hearted manner, they would reminisce the past, their youth, their warrior days, major battles and skirmishes they won or lost, women and good and bad years. Inevitably, the *romon* turned to what was happening and the future of their clan and tribe. Unlike other boys of my age, I was allowed to hang around, sitting behind my grandfather to stoke the fire and add firewood to the angst of my many cousins.

'When he did not have elders around, younger men and boys within the village would sit around him. He would tell spellbinding tales of his youth and sometimes of his travels as a warrior in foreign lands. "My son, pour me some wine," he asked me on one such cold evening, as we sat around the fire. Using a scoop made of a gourd cut in half, I filled his wine horn. He took a long swig of the sweet, sour booze and cleared his throat. In a solemn voice, he announced, "boys, today, I will tell you about my time as a warrior with the white man's army."

'I saw the other boys creep closer to my grandfather in anticipation. They had longed to hear the story. My face lit up, I knew this one was going to be a nice one—a tale of war and adventure, brotherhood and death—the stuff of legends.'

After a short pause, Mr. Fungai took a long gulp from his horn or rather short glass, half-full of his favourite single malt whisky, mimicking his grandfather's action.

'"When the Great War broke, the white man instructed all the chiefs to select warriors, to be trained to fight for God and King." My grandfather started telling his story in his calm, composed voice. "By then, I was the first warrior of the clan, the tip of the spear, head of a fighting force of several hundred strong. The warriors had not practised their trade for a long time, except for minor skirmishes during cattle rustling with adjacent tribes.

'"By a white man's order, the clan force had been disbanded. No one will carry weapons other than a handstick and a machete to protect one's self from wild animals, the order had stated. But the warriors had continued training in secret places, deep in the thick forest and in caves high in the mountains. The invitation to join the white man's army was exciting to the warriors. They spent hours debating, imagining what it would be like. Any fight, regardless of reason, was an opportunity to prove a warrior's worth to the tribe and so many were willing to volunteer. Any chance to leave the drab life of the village, to fight, make a name, become a legend, was a blessing, an opportunity not to be missed. The reason for the war was not important."

'I stoked the fire as my grandfather continued to tell his tale.

'"I was excited about the prospect of learning how to fight with guns, the stick that spit iron, killing at a thousand paces. But my father, the Chief, had other ideas, stubbornly declaring I was going nowhere. 'You are the first of my sons, the next Chief after me. Let others go and fight for the white man. Your first duty is to take care of our clan,' he had said.

'"As I lay on my straw bed that night, I knew there was no way my father would allow me to go away from the village unless ... I could come up with a very compelling reason. I had to show him why going to fight for the white man would benefit his people. That was my last thought before sleep overtook me. I knew my father's weak point: commitment to his people—his family, clan, tribe.

'"The next morning, I approached my father. In as serious a voice as I could master, I spoke. 'Father, the great and wise Chief, I know you don't want me to join the war but please give me a moment of your time.' I continued on, before the Chief had a chance to stop me. 'You once told me that a time would come when we will need to fight for our land ... when we must fight back against the white man. I know this time will come in my lifetime. Already, I hear people talking about how most of the good land has been grabbed by the white man. They complain that there is not enough land to plant their sorghum and millet. I see squabbles over communal pastures. I feel the hatred people have for the white usurper.

'"As sure as day becomes night, the time will come when we will have to fight back for our lands. Then, we will need to know how to fight like they do, or we will have no chance. This may be the only opportunity we have to learn how they fight their wars, use their weapons, how they defeat their enemies and therefore how to defeat them. When my time comes to be the Chief, I want to be a leader who will command respect from my people. I can only get respect if I stand shoulder to shoulder with my brothers as a warrior in this war of the white man.'

'"My father's face told me I had hit the right cord. He cleared his throat, 'Ramla, you speak like a great leader. Like your namesake, the great Ramla, the son of Fumi, you see what shall be, indeed, what you say will come to be.'

'"So, did he allow you to go?" One of the boys asked excitedly.

'"No, my son but he promised to talk to the other elders of the tribe."'

Mr. Fungai continued, mimicking his grandfather's sombre tone. '"That afternoon, my father had called a meeting of the elders. 'I know we as parents don't want our young men, our protectors, to go to war for the white man. You think, why should they go and fight a war that is not ours? That is of no benefit to us, why? You ask.' After a long pause, he continued. 'My son

Ramla has convinced me it will be good for our people if our warriors were to go and fight with the white man.'

'"He had stopped talking as a group of women brought five pots of wine.

'"What is the occasion?' One of the elders had asked.

'"As the women retreated, my father answered, "Our warriors are going to war. As is customary, we need the blessings of our ancestors, that they may live long."'

The recording rolled on and Mr. Fungai continued with his movie star oration of the story of his grandfather, he raised a whisky glass again, as though saluting Fumi.

'"My grandfather continued on, as the elders imbibed the sweet wine. "Ramla, my grandson has seen a vision. A vision of our people fighting the white man for these lands where our ancestors lie. In this vision, our warriors fight not with arrows and spears, they fight fire with fire, guns with guns, words with words.

"You all know as well as I that no one is happy when their land is taken. When our men and women work on the white man's farms, toiling from daybreak to sunset for a pittance, not even enough to buy grain for their families. They are abused, sometimes beaten and maimed by the white man's guards. The white man has weakened our elders. Most of you have lost respect for me, the Chief, for I have no authority over important decisions. Over time, my authority and dignity wanes even more, and our identity with it.

"Ramla believes we have to prepare for the day when we will have to fight the white man to get our land and our dignity back. So, I say, let our sons go to war, not to fight for the white man, but to learn how to fight the white man." The elders clapped three times then raised their wine horns in agreement with the Chief's decision.

'"An old woman walked in, wearing the regalia of a healer and seer. She faced the mountain capped with snow, sprinkling wine onto the dirt floor, asking for favour from the god of our people. "Great god, who knows all and sees all, now and into the future, we assuage you with our humble wine. Oh! ... great god, who lives high on the mountain tops, flows with the wind and the rivers, protects our lands, our cattle and our people, we beseech you to look over our sons as they go to foreign lands to fight a war that is not ours. If they must die, let them die as heroes."

'"To our warriors,' the Chief shouted for all to hear. 'To our warriors, the gathering of elders responded.'

'"So, what happened next?" Another boy asked.

'"The next morning, thirty-five of our best clan warriors reported to the District Administrator, joining recruits from other clans. There, our long journey to foreign lands started."'

Fumi paused the computer to take a break and internalize the message, leaving Mr. Fungai's face frozen on the screen, a portrait of an African elder, a leader, honourable and wise.

Tapping the Mac again, Mr. Fungai unfroze and continued with his narration.

'"Believe me, the world is bigger than our village and to travel is to know,"' my grandfather had continued with the story, quoting a saying from our tongue. "During the war, we learned the language of the white man. Now you boys go to school and spend hours learning the language. We had no time to read books, we just learned," my grandfather said jokingly. "We learned how to fight with swords, knives, bare hands and all kinds of guns, how to make and rig bombs and how to read directions from the maps, the sun and the stars. But most importantly, we learned how to fight as a group, order, chain of command, control and how to lead others." At this point, my grandfather paused, taking a deep breath before continuing.

'"By the end of our training, I was given the rank of sergeant, the highest title a black man could get. The white man said I had natural leadership talent. What he didn't know was that, even as a recruit, the warriors from my clan and our tribe gave me respect, as their tip of the spear, their Chief.

'"Initially, we fought under the banner of the King's African Rifles but it did not take long before we joined other warriors from Europe, India, Pakistan and even from lands far to the east. We travelled where no other person from our tribe had travelled. We rode on camels, donkeys and ships so large I once got lost while in one. We traversed deserts and walked for months in tiger-infested marshlands and jungles in Bengal. This scared others but it was never a problem with us. We were used to living with lions and leopards, how could a tiger be more dangerous? We told each other.

'"I distinguished myself in war. I became a leader of men, but only black men, never white or other races. That was reserved for the white soldiers. I always believed in our proverb that says, "If you want to go fast, go alone, but if you want to go far, go together." I translated this to mean ... if you want to die, go alone and if you want to live, gather others in your quest, and that is what I did.

'"We learned of the brotherhood of men in times of war but also the absolute brutality and the evil nature of men in the name of war. In the jungle, we were brothers, eating together.

Looking out for each other. However, it never ceased to amuse and annoy me in equal measure how my 'white brothers' always became aloof and above the black, Indian and Chinese men when we came out of the jungle. It seemed to me they were brothers when they needed us and their servants at other times.

'"I saw many of my friends, black, white and Indian go down. I then understood the equalising power of the gun, the advantage knowledge and intelligence gives you in times of war, and most profoundly, how far we as an African people had to go to be equal at war with the white man.'

'My grandfather had raised his horn again. I promptly topped it as he continued with his story.'

'"You know, boys, the war taught me that the white race is not invincible. I witnessed many white men die, being blown to pieces by grenades. In battle, the will to survive gave me the strength to keep on going when others lagged behind, to be alert even when asleep and to shoot faster than my enemy.

'"I have to say though, that the army with the biggest artillery, the most trained and best-organized wins battles, and ultimately, the war.

'"Five of us from the group of thirty-five survived and came back to our village as heroes. Yet I cannot forget our brothers who fell, who never came back. Your father was one of them," he said, pointing to one of the boys who had tears in his eyes.

'"I understood from the war why the white man considers us uncivilised and weak. Having seen and experienced their world, I came to appreciate their point of view. We do not have large cities, written words or large armies like the tribes of China and Mongolia who have been fighting for centuries. But a seed grows into a big tree when taken care of. We will grow strong, we will organise and we will fight with arms and words for this land where our ancestors lie.

'"Now, my boys, it is time to go. Tomorrow is another day." My grandfather had concluded his story of the great war.'

The Mac screen paused but the recording counter continued.

Ramla: The Jackal's Dream

After a moment, the recording resumed. Mr. Fungai was now wearing different African attire, he looked refreshed, too.

'According to my grandfather, it took him one whole year to get himself together. The war had messed up his head. He frequently saw his friends dying in the marshlands of Ceylon and the jungles of Burma. He heard screams of anguish from the wounded, he relived the commotion and confusion of bombs exploding. He would wake up at night screaming, soaked in sweat.

'They say time heals, and it did. These visions and nightmares gradually dissipated. He survived, albeit battle bruised, hardened and wiser.

'Ramla's father, the Chief, died soon after, gored by a buffalo while walking home one evening. My grandfather took over as the Chief the next day. As Chief, he was my people's conduit to the colonial government, more specifically, the District Administrator. One day, he was summoned by the administrator, who appeared to be barely twenty. The administrator had somehow learned that he had served with the Royal African Rifles. In a rather condescending tone, he asked my grandfather in broken Funi, "where did you serve, boy?" *Did I come here to be insulted by this insolent boy?* He had asked himself but his head told him to bear the insult—for now.

'Deciding to play nice, he answered, "I fought in North Africa, Burma and Ceylon." He told him how the Royal Army gave it to the enemy. This made the young chap particularly happy. My grandfather, now the Chief, remembered his father's saying, "a tamed wild dog will only bite you when it is hungry." He had learned to tame the ego of the white man, especially those who felt threatened.

'The next afternoon, my grandfather had asked me to accompany him to graze our cattle on the glades on a plateau high above our village. "My child," he started, "troubled times are coming but we are weak and unprepared."

'As the cattle navigated through the dry forest with sparse undergrowth, up the hill towards the high plains where soft green grass and herbaceous plants grew, my grandfather continued talking as though to himself.

'"White men have been fighting battles with all manner of weapons, using fighting vehicles, hoses and even elephants for centuries. They invaded and conquered black peoples' nations to the north and west. The people of the far east have been fighting wars with guns and gunpowder for many generations. I have heard that one of their great generals named Temujin almost reached our lands. Yet, for generations, we have only used spears, bows and arrows and other rudimentary contraptions.

'"Imagine if we had the knowledge to make the kind of weapons they have. Vehicles that float on water and travel long distances using the wind. Imagine if our forefathers could read and write. How far would we be? Imagine how strong we would be, with our courage, the knowledge of our lands and the tenacity of our warriors.

'"My grandson, their wars and history are written in their books. Each generation of warriors uses the books of war to plan battles, organise their armies and engage in warfare. I fought for them and with them, and I understand how they think."

'We reached the high plane and made sure the cattle were grazing contentedly, no longer on the move. My grandfather continued. This time more animated. "I am hearing news from the West and the East that people of these lands are agitating for their lands. We, on our part, must be prepared for whatever will come.

'"The white race is a cunning and greedy lot. With all the riches our land brings them, from timber, ivory, coal, coffee, tea, cattle, gold, diamonds and other rare minerals, they will not leave these lands willingly, they will not go without a fight. But one sure thing is, like a buffalo surrounded by lions, we have little choice but to fight with the determination to get back our dignity and what belongs to us. With our resilience, knowledge of the landscape and the tenacity of our warriors, we will be a thorn in their backside for as long as it takes—to get them to pack and leave."'

Fumi was glued to the screen, transported back in time to the years of his great-Grandfather, to a land he could only imagine.

On the screen, Mr. Fungai hesitated, like he was thinking of what to say next. 'It is time for a short break,' he announced. 'Go get a coffee while I take a toilet break.'

For the second time, Fumi walked to the kitchen. The wall clock indicated it was 12.20 am. Time for another snack, he thought.

After a quick snack and a cup of tea, Fumi was back, looking at the face of Mr. Fungai, his father. He double-tapped the pad and Mr. Fungai unfroze and continued to narrate the story of his grandfather.

'"Hard times will be upon us," my grandfather had continued as we sat under a tree watching his cattle graze. "We fight because we have to, not because we want to. In the end, what we really need, is the freedom to build our own nation and to rule it the way we want.

'"To rule well, we must have educated leaders, people with knowledge of other nations of other people. We need people with a dream, who can see ahead and who can inspire others to follow their dream. I want you to be one of those people. You are young and your mind is eager to learn. You must learn the white man's ways.

'"You see that valley to our right?" He pointed far into the distance. "There is a natural spring. Water springs from the depths to become the stream where we take our cattle to drink."

'"I know it well, Grandfather," I had said.

'"You know, as the stream flows to the south and east, it joins other small streams, becoming one great river. I am told the river joins other big rivers to become a huge river that travels even further south towards a great sea."

'After a long pause, a sniff of his tobacco powder followed by a rather boisterous and loud sneeze, he continued. "Now, you must be the spring that must journey towards the big sea, you will be joined by others in order to reach your destiny—a great fighter, a Paramount Chief."

'My grandfather always concluded with a saying, a parable or a philosophy but this was deep, yet his meaning was clear and inspiring, even to a ten-year-old boy. I imagined travelling to foreign lands and ultimately becoming a great Chief, just as he had. I felt as though I could fly, riding the currents, heading wherever the wind took me. I could not have imagined how apt and accurate this vision would end up to be.'

Mr. Fungai continued his narrative with a sonorous and emotive tone. 'The next day, I was shipped off to a mission school run by the catholic church. My grandfather, with his broken English, dropped me off at the school. "I found this rascal roaming in my village. He must be an orphan without a known family," he told the Head Master. From there on, I became the ward of the mission school.

'Shortly after that, a group of freedom fighters, among them my grandfather, called upon all true Africans to rise and fight for their freedom. My grandfather would lead a legion of fighters, partaking in hit-and-run raids against the colonialists.

'I followed the news of the terrorists as the African warriors were referred to by our white teachers. But, admiringly and in hushed tones, as Freedom Fighters (FF) by the African night guard, cleaners and gardeners who, once in a while, I sought news from. One evening, the night guard called me as I passed by the gate towards the dormitory.

'"Pss ... hey Francis,' a boy who called me by the name given to me by the school priest. "I have some news for you."

'In a hushed voice and with the reverence of a priest on his knees, he said, "one of the freedom fighters has been captured. You know, he is a Chief and a true hero. Have you heard of Ramla, also known as *Bweha* or the jackal by his fighters? He was captured when he raided a police post at the foot of the mountain. Rumours say that he stayed behind, defending the rear of his fighters, as they escaped with a cache of guns, bullets and explosives. The Chief of Police has declared him the most notorious criminal in the land. They say he will be judged in the white man's court but there are already rumours that he has been tortured to death."

'In shock, I had collapsed. I had woken up to the face of an African nurse staring at me with kind eyes full of worry.

'"I know my son," is all she had said before sending me off to the dormitory.

'After two months, Ramla had not been taken to court. The colonial government had instructed all newspapers to stop mentioning his name, hoping the story of the freedom fighter who stole guns and bullets from the white man would go away. To the contrary, rumours grew with his absence. The stories of the jackal, his cunningness, might and prowess in battle became legendary. Each iteration of the story, more embellished. He was a six-foot, wide-chested, rasta-haired hero who, it was said, could never be killed by a bullet. In another version, he was the war hero who had survived the great war fighting for the white men only to fight them for his homeland.

'He became a hero by his absence and, ultimately, a martyr, a driving force in death. His name, Ramla the Jackal, spoken in hushed tones, became the unifying force for African freedom fighters across the land. Fighters took an oath in his name and his motto, "this land is mine, nobody can take it from me, like Ramla, die for it I shall." The motto became a rallying call for freedom across the African continent.

'"*Now, you must be the spring that must journey towards the big sea; you will be joined by others to your destiny, a great fighter, a paramount chief.*" These, the last wise words from my grandfather, my hero, the Jackal, were etched into my head. Tattooed into my psyche, they became my compass, guiding and goading me to be the best in school, to be a leader of men or boys at the time.'

Mr. Fungai seemed to look directly at Fumi. 'It is your time now. I have done my job, prepared the way for you and all the building blocks are set. You have learned well. We have the resources and the organisation. The soldiers are waiting. My death was the sign of your beginning, you must continue the journey. It is all written. Fumi, son of Fungai. May our God look down upon you from high places. May the Ancients shower you with wisdom when you're in doubt and bless you with the vision needed to be a great leader of our people, my son.

'Remember the words of your great-grandfather Ramla, whose blood flows in your veins, whose name you carry and whose aspiration you must bring to fruition.'

Mr. Fungai paused, his index finger lifted, pointing at Fumi as though admonishing him. He looked tired.

Fumi could still not believe that this man, the man he referred to as Mr. Fungai and sometimes fondly as *the old man*, was actually his father. This realisation also explained a lot of things that had happened to him, among them his meteoric rise to the top of The Futures Group. 'I bet you have always been there for me. I think I now know where to begin, where I am heading, Mr. Fungai ... baba.' Fumi waved to the screen as though saying ... *see you later*. He was exhausted emotionally by the story and the revelations but now he knew where his destiny was. 'I will follow the path that you have meticulously crafted for me, old man. That I promise,' Fumi said. Tears in his eyes, he turned off the old Mac.

Africa: A Sad State

'When you follow the path of your father, you learn to walk like him.'
(African saying)

Fumi had stayed until 3 am, getting a lesson on his family history and a lot more from Mr. Fungai. He slept in, waking up at 10 am to a breakfast of omelette and croissant, thanks to Matadi, now not just his friend but his head of security.

'You know Mr. Fungai used to lock himself up in his office for hours,' Matadi said as they sat on the kitchen table. 'I see you're not unlike him.' He looked at the tired-looking young man with concern.

'Yep, what a life! And I am back at it again. Let Melissa know I will see her at 6 pm,' Fumi responded as he stood up and headed back to Mr. Fungai's office. He strolled across the room to the old Apple computer. The silver computer with the trademark bitten apple looked as archaic as the old man to whom it had belonged. Yet, in his wisdom, Mr. Fungai had used it to store his most secret of secrets, his story, his plans and his dream.

He tapped on the keyboard. The screen flickered as though coming out of a deep slumber and requested a password. Fumi had forgotten how cumbersome old tech could be. Nowadays, everything from his oven to his ultra-thin wrap-around-your-wrist micro-computer-telecom device is voice-activated.

'But then, the dead can't speak, face recognition and fingerprint-reading technologies wouldn't work. There is something to be said about old tech.' Fumi realised he was talking to himself again.

!Ramla.ra.Fumu☺ the King who could read the future, the old man had written. He was finding it difficult to refer to Mr. Fungai as his father. Besides the image file that he had seen, there was one more folder, 'FUTURES', that sat alone on the computer screen, an orphan begging for attention. The folder contained one document in MS Word, a computer software now long gone. Luckily, his IT professor had insisted that his students learn old software, arguing it helped understand modern computing programs.

Fumi double-tapped on the FUTURES.docx document. He had expected an elaborate document with a title page, table of contents, pictures ... the works. To his surprise, the first page was a rather apt and instructive quote.

'When you follow the path of your father, you learn to walk like him.'

Below was a simple family tree drawn free hand. His name, Fumi, was right at the top and his lineage was clear to the fifth generation. The men in the third and fifth generations that preceded Mr. Fungai had a *Mokonzi* or King title.

From that first page, Mr. Fungai had made Fumi's lineage and destiny abundantly clear. The use of the title Mokonzi was certainly not by mistake. Like his father, he was in line to become King, but of what? His father had patiently waited, laying the groundwork to ensure he became what was written. His fate had been sealed the day he was born in Noah's slum in Zimai. *'It is written,'* he remembered Mama Maria and Professor Osman telling him. It had all been orchestrated by this old man, who was his father.

'You need to shape up and quickly, if you have to walk like him,' Fumi told himself. He scrolled to the next page, this time with no predetermined ideas of what to expect. A copy of a document, neatly handwritten, met his eyes: a poem that he proceeded to read out.

Africa: A Sad State

What a sad State!
For centuries, a source of gold and other gems
African chiefs tell the foreigner
Take what you can: gold, ivory, ancient artifacts, timber
I will throw in slaves to help you dig the gold and carry
*   the loot.*
In exchange, you will give me silk and gold trinkets so my
*   wives will adore me.*
Guns and powder to fight and enslave my brothers across the
*   river*
To supply you with more slaves next time you come by
And by the way, I agree. Your men of God can preach to my
*   people about your God.*
Promise them a better place in heaven
Make them accept their miserable existence under my rule
Teach them to be subservient to your God and their King.

So many years
Liberation wars have been fought, 'independence' has come
But what has changed?
On international news, only when its people are dying of
*   Ebola and Cholera*
Or hundreds of thousands die as two puppet Chiefs
*   disagree*
On their share of peanuts from the foreigner

Whose only interest is the wealth under their feet.
The tourist sees the spectacular elephants, rhinos and gorillas
Rarely noticing the emaciated woman
Walking on the road-side, with a bundle of firewood on
*   her head*
A child slung on her back.

Like centuries before, a market for guns, a source of raw
*   material, an exotic destination.*
To be plundered and enjoyed
The chiefs are happily gorging themselves with peanuts
*   from the foreigner.*
From the sweat and misery of their people
What a sad State!

The poem transported Fumi to the histories of Africa he had read. He knew the old man never did anything without a goal, so where was he leading him to? He scrolled to the next page. There was a short paragraph, this time typed.

"I wrote this poem when in high school with the intent of sending it to the newspapers, but my teacher advised me otherwise ... 'It will get you marked by the security forces,' he had said. 'You can publish this when you are in a position to defend yourself.'"

It was a cry for action, a political masterpiece as relevant today as it was post-colonial era characterized by dictators. But what does this have to do with me? He scrolled to the next page, hoping to get clarification. This man is full of surprises, another poem? Was this the explanation?

Like jellyfish of the deep, we are amorphous, pliable, flexible.
Yet, symmetrical, structured and organised, like the
  capsid virus
We split into smaller forms
We grow and multiply
Forming armies, numerous but invisible
We are dangerous and deadly
We infiltrate, becoming one with the host
Surreptitiously living within as we learn and grow.

We are 'Antu' with a common purpose: to create that is whole.
  That is Africa and African.
An Organism that can compete, defend itself and secure
  its people from the evils of others.
Otherwise, our host will continue to be raided, exploited,
  mined, raped, defiled, devoured.
Like a dead buffalo in the wilds of the Serengeti.
What will remain?
A carcass, left rotting, at the mercy of scavenging hyenas,
  vultures and maggots?
Do you want that?

'Bloody hell!' Fumi cursed loudly. *How could I possibly disagree with him when he poses such a question? The old man has just checkmated me.*

He now understood where his father was leading him and what he wanted him to do. What remained was guidance on how. Within the course of an hour, he had been reprogrammed, changed from a tie-wearing CEO of a global corporation to the head of a revolutionary organisation whose name he had just figured out—*Antu*. What it meant, he didn't have a clue but he would know soon enough. After all, his father never left anything to chance.

It took him a quick glance at the next page to understand the metaphor *Like jellyfish of the deep* and the *capsid virus*. His curiosity, aroused by the tantalising diagram on the page, begged him to continue on but his tummy, now rumbling loudly, demanded to be fed.

From the secret basement, Fumi stepped into the small box-like lift with the old seat and slowly ascended to Mr. Fungai's study. He found himself staring at the antique table, feeling as though he had just come from another universe, a subterranean cave full of mysteries from another era.

Then, he felt a vibration on his wrist bringing him back to reality. He looked down at the smart Holo-sp5 as he instinctively opened his palm. A list of messages popped up as if sprouting from his palm, one was from Melissa.

"Where are you? Are we still having dinner?"

The message had been sent at 6 pm and it was already 6.30 pm. He realised that the secret basement was insulated from smartphones. 'A smart move, Father.' He muttered to himself.

He needed to finish reading the dossier to get a full picture of his father's thinking and wishes. Besides, it was already past date-time, there was no way he could drive back to Bondi in time for dinner. He had to excuse himself.

'Audio type,' he commanded his Holo-sp5 smartphone.

'I am sorry honey, still sorting out Mr. Fungai's stuff. Proving more complicated than I thought. A rain check for this once, please! Will sleep over here. Love you.' Fumi dictated.

The draft message appeared on his open palm: To Melissa Chan. 'Send.' Fumi commanded.

The holographic screen displayed: message sent.

Fumi ignored all the other messages, over 20 of them. He headed to the kitchen, out through the back door to his new neighbour, Mr. Matadi. He knew he would get a decent meal from his father's head of security.

He had seen enough from his father's dossier to realise that he was now the head of the cobra, leader of an underground organisation and his security was paramount. He reasoned that his father's enemies would regroup and would soon be after him. He needed to discuss issues of security with Matadi.

Before he could knock on the side door, Matadi opened it from the other side, quickly ushering him into the house. 'Sir, coming here to our house is reckless,' Matadi whispered to Fumi with a polite but firm tone. The security lessons had commenced.

'What's for dinner? Fumi enquired.'

Matadi broke into a broad grin. 'You're lucky, boss, goat tripe curry, served with kale and maise meal, my mother's favourite dish. She used to say "Eat well, my son, this may be the last meal before an earthquake."'

Fumi devoured it. 'That was the tastiest meal I have had in a long time.' He complimented Matadi.

'Now we can start discussing se—' before he could finish, Matadi put a finger to his lips and looked around as though there was someone in the room. He coughed loudly as if choking. 'Excuse me, the school my girl Semi is going to go to? Is that what you were about to ask?'

Lesson two: never assume a location is secure. Fumi took note. They bantered for a short while, talking about nothing important, before Fumi offered to wash the dishes.

'No, no, I can do that later. I need fresh air now, care for a walk?' Matadi suggested. But instead of heading out, Matadi walked casually to the next room, he switched on the TV while directing Fumi to the security screens on the far wall.

'I have news from Zonga.' Matadi stated as they sat in front of the screens.' President Onim is unhappy his soldiers did not come back home. He seems to have very good intel. He knows Jose, my partner, is on the run and he also knows I survived. He is sending his thugs after me. We can also assume, like a dog, he has been sniffing around to find out what Mr. Fungai was up to. He was obsessed with him and I am told he almost went crazy when he found out that Mr. Fungai was alive and well almost thirty years after the bombing of his office.'

'Start from the beginning.' Fumi asked Matadi. 'Who is Mr. Onim, and what has he got to do with Mr. Fungai?'

'In order to understand my job, Mr. Fungai demanded that I understand his enemy, Mr. Onim the Crocodile, the President of Zonga. He told me they had been friends before they became enemies,' Matadi summarised.

It would take close to an hour for Matadi to narrate the story of a man from a small desert village near Sukuta who, through sheer will and ruthlessness, became one of the most feared men in Africa. Fumi remembered Zonga's Ambassador in Canberra saying, 'a storm is coming.' It was clear now that he had been warning Fungai.

Chapter 16:
The Dream

His stomach was full of goat tripe, kale and maize meal dinner, courtesy of Matadi's excellent cooking, Fumi focused on what was at hand. His head was swirling with new information, more questions and possibilities.

Matadi was an impressive storyteller. He had beautifully recited President Onim and Fungai's story in detail, bringing it home by explaining his new status as the head of what he referred to simply as *The Organisation*. 'This means you will be the main target now,' he had concluded.

'We can assume that President Onim will send more troops to tidy up. To remove any evidence against him, we have to move you. Luckily, Mr. Fungai had anticipated this day and made arrangements,' Matadi confided to Fumi.

'I have to call Melissa,' he told Matadi.

'You know you can't use your Sp5 phone now?' Matadi responded.

With that statement, he realised that the earth had shifted, his life had just become a nightmare. But somehow, he felt as though he had been programmed for this very day throughout his life. His mind went into overdrive.

'Alright,' he started. 'Get your personnel here ASAP. I want to know everything the Crocodile is doing, and I mean everything.'

Matadi came to attention, recognising the tone of a leader.

'I noticed you had one of those ancient Nokia cell phones in your desk drawer. Get me one that has never been used.' As Matadi went to fetch the phone, he copied important numbers from his phone into a notepad. *Old style is always best under these circumstances,* he thought. He also jotted down what needed to be done.

Matadi handed him a Nokia cell phone, charged and ready to go. It seems Matadi had anticipated this, Fumi thought. The cell phone really belonged to the Museum of Ancient Communication Devices. It indicated it was already 9.32 pm.

'Prepare to move out in two hours,' he said instructing Matadi as he opened the back door and headed back to Mr. Fungai's compound.

Things were starting to become clearer. Mr. Fungai, his father, had thought of every eventuality, like an orchestra conductor, orchestrating everything, including his past and his future.

Back in the basement bunker, Fumi continued from where he had stopped. He restarted the old MacBook Pro as he recalled the phrase, *Like jellyfish of the deep.*

He studied the hand-drawn diagram. It was a rather intriguing spider web with coloured lines, a spiral and numbers from one to thirty-seven. It looked familiar. *Have I seen this before somewhere?* He wondered.

Fumi's attention was drawn to a hyperlink at the bottom of the page. He clicked it and Fungai's weathered, wrinkled and pockmarked face appeared again on the centre screen.

'There is an African saying that goes like this: "A bird will always use another bird's feathers to feather its nest,"' Mr. Fungai spoke. *How typical,* Fumi thought.

'It's okay for you to use my feathers to build your nest, as I used my grandfather's. To understand me is to understand who you are, where you come from and how you have ended up in this room.' Mr. Fungai stated in a matter-of-fact way. *He looks so old, why didn't I notice this before?* Fumi was thinking as he continued listening to his father.

He made himself comfortable, leaned back against the weathered leather seat, closed his eyes and wondered, *where are you leading me to, old man? What is the end game?*

'On my last day in school, the Head Master called me into his office,' Fungai continued. '"My son," he said, "your grandfather was a hero to your people." The Head Master saw the surprise on my face. He looked at me with compassion as he continued. "You think I didn't know? I have known all along. I saw how it affected you when he was caught. I followed the news and was privy to what was happening to him in jail. Know that he died with honour, never revealing his associates in the armed struggle for your self-determination."

'"It is time now you went on to fulfil his dream. Study hard and make us proud. As we have discussed, I think you should study economics or politics, because that is your destiny. May thy Lord give you the wisdom of your ancestors." With the short prayer, he had finished.

'And so, I headed to the big university to do economics and politics. One evening, a few of my friends from my district came by my room to play a game of cards.

'"What is that you have pinned on your wall?" One asked. I stood up, pulled the page off the wall and passed it to my friend.

'"That, my friends, is a poem that I penned while in high school. I planned to publish it in the local newspaper but my language teacher thought it would rub the authorities the wrong way. So now I use it to remind myself of who I am and what I don't want to be."

'The other students had stopped playing cards as the poem passed around.

'"This is a great piece," one of the boys said.

'"It's so ... like what is happening. You have to publish it in the University Scholars' Newsletter." Or the USN, as it was commonly referred to. And so, the next day, I walked into the Students' Association room, which housed the USN.

'"Hey young man, what have you got for us? I am the Editor of the USN." He was a student just like me, barely a year older. How condescending? I had thought. I handed my poem over. As he read it, his face transformed into a huge smile. "This is really something. Did you write this?"

'"Yes, I did, comrade."

'"It seems we have a politician among us." the Editor lamented.

'That was the starting point of my political career. The poem became a hit with the students, many accolades were heaped on me in the preceding weeks, including by some of my lecturers and tutors. One evening, after supper at the university dining hall, a delegation of students, mostly from my district and a few from my class, approached me.

'"I am the Student Union's Treasurer," one of them said as he offered his hand. "We want to propose that you stand for the position of Secretary during the coming elections. It will be a tough fight but we think you have got what it takes."'

On the screen, Mr. Fungai looked directly at Fumi as though sitting right opposite him as he continued with his life story.

'My son, thanks to my grandfather, I had learned how to captivate an audience. I could spin a yarn with ease, using my grandfather's quotes, poses and even demeanour. I could build a case and fuel passion. I could also read the mood of the mob, fire or diffuse their desires.

'I won the elections outright. By the end of my studies, I had become the Secretary General of the Student Union. Within the Ministry of Education, I was referred to as the Negotiator. This gave me great exposure to the media and government officials. One paper had even dug up my heritage, comparing me to my grandfather, Ramla.

"Mr. Fungai, the Secretary General of the University Student Union, like his grandfather the great Chief Ramla, a general, a leader of men, a war veteran and national hero who died as a freedom fighter—is a young man to watch." One paper had written.

'It was no surprise that I had caught the attention of politicians. Some of them saw me as a tool, a machete, new and blunt, that could be sharpened to achieve their goal. To others, I was like a looming bushfire, a potential political threat that needed to be contained.

'"Mr. Fungai, what are your plans now that you have graduated?" the Vice President of the Republic asked, facing me from his massive mahogany timber table. The only item on the table was the bright-coloured flag of the Nation of Impula.

'Though not surprised, I was kind of perplexed. Why would such an important person invite me to his office in the first place?

'"What do you have in mind, your Excellency?"

'I saw the surprise on the VP's face. He had not anticipated, nor was he used to being talked to, especially by a young man. But he was a good actor. He hid his surprise with a boisterous laugh as he countered, "What do I have in mind? Your welfare, of course."

'"Your grandfather made a great contribution and sacrifice for our independence. We want to pay back this contribution through you." The VP stated. He stopped, waiting for my response. But my grandfather had taught me well.

'"First, understand the playing field, fight from a position of knowledge." I remembered him saying. So, I played the waiting game. I stared at the VP with a questioning face, as though telling him, go on, give me more information.

'After a long pause, the VP realised I wasn't going to budge.

'"Okay, son, I will be honest with you. You're a natural leader, we want you on our side. The President himself has offered you a scholarship to Cambridge, fully funded, of course."

'Am I a new machete to be sharpened for their future use, or am I a bushfire to be contained, or do they see me as both? And why Cambridge? I had wondered.

'"Understand your adversary's intentions." I remembered another lesson taught around the bonfire. They want me out of the way for now, but in a place where they can observe me.

'"Well, Sir, I had thought of going into politics," I goaded the VP even though I hadn't even thought of becoming a politician. I needed to explore their limits.

'"Listen, you have time on your side, son, wouldn't you say?"

'"Your Excellency Sir, you may be right. It may be of benefit to get to know the world. Would it be too presumptuous to suggest a different university? I have planned to pursue my Masters at Harvard. I am made to understand that their economics faculty is one of the best. In fact, they have accepted my application pending a scholarship."

'The VP took his time, seemingly contemplating, as wise people tend to do. "You are indeed the son of your father. You haggle like a fishmonger, yet you speak like a diplomat, I like that. You will be an asset to this nation."

'The VP dialed a number. After the usual pleasantries, he made a booking for me to go and see the Minister for Education. From a drawer, he fished out a business card and passed it to me. "Please keep in touch and let me know of your progress. I will also do the same."

'And so, I headed to Harvard, where my life's work would start.'

The face that looked back from the screen was haggard. Fungai started coughing. Fumi could tell he wasn't well. Two or so months earlier, Fumi had tried to ask about what ailed him. 'I will live a fruitful life,' he had responded evasively.

'You have no time to waste. You must act swiftly.' Mr. Fungai, quite obviously disregarding his pain, continued on the screen. 'Do not feel sad for my death. Know that it happened the way I wanted it to, in fact, I planned it. I leaked the information that led Onim to me. Why, you ask? Because my time was up and my death needs to serve our dream. Know this: I had only a month to live. I had terminal cancer. By dying by the hand of Onim, I become a martyr, I will awaken my people. Your people now.

'With my death, a series of motions have been activated on three continents. You are now the head of the cobra and your people are waiting for you. The way is written in the pages of your life. My diary will give you the answers you seek to understand where to start and the way forward.

'For forty years, I have dedicated my life to *'the dream'*, a better and united Africa, it is your turn now to see the next phase through. May the knowledge of our ancestors and the gods of our people guide you through your journeys. May they furnish you the strength, vision and wisdom to continue with what has been started. Goodbye, my son.' The recording ended abruptly.

The room went quiet. Fumi had been so focused on the screen he had forgotten that the old man was actually dead. The silence reminded him that, indeed, he was gone. *You, the Chairman of the Africa Futures and The General of the clandestine group, Antu, have just made me the head of the 'cobra', committing me to your dreams? Now I have to figure out what you mean by 'the way is written in the pages of my life'?* Fumi was almost in tears, emotionally exhausted and overwhelmed by the responsibilities thrust on him.

Ma Beki: The Spider

"If the opolo frog leaves the swamp for the mountains, it means it is in danger."
(African proverb)

President Onim could not hide his excitement. An old memory came back to him, the day he saved himself from the shackles of the horrible Ahmed, the salt trader, so many years ago. He felt the same satisfaction as when he experienced Ahmed and his family choking, wriggling like worms, before taking their last breaths. The feeling was exhilarating. 'Oi, oi, ai, ooh... All my enemies, gone...' the president shouted as though he had won a million dollars.

'Why are you so happy?' Ma Beki enquired.

'I have done it! At last, my most formidable enemy is dead, gone, finished. Now I can sleep in peace. No more nightmares.'

Mama Beki knew immediately who he was talking about. She felt sick—nauseated. She knew she had to take hold of herself. *This is the time you become the actor extraordinaire,* she told herself. Before he could see her shock, she rushed to him, hugging him tightly, hiding the tears that were now running unrestrained down her face.

'What has gotten into you, woman?' Onim asked. 'I can't remember the last time you hugged me. Come to think of it, you have never hugged me.'

'Thank the heavens,' she replied, still clinging to him, buying time so she could get hold of her emotions. 'While I am a bit sad, I am happy for you. Now we can move on with our lives.' She sighed, pretending relief. 'I have to go organise for your victory.' She pulled out of the embrace, curtsied, quickly turned and left the room. She headed for the bathroom to properly shed tears for her love, friend, and the father of her son.

As she oversaw the party preparation, she heard voices, boisterous and joyous.

'You have done it, Mr. President!' She knew the voice well—that of President Nima. 'You have to tell me the whole story.' Ma Beki heard him shout as they retreated to the men's chamber. She was sad and heartbroken. She felt like screaming, breaking something, even killing. She remembered one of the African sayings her mother was so fond of, "If patience hides something, anger cannot find it." She had to restrain herself, play the happy wife, find out what had happened, and then act.

'Chef, we expect a large number of people, and soon. Please make the usual arrangements for catering.' She told the old man who had been the President's chef for as long as she could remember. She looked around at the young man wiping glasses at the other end of the huge kitchen. 'You, Bekele, prepare finger foods for the President and his friend. Roast peanuts, sesame biscuits and a bowl of fruits will do just fine. And stay by the President's side in case he needs to send for anything.' Beki instructed as she removed her spectacles, taking time to wipe them with a white handkerchief.

'Right away, ma'am,' Bekele responded. *What is happening?* He wondered as he headed towards the President's men's chamber. Mama Beki rarely made requests for him to spy for her but he was happy to do it. She had done so much for his family and people. He remembered the day she flew his mother from his village, perched on the plateau of the highlands of Habesh, for a life-saving operation in the main city.

Walking casually, a fake smile on her face, Beki retreated to her private suite. She locked the door behind her. She knew more men would be coming to celebrate the President's victory. It was her duty to keep the women entertained as the men drank and talked of their exploits. But first, she needed to know what the two men were discussing, even though she knew Bekele would feed her the information later. She placed what looked like a hearing aid in her right ear, then tapped it twice, then once. The gadget, given to her by her father, Professor Osman, came alive. She sat down on her dressing table, lipstick in one hand. She heard the chatter in the kitchen, the Chef was issuing instructions to his minions. She tapped the earbud again, a different channel came through, the President's voice boisterous and clear.

'I heard the bastard's last words and saw Fungai go down like the dog he was, thanks to the transmission from Juma's body camera.'

'Let's drink to this great day. To you, my friend, now you can sleep in peace,' said President Nima. Beki heard the clinging of glasses.

'Cheers to that, my friend. For almost four decades, the bastard has tormented me. Like the devil himself, he has visited me every night, he was my nightmare,' responded Onim. 'But I am still worried. Fungai has always been one step ahead of me. I will not rest until I destroy his bases, his organisation, his clan and everyone around him. I hear he has recruited a young man to run his company. I want him dead or alive. Tomorrow, my soldiers arrive in Sydney, the day after, the operation *Finish Fungai* will be completed.'

Beki's heart skipped a beat, it constricted. She was about to have a heart attack. She grabbed her handbag, quickly retrieved a small vial, got two tablets and swallowed them without water. She held on to her chest, which felt as if it was being crushed, clumped by a vice so strong she could barely breathe. 'Breathe ... one, two, three, four, breathe ...' she counted as the tablets did their work.

Kill Fumi, my son ... she found herself thinking. 'Over my dead body,' she whispered as her heartbeat slowed down. She knew what she needed to do.

'Shouldn't you take the win and direct your focus onto other things? I hear the Americans are after the neodymium-rich mines to the north of Zonga. You could make a deal with them to become the richest and most powerful man in Africa.' From her high-tech earbuds, Beki heard President Nima say, his tone that of a man pleading.

'What is wealth when vultures circle above your head?' Onim responded. 'Besides, I will use the Americans' greed to help me finish Fungai's empire. It is how they do business. Scratch mine, I scratch yours, you know.'

'What a despicable person!' she heard herself say. From her window two levels above the driveway, she heard a convoy of vehicles. Military, she knew from experience. The Generals are flocking like hyenas to congratulate the President. She stepped out onto the balcony. An immaculately dressed, youngish-looking Lieutenant General stepped out of a military Landcruiser troop carrier. He looked up towards her balcony as though he knew she would be there. Beki touched her forehead before adjusting her headdress. He adjusted the collar of his army-green dress jacket. The message was received. *Get your wife to talk to me,* it said. Like Bekele, Sani owed his position to Ma Beki.

Time to get back to the kitchen, then to the President's side, Beki thought. The kitchen was frantic. She quickly made sure everything was in order before heading out to the main entertainment hall, now almost full with visitors, high-ranking military personnel and ministers. There was a discernible hush as she walked in. Even at her advanced age, her beauty and poise mesmerised even the younger women. A young woman with a distinct tribal mark on her face approached. 'Good evening, Ma Beki,' she curtsied as she shook Beki's hand. 'Sani, my husband, passes his greeting. He is busy organising the military catering for the party.'

'I have not seen you for such a long time. Did you know the *opolo* are leaving the swamp for the mountains?' Beki spoke in a low but confident voice. Anyone listening would think she was jesting the young lady, Didi.

Didi looked stunned but she quickly composed herself. She understood the coded message from the African proverb: "If a frog (*opolo*) leaves the swamp for the mountains, it means it is in danger". *Opolo* ... Fumi was in imminent danger, which meant Mr. Fungai was gone. 'No, Ma, I have just been a bit busy. I will make sure I visit you more frequently. I have to go and see how my husband is doing. Keep well, ma'am.' She left quickly, looking around for her husband, Lieutenant General Sani.

'I am not feeling so well,' Didi told her husband, who had just returned to the entertainment hall. 'I will see you at home.' Sani was about to ask what was happening when Ma Beki approached.

'How are you, General? Care to pour me a drink?' Beki requested as Didi tiptoed out of the hall to go relay the urgent message and prepare her girls.

'Head for the Red Lipstick, please.' Didi instructed her driver, who had appeared immediately after she stepped out of the hall. While the driver weaved his way towards Oko city centre, Didi fired off a quick message on her smart phone, "Red Lipsticks in 30."

Using the VIP entrance, Didi entered the high-end club and headed for the VIP lounge. She knew the three young women would be waiting for her. They spent most of their evenings in the club, owned and operated by her, compliments of Ma Beki.

'What's happening, boss? Why the urgency?' The oldest of the three women asked.

'Big party at the palace today. You know what that means. Most of those big-wig generals will end up here later. Listen for Sydney. The usual: who, what, when, how. I will be waiting. Now start preparing.'

Ma Beki gave her instructions before heading upstairs to her office while sending the message, "The *Opolo* leaves the swamp for the mountains ... tomorrow evening".

She looked at her watch. It was 10 pm. She knew the old man in Boston, USA, would be going for his afternoon walk. Her phone beeped back almost immediately with a thumbs-up emoji. As she sat down in her cozy office, she placed her phone on what looked like a glass placemat with a colourful spider web design. The smartphone vibrated before restarting, wiped out clean, like a new phone. No numbers, messages, photos or Apps, except for one, the one with the spider web icon.

At 2.00 pm, the now retired Professor Osman stood up from his desk, ready to start his usual one-hour walk around his leafy suburb. He looked out through the large window of his home office to see the Charles River at a distance. It was a gloomy day. *I need a raincoat*, he decided. His smartphone vibrated before he had the unique ringtone, the song Malaika by Miriam Makeba, endearingly referred to as Mama Africa, that signified an urgent incoming communication from Beki. He quickly put on his earpiece, similar to Beki's. He heard the raspy voice of the President. He was gloating about how his men had eliminated his main rival. 'Cheers to that, my friend,' President Nima responded.

'Beki, my daughter, like the black space between the stars, living in the dark and unseen, you provide us with things only you can, without you, we would be half blind.' The Professor spoke as though Beki was right there next to him. A tear dripped from his right eye. His only daughter, with her cells of young women and men, had given up so much for the cause.

The smartphone pinged; the ringtone was the song Malaika. Dr. Putumayo was half-awake, just about to get up. He looked at the old analogue clock next to the bedside table. It was 5 am, Sydney time.

"*Opolo* ... Crocodile hatchlings are on their way. Details to follow".

This is not unexpected, he reasoned. From his network, he had heard rumours of a follow-up attack. Still, the confirmation was welcome. He knew there was no time to waste. He decided it was time to pass on the information to Ms. Elysia Broughton, the Australian diplomat in Canberra, Matadi in Patonga and Mr. Chan, whose whereabouts at any one time was a secret. He knew it was going to be a busy day. The wheels of government would start churning, courtesy of Ms. Elysia.

In Oyo, Madam Beki, like in the times of old, would be gathering not wild vegetables and fruits but intelligence. Her network of informants, like the rays of bright light, were dazzling. 'Kudos to you, Madam,' Dr. Putumayo spoke, complementing Beki's good work. His wife, still half asleep in bed, smiled. 'Thanks for the compliment, darling,' she responded.

Didi decided to do the rounds. The club was packed, the lights dim and cozy, the music slow, romantic African rhumba. She spotted the head waitress, a smallish and exceptionally beautiful woman with long red braids flowing down to her waist.

'So how are we doing?' Didi asked, loud enough to be heard by a few of the clients.

'I will bring the accounts to your office in a moment, ma'am,' the young woman responded.

'A pax of 4. Tomorrow night. Here are the accounts.' Didi quickly read the four names on the piece of paper from the waitress.

'Are you sure?' She asked.

'The three of us got the same results from three senior officers. So yes, I am sure. I am sorry, ma'am.' The woman understood that the four men may not come back.'

Her knees felt weak. She sat down and heaved heavily like an old woman as she contemplated what to do next. 'To be a woman is to be soft as a feather and as strong as a buffalo,' her mother used to say. Didi tapped the smartphone, waking it from its slumber. She tapped the spider web App. It opened out like the spider web it was. The image of a spider started moving along one strand of the web. 'Didi to spider,' she spoke softly, as though she feared the spider would bite. A memo-like page appeared.

"Four Pax sent to destroy Base. To finish *Opolo*." Friday night Base time. Lieutenant General Sani, the lead.' She dictated, then listed the other three names. 'Send to spider.' The message disappeared as the spider moved back to the centre.

"Pack for Base. Connect with 36. Save S." The return message read. A wide smile spread across Didi's face. She knew Sydney well. She had operated under Cell 36. Dr. Putumayo would know what to do. Ma Beki sure took care of her people, she concluded. She was not prepared to sacrifice Lieutenant General Sani, her husband and a member of her cell.

Back in her chamber, Beki activated the spider web App as Didi had done and fired a message. "Three Pax sent to destroy Base. To finish *Opolo*. Friday night Base time." She attached pictures of three assassins. Lieutenant General Sani's picture was not one of them. The smartphone indicated it was 2.05 am.

At 7.07 am in Sydney, Dr. Putumayo passed on the message to Elysia, Matadi and Mr. Chan. He decided Melissa would be obliged to inform Fumi if she had the information. This, he did not want.

"What would we do without you? Thank you. Leave the rest to us." Dr. Putumayo responded to Beki's message. In Boston, Professor Osman received the message. "Cell 36 on it." It was past 4 in the afternoon.

"You, my daughter, are a gift to mankind. May your ancestors bestow you with the wisdom of an owl." The message from her father, Professor Osman, read. As she crept into bed, she wondered, will my son Fumi survive?

Fumi: Infernal

Fumi heard the iconic ringtone, like the old telephones that used copper wires to relay messages before mobile phones and other wireless technologies. He had been lost in thought, contemplating his father's recording. In a dreamlike state, he searched for the source of the ringing. At the far-left corner of the room, a red light blipped in sync with the ringtone. He hadn't noticed it before. The ringing was from an archaic telephone handset connected to a black cable, like those roadside phones in the old movies.

'Boss, the house is on fire, we have to move—now!' It was Matadi on the other end of the line.

As Matadi spoke the series of screens along the wall came to life, as though activated by the ringtone. Each screen spat out an image of a house engulfed in fire—his house. Just recently inherited from Mr. Fungai. In the kitchen, there was fire everywhere. Fumi saw and heard mini explosions as bottles with various contents burst from the heat. The ceiling trusses caved in and the terracotta tiles cascaded into the fiery kitchen. Fresh air coming from the collapsed roof intensified the fire into a huge fire-ball reaching out several meters above the roof. From another screen, he saw his living room clogged in smoke that swilled around like ghosts looking for an escape. On yet another screen, Mr. Fungai's office was filled with smoke that had seeped through the gap under the door. His escape route was now a smoky cavern.

Fumi heard police sirens coming from all the screens. On the centre screen, two dark figures, heavily armed, started firing. He heard the return fire even though he could not see by who. They move like trained soldiers, covering each other as they retreated towards the back of the house. Then he saw Matadi with two others, a woman and a man, looking out from a window. 'Let's meet at the Patonga Beach Hotel in 30 minutes. The thugs must have started the fire and I'm sure they're watching to see the mole scurry from the hole,' said Matadi in a hushed but urgent voice. 'I have to go, we're under fire. See you soon.'

Why is Matadi in police uniform? Fumi pondered.

Matadi disappeared from the screen, then reappeared on the next screen, crouching low. 'What the hell?' Fumi exclaimed. The policewoman beside Matadi was none other than Elysia, the diplomat from Canberra. 'How is she involved in this?' He saw Matadi aim, take his time, then squeeze the trigger—a single shot. One of the dark figures cried out in pain. 'The son of a bitch shot me,' he shouted before folding forward and collapsing into a heap. The other assassin looked bewildered. 'It's an ambush, he shouted.' In fear, he took off, running towards the river and the bush behind the house. Big mistake. Elysia took aim, calm and composed, she seemed to take forever. She tapped twice. Fumi saw the man, now almost disappearing into the bush, collapsing face first. The would-be assassin tried to push himself up but went down again, managing to crawl into the bush.

'He will not get far. Pete will be onto him, hopefully alive. We need answers. Great job, by the way.' Matadi's voice came from the TV screen.

'I have to get out of here, but how?' Fumi said, talking to himself. Mr. Fungai would have anticipated this scenario. He looked around. *Where would I put an escape door? To where?*

The escape would have to be towards the river, he reasoned. He walked to the far end of the large room, towards an old hardwood bookshelves which he noticed were in-set, built as part of the wall and packed with all kinds of rocks. All dark and boring looking. As he came closer, he felt a pulsing on his finger, the one that had his grandfather's ring. As he looked at the ring, the small dial of Mr. Fungai's old watch with Amharic-like alphabets started ticking, becoming faster and faster as he approached the bookshelves.

Fungai, now next to the shelf, looked at the rocks. The watch dial went round and round. He felt the pulses from the three-stranded ring become stronger. He felt the pulses course through his body to his brain. 'What is happening?!' He shouted to himself.

Then he noticed the stone. One stone amongst all the dull black and earth-brown stones started pulsating, like a living breathing organism, in tandem with the pulse from the ring. It started lighting up, becoming a dim bulb amongst the nondescript stones. He couldn't resist touching it. It was as though his hand was moving on its own volition. *This is crazy,* he thought.

As he picked it up, he felt his body stiffen and then his mind became charged, like it had been hit by a mild electric charge. Everything became clearer, his eyes became sharper. He knew the stone was the key. He picked it up without hesitation.

Fumi heard a faint click and a crack like an old knee joint on the right side of the shelf. Overjoyed, he pushed at the end and the shelf started rotating from the centre point. He pushed harder, it creaked, then opened. There was barely enough space for him to squeeze through. He found himself in darkness but immediately, tiny lights came on. They ran down a tunnel of what looked like a mine shaft.

The stone had stopped pulsating and had lost its dim light. It now looked just like the other stones in the cabinet, dull and devoid of life. He refocused on the task at hand. Adjusting his backpack containing the old laptop and the only paper file in the room, he took long strides, covering the 40 paces in a few seconds. He was confronted by a huge floor-to-ceiling, rough-hewn hardwood timber door with no visible handle or lock. *This must be the way out but how do I open it?* He wondered. Before he could finish his thought, he felt it again: the pulse on the finger with the ring. Involuntarily, his hand moved, touching the stone now in his pocket. He felt its warmth with each pulse. It had come alive again, somehow responding to his needs. He heard a faint whooshing sound and felt a slight breeze before the thick wooden door slid open, smooth and soundless. *What is this stone that responds to my mind?* Fumi wondered.

With the door wide open, he had expected to be greeted by moonlight, but all he saw was a solid rock wall blocking his way, a dead end. He moved closer to the rock, wondering, *why would you build a door in front of a solid rock wall?* On further inspection, Fumi noticed a small crevice to his left, a light breeze confirmed it was an opening to the outside. It was just large enough for him to squeeze through. He found himself inside a bushy scrub. Through the bushes, not more than 20 meters away, he saw the waters of Patonga Creek reflecting moonlight and the bonfire further uphill.

He felt the heat and smelled the smoke from the fire billowing high into the sky. Looking back towards where he had come from, he saw the inferno. A massive bonfire engulfed Mr. Fungai's beautiful home.

Shouts and sustained gunfire reminded him of Matadi's warning. 'You are in danger from Onim's agents,' he had said. Making sure he wasn't seen he crawled downhill towards the creek. He followed it to the campsite then made his way to Patonga Beach Hotel. As he walked the stretch of Bay Street to the junction with Patonga Drive, he felt tiredness creep through his body. He was angry that someone could be so daring as to burn Mr. Fungai's home after murdering him less than a week ago.

The Future is alive

Lieutenant General Sani heard the gunfight. He was sitting in an unmarked car a hundred meters from Mr. Fungai's residence. He had seen the smoke, then the blaze as the house became engulfed in the fire. From his UHF handheld radio, he heard one of his men scream in pain, then heave heavily as he fell. 'Fuck this,' another said, followed by the rustling of bushes, then a splash of someone diving into the water. Sani stepped out of the car.

'One pax in the river,' he whispered into a cheap mobile phone passed anonymously to him at the airport. The phone contained a single name—Fungai. Sani felt annoyed that his army mates had to die doing the bidding of the despicable President Onim. He felt like he was a sell-out. For the greater good, for the cause, he consoled himself.

'Message received. Move out now. Let the President know his wish is fulfilled. Three men went down in the process.' Matadi responded.

As he drove off heading out of the village-like settlement, police cars and two fire trucks raced by.

Didi saw her husband, driving rather casually as though he had no worries in the world. She was parked on the roadside, allowing the police cars, ambulances and fire trucks to zoom by. With a smile on her face, she followed one of the fire tracks at a safe distance. She needed to see Fumi to confirm he was alive. As she passed the Patonga Beach Hotel, she saw a tall figure walking slowly along the street. It was that of an African man who looked tired but alert. Didi noted his gait and appearance—late twenties to early-thirties, a thick afro, as black as night. *It is Fumi, alright.* Ma Beki had shown her his picture. Didi parked on the side of the road and watched him as a Mercedes Benz sports car stopped next to Fumi. She was about to pull out her gun when she saw Fumi smile as he quickly entered the car. Tyres screeching, it dashed off towards the creek. She knew where the car was headed. She had scouted the place earlier on. At a slower speed, she headed towards the Patonga camping ground, where she knew Fungai's small boat was moored.

Fumi and a young Chinese-looking woman were already boarding the boat by the time she had arrived. Matadi, whom she knew well, started the outboard engine. The boat took off, heading towards the opposite bank of the river.

Back in Oyo, Ma Beki heard her smartphone's Malaika ringtone. The spider App lit up and self-activated. A message appeared.

"*Opolo* lives."

The message was followed by a rather dark picture of a man and a woman boarding a boat. She magnified the picture, a smile appeared on her face. 'The Future lives,' she whispered to herself in the privacy of the First Lady's chamber.

A black Mercedes Benz sports car pulled next to him. Thinking the worst, he was about to take off when he heard a familiar voice. 'Hurry up, you buffoon, quick before someone sees us.' Only one person dared call him a buffoon. Not even his father would do that. How she knew where to find him was a mystery to Fumi.

The car took off before he could close the passenger door.

'Melissa, what are you doing here?' Fumi asked.

'You look terrible,' she said ignoring his question. 'When was the last time you slept?'

'About 36 hours ago, I guess.'

Melissa did a U-turn, doubling back towards Fungai's residence. She slowed down as she approached the Patonga camping ground, where a small tinny boat sat on the sandy beach. Matadi appeared as Melissa parked the car.

'We're going fishing,' Matadi said, handing Fumi a fish tackle box and rod. 'Leave the key in the glove compartment. And hurry up before someone sees us,' Matadi rushed them.

He started the outboard motor, riding off across the creek to the Patonga Beach House. After a few minutes, they crossed the river and switched into a 4WD with a large 'Budget Car Hire' badge on the side. Matadi seemed relaxed, like nothing had happened, as he drove on a lonely back trail verged by trees and thick bush. Melissa sat beside Fumi, composed like it was just another night ride. Fumi remembered the inferno and the gunfire. *Nothing peaceful about that,* he thought.

'Don't look at me like that. I know exactly what is going on in your mind,' Melissa said. 'All your questions will be answered in due course. For now, enjoy the ride and the full moon.'

'What is this road? Where are we headed?' Fumi asked.

'This is the Pacific trail, a bush trail that I regularly use when I want to clear my mind,' Matadi responded. 'We're headed for North Sydney, your father's Plan B residence.' Fumi looked at Melissa, then Matadi with a quizzical face, mouth agape, hands raised halfway in the air. *How did they know Fungai was my father? How much more do these two know about Mr. Fungai that I don't know?*

Melissa looked at Fumi with a face that relayed love. She reached out for his hand. The gesture and the smile on her face seemed to say—just wait, in time you will know.

They followed the deserted track, past Brocken Bay Sports and Recreation Centre, then took a tight right turn heading north, soon arriving at a small settlement. A series of jetties lined the river bank. Matadi parked the car on the side of the road next to the first Jetty. Melissa stepped out of the car and approached a man who was securing a medium-sized yacht to the jetty. On seeing her, the man smiled and gave her a warm hug. From inside the car, the man looked familiar to Fumi. Matadi pulled out a pair of gloves, a cleaning cloth and spray. 'You go ahead, I need to wipe the car clean of our prints.'

As Fumi approached the yacht, he saw that it was Mr. Chan. The man walked towards Fumi with an outstretched hand. 'Good morning, Mr. Crawford,' he said addressing Fumi formally before bowing politely. This made Fumi feel uncomfortable.

'Please call me Fumi, Mr. Chan.' Fumi responded as he bowed.

Quickly, they boarded the yacht and went down a few stairs to a beautiful lounge area. Fumi could not help but notice the lovely timberwork and the chrome finish that adorned the inside of the yacht. A large sofa bed occupied one side of the room. A small kitchenette, a bench and bar stools on the other side. Delectable aromas of coffee and warm butter-rich croissants reminded Fumi that he had not eaten anything for some time.

'Hey boss, coffee or tea?' Melissa asked as though reading his mind.

'Coffee, please.'

She passed a takeaway coffee cup and then placed warm croissants on the kitchen benchtop. 'Your favourite brekkie is served, sir,' she said jokingly.

He felt the rocking movement of the yacht as it made its way across the wide Hawkesbury River. Looking through the window that was almost at water level, he noticed they were midstream, heading towards a point jutting out into the river. The captain, Mr. Chan, guided the yacht expertly to a pier. After half an hour of riding, they moored at the Parsley Bay Boat Marina. Melissa disembarked from the yacht, heading to an adjacent parking lot. Matadi was busy vigorously wiping the yacht clean, as he had done with the car.

'Is that really necessary?' Fumi asked.

Matadi ignored the question. 'Boss, from here, we drive back to Sydney,' he announced.

Fumi alighted the yacht, making sure he touched nothing in the process. He did not want to undo Matadi's work. Melissa, now in the driver's seat, headed towards the M1 and the city. Clearly, she knew where they were going. *It seems it is only I who is in the dark*, Fumi contemplated, not a position he was used to and one he had to change, and soon.

'Where are we going?' Fumi enquired again.

'We're going to Mr. Fungai's second home in Mosman bay.' Matadi responded.

'Mosman? I didn't know he had a place in Mosman!'

'That was the wish of Mr. Fungai, boss. He said and I quote ... "There is no need for Fumi to know our plan B. If ever I should go and you are in a crisis, only then should you use the plan."'

'It seems he had anticipated our current situation, in fact, if you ask me, I would say he may even have played a part in making it happen. But I am speculating now,' Fumi responded as they headed south towards the city.

'Where are we?' Fumi enquired as he stared through the tinted window of the Toyota, they had been riding in. He realised he had dozed off.

'We're home.' Melissa responded as though saying, isn't it obvious?

Fumi saw a large, modern two-story home with a well-developed garden. He lowered the window to have a better view, there was a distinct sea smell in the breeze. From the garage and through a laundry room, they entered a huge modern kitchen that opened out into a large dining room.

'This is it, boss. You rest while I go tie up some loose ends,' Matadi told Fumi. He heard the sound of a motorbike, then a garage door open and close. His body needed a bed, a shower and then a coffee. His ego wanted an explanation as to how Melissa and Matadi knew so much more than he did. He decided to have a quick tour of the house before the shower. He could not help noticing the similarities with the Patonga home, except for the decor, which was more ... feminine and modern, more like his Bondi Beach apartment. No doubt Melissa had something to do with that.

'What the hell!' he whispered as he entered the office. It was an exact replica of Mr. Fungai's office in Patonga. A desk sat prominently at the end of the room and a round table outlined with Chinese calligraphy was next to the wall. Both were exact replicas of the ones in Patonga. Next to the round table, an old chair, also similar to the one in the Patonga office, invited Fumi to have a seat.

'Honey, where are you?' He heard Melissa's voice from the kitchen. He had seen enough and knew what he would find underground.

'Just checking out this place.'

'You need to sleep,' Melissa said. 'Take some time out. You should be fresh for whatever is coming.' Fumi knew she was right, his body needed to rest for a few hours. He headed for the bedroom.

He heard music: soothing, melancholic, familiar yet nameless. A canto that kept repeating time and time again and then he realised it was his new Holo-sp5. It had awakened him from a deep slumber. *How long have I been asleep?* He wondered as he looked at Mr. Fungai's watch—now his. It was already four in the afternoon. He opened his palm and saw Melissa's hologram, a big smile on her face, cheerful and intoxicating.

'Good afternoon, I thought it was time to wake you up. Things are happening that you need to know.'

'Give me ten, I need to shower first,' Fumi responded. As he took a quick shower, the single question in his mind was, what next? He now understood the big issue, the end game so to speak, but he needed to find his way forward. But before that, a few answers from Melissa were overdue.

Melissa Ai Chan

"Without an opposing wind, a kite cannot rise".
(Chinese proverb)

Melissa was browsing her Holo-sp5 while watching the holograph projection displayed above the glass-topped coffee table.

'Mr. Fungai's death is all over social media,' she said as she stood up and gave him a warm hug. 'I miss you so much,' she whispered close to his ear as though there were other people in the room. Fumi responded in kind, holding her close for a moment longer.

'I'm starving. What's for dinner, or is it lunch?'

'First, coffee, then congee soup with extra ginger to give it that kick you so much like. Then dinner later.'

As Fumi devoured the thick rice soup, his mind was on one thing only ... *who is Melissa?* He could not wait any longer.

'There is more to me than you know,' Melissa started suddenly before he could pose the question. 'I want you to know I would take a bullet for you, because I love you but also because it's in my job description. Mr. Fungai saw to that. That is how important you are to me and to others.'

Now this is becoming interesting, thought Fumi, keeping taciturn he looked at her, eyebrows raised as though asking ... *what!?*

Melissa took a deep breath. 'Okay, the story goes like this: the person you know as Mr. Chan is actually my uncle, yes, brother to my mother. I consider him more like my father. I grew up in his household.

'When China was under strict communism, the government was very harsh on anyone who had alternative views. My grandfather, Mr. Chan's father, was a factory worker and an activist in Northern China. He made the mistake of speaking his mind too openly, demanding better working conditions for himself and fellow workers in a government-owned garment factory.

'One afternoon, he was called into a meeting with the factory management as a representative of the workers. It is said that they tried to corrupt him by offering him a senior management position but he refused. Well, that night, his home, which had been in his family for generations, was burned to the ground. Mr. Chan's father, my grandfather and all members of his family were trapped in the fire. They locked the doors from outside. Luckily, my uncle Chan, then a boy, had been sent to visit his ailing grandfather. The news found him next to his grandfather's bedside.

'When his grandfather heard what had happened, he had told him, "now you're the only one remaining of my bloodline. You have to survive at whatever cost. You must vanish, become someone else." Discretely going back to the family home, Mr. Chan saw black body bags lined up in a row. Ten of them of different sizes, all members of his family. His mother, auntie, sisters and brothers—all burned to death. With that image imprinted in his mind, he moved to Shanghai to live with distant relatives. He never forgot what the government had done to his family. From then on, he decided to dedicate his life to changing the government system. He was intelligent enough, though, to know that the only way to do that was by being part of the system. So, at a fairly early age, he joined the student wing of the communist party at his university. He was a brilliant student, a senior member of the student wing of the Party and, in the eyes of the Party, he was a future leader. After his first degree, he got a scholarship to study economics at Harvard. That is where he met Dr. Fungai, then a Senior Lecturer in economics and technology studies.

'"I was utterly surprised to see a black man, wearing African looking attire standing in front of the class, talking about the technologies that would change the world. All my life, I had been told stories of how Africans lived on trees, hunting and gathering wild animals and plants. So, to see a black lecturer with a strange name teaching a postgraduate class, let alone a technology class, was simply unreal." Mr. Chan had told me while talking of his first encounter with Dr. Fungai.

'After that class, Mr. Chan had approached Dr. Fungai, wanting to know more about Africa and Africans. Your father had invited him to his house, where he was hosting a small gathering. Their friendship grew from there, especially after Mr. Chan told your father of his childhood.'

'So, what has this got to do with you and me, Melissa?' Fumi asked in a serious tone as though saying ... *get on with it.*

'Patience, my dear,' Melissa responded. 'It's a long story, best told over dessert. Would you like a chocolate fudge?' She knew Fumi could never resist chocolate.

'As I mentioned, Mr. Chan is my uncle. How? You ask, while all his brothers and sisters were burned on that fateful night.' Melissa continued as Fumi munched on his chocolate fudge. 'Well, it turns out that his father had an affair with a woman from a neighbouring town. My mother had been the product of that relationship.

'One day, a big black car parked next to our small two-roomed home. I had been playing outside. I wondered, whose car is that? I was only six years old then. A man, obviously a high official from the look of his clothes and the car he was driving, knocked on our flimsy front door.

'"Is this the home of Ms. Jing?" The man asked.

'"Yes. I am Ms. Jing, how can I help you."

'"Can I come in Ms. Jing?"

'I remember my mother had been so embarrassed. "Oh, sorry for not inviting you in, please come in but we're not prepared for visitors." I heard her say as I continued playing with my friends.

'After a short while, I went into the house. My mother had a huge smile, tears of joy dripped down her cheeks. I had never seen her so happy.

'"This is my daughter, Ai," she had introduced me.

'"Hi Ai, I am your uncle Chan." He had said, looking at me with a directness I was not used to. It was as though he was looking for similarities with his family.

'"You look as beautiful as my sister when she was your age. I bet you're just as clever as she was." Nobody had ever told me I was beautiful or clever before. From that point on, I loved him as though he was my father, whom I had never met. Often, I would pester my mother. "When is uncle going to come?' And he did come regularly, always bringing me nice clothes, chocolate and other sweet things from the city.

'One day after such a visit, he asked my mother if she would like to come visit him in Shanghai. "Is next Sunday okay with you?" He had asked. My mother and I could not wait for Sunday. So, when the car came, we were ready for the trip.

'And that was it. My mother and I moved permanently into his large home in the big city of Shanghai. Living with my mother and her half-brother—my uncle, I could never have been happier. Then my mother died. A car had struck her when she was crossing a road coming from the market. My uncle had taken her to one of the best hospitals in Shanghai. After a week or so, he had come home looking very sad. "Your mother has gone, she is with the angels now," he had explained. Though I was seven, I understood what he was saying. "It's now my job to take care of you," he had told me as I sobbed, wanting my mother to come back.

'After that, Mr. Chan became my guardian.'

'So, how did you end up in Sydney?' Fumi asked Melissa.

'As I said, it a long story.' I am getting there my dear.

'When I was thirteen, I became restless, as most teenagers do. I lost focus and felt like I didn't have a purpose. I was convinced I was fat and ugly. I was always angry, especially when I thought of my mother. My uncle noticed this when I became, what he termed as, disrespectful.

'One Saturday morning, my uncle asked me to go for a walk with him. This was the first time we had walked in the neighbourhood together, and I was excited and happy that he could find time for me. We walked in silence for some time before he stopped suddenly, in deep contemplation, or so it seemed.

'"Are you okay, uncle?" I asked him.

'"My daughter, we Chinese say that, 'If small holes are not fixed, then big holes will bring hardship.'"

'"What are you talking about, Uncle Chan?"

'"In the last twelve months, you have grown very fast. You have changed. You are now almost a young woman. Change brings many things, one of them is strength, and as we Chinese say, "Unless there is an opposing wind, a kite cannot rise". I have decided you need something that challenges you."

'Then he pointed to a building across the street. The Five Brothers Dojo. I heard the usual sounds of young men and women shouting as they practised kung-fu. I looked at him, confused.

'"Let's go in and see what happens there," he said. A man waved at my uncle as soon as we entered the dojo.

'"This is the girl I told you about, her name is Ai."

'The Dojo master was a big man, broad-shouldered, slim waist and a strong-jawed face. His hair was tied back with a rubber band. I remember he was sweating so much that he had to go get a towel.

'"And this is Master Ling, the owner of the dojo. I have asked him to give you some basic training. I will be back in an hour. Try and enjoy yourself." My uncle had told me as he handed me a black bag he had been carrying. "Everything you need is in the bag."

'"Well, Master Chan, we will take care of Ai."

'My uncle bowed, using the classical martial arts fist-over-palm salute. I wondered whether he was also a martial artist.

'I was not given a choice but I was excited. I had always wanted to learn how to fight. After that, I got into it so much that I decided to join the military when I finished studying IT at university. I had thought that my uncle would resist this move but he was very supportive. In fact, I was surprised at how happy he was. "This is the best way to start your career," he had told me. When I think about it now, I wonder whether he had planned this all along from the moment he took me to the dojo.

'One day, after the mandatory military service period, Uncle Chan asked me to join him and celebrate my accomplishments. Right in the middle of dinner, he asked, "would you like to work with me in my company?" By then, I knew that he was the head of The Futures Group China Ltd., a company that invested in information technologies and finance, among other things.

'"We need an IT security adviser and you would be perfect, with your military and IT background. You can take time to think over it but your salary would be … let's say … ten times what you're earning now!"

'I was flabbergasted and he knew it. I couldn't contain myself. I didn't need to think it over, I just needed a moment and a deep breath before I spoke. "A chance to work with one of the greatest minds in China, who would say no to that, uncle?" Here I am now, still working as a security adviser to The Futures Group, though now assigned to secure the man who will change the world.' Melissa searched Fumi's eyes as though imploring understanding, saying, please accept me.

But Fumi was not about to let it go just yet. 'For the last two years we have been together, you haven't said a thing about this. Anyway, what I don't get is how Mr. Chan ended up working with Mr. Fungai and how you ended up working as my security?'

'Well, I was coming to that,' Melissa answered. 'One evening after dinner, we were watching TV. An elderly, regal-looking black woman was being interviewed. Suddenly, my uncle became all alert, silencing me mid-sentence while he increased the volume.'

'"As an example of what we can achieve if we work for the future of our people, my husband, President Onim, is committed to building a strong and powerful nation." The woman spoke with a distinct American accent. "The dream of Africa must live on." She had said, directly looking at the cameras as though sending a subtle message out to the world.

'For no apparent reason to me, my uncle had started pacing the living room, deep in thought, then abruptly, he had said, "let's talk in the study. How much do you know about The Futures Group China?" He asked me.

'I thought this was a rhetorical question but I responded anyway. "I know we invest a lot of money into research for new and emerging technologies. That it's a private and secretive entity with no information in the public domain, the fact that we are allowed by the government to operate in China means there is government blessing to TFG-C's work."

'"Good, you're correct. Now, I will tell you a bit more. You remember I mentioned to you that I met an African lecturer at Harvard. Well, he was more than a lecturer. He had great dreams of Africa and the world. Dr. Fungai is the founder of The Futures Group, a global organisation with over seventy subsidiaries and worth more than I care to mention. That woman you saw on the TV was to be his wife. It never came to be," Uncle Chan explained. "With her coded message, she just told us that Africa is ready for change. You have to go to Sydney—tomorrow."

I could not believe what he was saying. "What are you talking about?" I asked him.

'"You will learn more in Sydney," was all he had said.'

'I see,' Fungai interjected. 'So you're telling me, without hesitation, you came to Sydney?

'Yes! I trusted my uncle's judgement and who would not want to come Sydney? Melissa responded. 'In fact, I was having dinner with Mr. Fungai in Patonga the next evening. It was a Friday I remember because he always barbecued every Friday and it was my first time to taste Kangaroo meat, which I dare say was exceptional.

'"I have heard a lot about you, Melissa, and I am very happy that you could make it at such short notice." Mr. Fungai had told me. "We have been planning that you would join us but we did not anticipate it would be this soon."

'"We need to increase our surveillance and security capability. We reckon we're pretty good at it but you will make it even better. You will work closely with Mr. Matadi." As though choreographed, a tall man who looked like a bodybuilder or a boxer came over. *He must spend a lot of time in the gym*, I had thought. Matadi bowed politely to Mr. Fungai before shaking my hand and sitting down.

'"This is Mr. Matadi, my head of security."

'Around six months after that, Mr. Fungai told me, "I have a visitor arriving tomorrow from Boston. You will pick him up and bring him to the office. He will be staying at the Bondi apartment. Make arrangements for that." I remember asking Matadi who this person was being given VIP treatment. He had just looked at me and said, "you will see."

'A tall very black man who looked like a movie star, wearing a turtleneck neck, a Prada casual jacket and very expensive Oxford shoes appeared from the gate. The picture I held in my hand did not do him justice. I felt giddy, like my stomach felt funny and I was a bit light-headed. No one had made me feel this way before. He was the most handsome man I had ever seen, I thought. I'm sure you know who I'm talking about.

'I was actually really happy when I dropped you off at your apartment. I needed time to breathe and reset my mind. But I was dying to spend time with you, mostly because I could not sleep without thinking of you. Somehow, my uncle and Mr. Fungai saw right through me.

'"I hear you have found love?" My uncle asked me. I thought he was about to scold me but instead, he just said, "fate is a strange beast." I was happy that my uncle did not have an issue with it. I had thought he would see it as a conflict of interest. "By the way, your job now includes the safety of our CEO," he had added.

'I would like to imagine it was not intended to be this way but I have a strong feeling that my uncle and Mr. Fungai had planned this all along. Mind you, I am not complaining.'

'Why didn't you tell me who you were before? Why did you keep me in the dark?' Fumi asked.

'Please forgive me, my uncle and your father gave me very clear instructions. "There is no need for Fumi to know all the details," they had said. Now, I can say I have a dream job. I make use of my skills as a highly trained fighter and surveillance technician to make sure that the man I love is safe,' Melissa said in a tone that was sincere and loving.

'So, how long have you known Mr. Fungai was my father?'

'Yesterday when my uncle told me that you are now the Chairman of The Futures Group.'

So, Uncle Chan knew, how about Matadi? Fumi wondered. 'Where were you yesterday when they set fire to Mr. Fungai's house?'

'I was there the whole time. We knew they were coming, we even encouraged them. Mr. Fungai wanted evidence of President Onim's involvement. Am I getting ahead of myself?'

'How much more do you know?' Fumi asked.

'I know a fair bit but I'm still trying to figure out what's happening or is supposed to happen,' Melissa responded. 'We have President Onim under 24-hour surveillance, our units worldwide are on high alert, ready to be mobilised by your orders.'

Suddenly Melissa paused and raised her finger to her lips. 'Someone is in the compound.' She pointed to her earbud. She could pick up waves generated from around the compound and isolate those that were from a human. 'It's Matadi coming in from the kitchen door, right about ...' the door opened.

'Hi boss. Melissa. I hope Melissa has answered all your questions. I am glad that we don't have to keep secrets from you anymore. It always weighed on me but as they say, orders are orders.' Matadi said as he walked straight to the fridge, pulling out a bottle of soda water.

'President Onim sent the crooks that set fire to Mr. Fungai's house. Two died in the attack, another one was found holed up in an apartment near Crows nest. Apparently, Ms. Elysia Broughton, who you met in Canberra, got a tip-off.' Matadi said with a smug smile, indicating he was somehow involved.

Fumi wanted to ask why Matadi was wearing a State Police uniform but decided that would lead to questions he might not be willing to give.

'How would you like to use that information?' Matadi asked.

'Sit on it for now. I need time to think,' Fumi responded.

Fungai: Pages Of My Life

"Let us trust God and our better judgment to set us right hereafter. United we stand, divided we fall"
(John Dickson, 1768)

Fumi stood up. Matadi and Melissa did likewise, a sign of respect. It was at that point, he realised he had taken over from his father. What exactly, he was not sure. The only thing he was sure of was that his life had changed, and considerably. He looked at Melissa with stern eyes as though saying, *we are not yet done.* 'Let's get to work,' he said as he headed to the subterranean bunker.

'The way is written in the pages of my life,' Fumi remembered Mr. Fungai's recorded message. He still found it difficult to think of him as his father. He rebooted the old MacBook opened the .docx file, 'The Futures', continuing from where he had left. He considered the caption at the bottom of the diagram, '*Antu*, The Organisation. Only you know the whole.'

The colourful spider web looked familiar, yet he could not place where he had seen it. Six radial strands connected to the centre pointing to six different directions. A spiral thread ran from the centre outwards, connecting the six spirals. A number marked each node where the spiral thread intersected with the six strands. The numbers started from one in the centre to thirty-six at the end of the thread. Each strand had six nodes.

'If this is a representation of *Antu*? It is quite neat, I dare say.' Fumi spoke to himself, admiring the simple yet the naturally strong arrangement. *I will come back to this later,* Fumi decided as he flipped to the next page.

What followed blew his mind. It was visionary and sprinkled with the dreams and hopes of a people who had gotten a raw deal, dating back to the slave trading days.

"Your name *Fumi*,' the document started, means, *the wise ruler* in the language of our people. As I have come to know you, I realise how apt it describes you."

Fumi knew what Fungai was talking about, his friends considered him groomed, aristocratic, even aloof. Within the business, he was referred to as 'The Strategist'. He was regularly compared to his mentor, 'The Elder', as some referred to Mr. Fungai.

Fumi continued reading the document.

"Early in my career, I attended a conference of leaders in Africa. Sitting in the back row of the hall, I looked around. I saw young people like myself, full of anticipation and hope. The majority, though, were what we call the Elders in Africa. I heard a cacophony of tongues: French, English, Portuguese, Shona, Swahili, Arabic, Igbo, Olof and other numerous African languages.

This was Africa. Many tribes, different histories. But we thought we had one aim, one objective, one vision and one dream. It was among the first gatherings of leaders from across the continent. I was young, open-minded, a Harvard doctoral student and full of aspirations. I was at home with my people.

I listened to the messages of our leaders. Heard them spelling out their dreams of making Africa great, African people free, rich and powerful. Over the course of the conference, the dreaming of our leaders became more poignant. I felt it. It became my dream, a dream to liberate Africa, to unite her, to make her great. To move her from being a source of slaves, ivory, raw materials, and labour to being a leader in the world.

I decided then and there I was the one who would make the dream of a united Africa, the most powerful Federation in the world, a reality. That became my aspiration, my end goal, inspiring me and guiding my decisions to my last day. I did not achieve this, but what I did was to set the way for you to see it through. My death was all part of the plan. A milestone towards the end goal.

You have heard parts of my story. You will hear more from others who know me well. For now, know this: before you put me into my grave in Africa, my people will call on you to lead them. This will result in chaos. You will face dangerous enemies but I have laid the path for you. I have created an organization that will help you to be one of the greatest men of your time. I have seen you. You are strong yet compassionate, proud yet humble, stubborn but flexible in equal measures. Like a river, you flow with ease. You bring along others to form a formidable power. You, more than anyone else, can achieve the goal of uniting Africa. Talk to the elders, men and women who have travelled with me. They will guide you and protect you. The plans are in place, and the resources ... well, what can I say? Take your place in bringing our dream to fruit. The ancients will guide you.

But first things first. Your mind must be preoccupied with the diagram you saw earlier. It is simple for you to understand but it is better when explained by others. Know this, though: The Futures Group is only one of the organs. It is only a means to an end.

You must be busy preparing for my burial. Make use of the situation that is about to unfold. Let people sing my praises, ride on the wave of emotions that will flow from my death and strike when the iron is at the right temperature. Goodbye, and may the God of your ancestors guide you."

Fumi realised the finality of his father's goodbye.

With the knowledge of what his father's dream was, his head became clear. He felt at peace. At that point, he realised that the story was the strategy, the way to bring change, to build the greatest nation on earth. Apparently, according to the old man, Fumi was not just a cog, a pawn, not even a knight but the kingpin of this great scheme.

He decided to confirm whether his new home had an escape route. So, as he had done in Patonga, he found the hidden exit and followed it to the end, where he found another hidden exit. As he exited the bunker, he saw the yacht moored not more than twenty meters away. The view of Mosman Bay was breathtaking, the salty sea breeze ... rejuvenating.

Fumi retraced his way back through the hidden tunnel, the long corridor into the subterranean bunker, before riding on the chaired elevator into his formal office. It was half past nine at night, time to get a security briefing from Melissa.

'Melissa, I am ready for the briefing,' he told Melissa over his holographic cellphone.

Fumi heard the knocking on the door. He looked at the projection in the centre of the wall and saw Melissa, hesitant, waiting for his response. 'Yes, come in, please.' *Since when did she require permission to enter his space?* Things had indeed changed.

He decided to play the game. 'Please sit, he said as she approached the large hardwood office table.' He pointed to the visitors' chair across the table. She raised an eyebrow, indicating her surprise that he had not invited her to sit on the more relaxed office sofa.

'You're now the head of one of the largest organisations in the world. This comes with considerable risk to you as a person but also to the organisation.' Melissa said as she briefed Fumi on the status of the security apparatus across their six main locations across the world. 'Dr. Fungai has created a state-of-the-art surveillance and intelligence system not only to match the security risk but also to simulate strategic geopolitical trends.

'Your current and most urgent threat is President Onim and the puppet Presidents he has groomed in some of the African countries,' she continued. 'We know he will come for you but you're secure for now. We know he will target you at your weakest point—during the burial. What are you going to do? That is the question.

'Your Father was always one step ahead of everyone else. It was like he saw things before they happened. I don't know how but I am sure you have his abilities.' Fumi did not mention that he had already found the bunker and the gadgets within.

'We are making preparations for Mr. Fungai's burial and I understand security will be a nightmare,' Melissa finished. Again, Fumi did not mention that he had already received instructions from his father about his own burial.

It was time to be the leader, he thought, and that requires keeping secrets, even from your closest confidantes. He wondered whether their relationship would survive.

$$\diamond$$

Chapter 17:
Fumi – "A Single Bracelet Does Not Jingle"

umi sat alone in his office, deep in thought, reviewing the security meeting. Something was bugging him. *Yes, that's it!* Melissa had said, 'Mr. Fungai was always one step ahead of everyone.' It was as though he had a sixth sense or secret intelligence that even Matadi did not have.

If there is a secret feed, then it must be in the bunker. Though it was past 1.00 am, he decided to find out whether this was the case. He sat on the old leather office chair. *Where would I place a secret button, a keypad?* For the first time, he noticed a small antique lounge chair opposite the wall that supported five large screens. *If I wanted to watch visuals, that is where I would sit,* Fumi decided.

He moved to the lounge chair and sat down. The screens booted and came to life without him touching anything. *This is interesting,* he thought. *It must be triggered by his image, bio-recognition! This is cool.*

A high-definition image appeared. In a sitting room somewhere, an old man with a massive belly, bald-headed and bloodshot eyes sat on a golden-coloured lounge seat smoking a cigar. The camera panned across to two men wearing dark grey military-type uniforms and red berets. They reminded him of a picture he had seen of President Idi Amin, one of the many dictators who have graced the African continent.

'Sir, there is trouble,' One of the soldiers told the man on the sofa. 'Social media seem to have gone into overdrive. The story is that *you* are responsible for Mr. Fungai's death and they are calling for all citizens to demonstrate, to show solidarity with the late Mr. Fungai. To demand for change.'

How did Mr. Fungai manage to get cameras in President Onim's house, one of the most secure palaces in Africa? Fumi wondered.

The old man stood up, stretched and yawned as though the message did not disturb him one bit. *He is big and ugly, no wonder people call him The Crocodile,* Fumi thought.

'We fight fire with fire. Get my public relations team to deny all these allegations. I want the name of Mr. Fungai in the rubbish bin of history. I want the media to know he was nothing, that he hid away, leaving his people behind. Tell the people what I have done for them. I will not allow group meetings or demonstrations in the streets. Give an order to that effect. Go now, you morons and deal with the stupid demonstrators.' He shooed his minions off.

'Ma Zendi, come here please.' A woman came into view, she was old, almost as old as Mr. Fungai. Her face looked familiar, as though he had seen it before. 'From your sources, have you heard anything about what is happening? When is Fungai's burial? I know you still love him and you are always well-informed.'

Now Fumi was sure he was looking at President Onim, the man who had murdered his father. He also realised he was looking at the woman who was once Fungai's fiancé, now Mrs. Bekizeli Onim.

'Baba Onim,' she responded politely. 'That was a long time ago. Remember, he also used to be your friend? By the way, what did you see in me that made you want to kill your own friend?' Expertly changing the subject and putting Onim on the defensive.

'What do you know, woman?' President Onim responded forcefully.

'What I know is what everyone knows, what is circulating in the media. Be warned, his assassination is raising the people's temperature. You should deal with it before it gets out of hand. Perhaps it is time to soften your stance against Mr. Fungai. Acknowledge him as a good statesman, give him his accolades, and be on the same side with the people.' She said this as she glanced at a hidden camera with a knowing look, hoping Fumi had figured out Mr. Fungai's surveillance system in Sydney.

'Never! I will never do that. He has made my life miserable. I can't even sleep without seeing his ghost. He has bewitched me and he paid for it,' President Onim whined to his wife. 'Go find out what is happening, Ma Zendi.' He dismissed her.

Fumi stood up to relax his muscles, stretched, arching his back. As he raised his arms, the screen changed to a new scene, it showed the White House from outside the grilled fence. *What is this?* he wondered. *How did that happen?* He waved his hand again, yet another feed, this time showing a large home at a distance, like a palace. This was followed by a close-up of an office. A woman, immaculately dressed in bright-coloured West African attire, was watching TV where youths standing in groups were shouting back at the police in riot gear. On her large oval desk was a flag of the East African Union. He waved his hand again, another office scene, another leader. *How did Mr. Fungai manage to do this? Will I ever know how he did it?* Fumi wondered.

Time to take a break Fumi decided. Rest for a few hours before shit hits the fan. He found Melissa in his bed, flipping across pages of social media on her new palm cell. 'Are you following the African news? Things are going crazy, there are riots everywhere across the continent,' she observed.

Fumi looked over Melissa's shoulders to see mobs of young men and women, mostly students. 'Who was Fungai? A visionary and a hero. Who murdered the General? Onim! The enemy.' The students shouted.

Fumi activated his new Holo-sp5, requesting news--'Africa, news, demonstrations in Baju, Bakoko, Oko, Zomba, Zimai.' "President Onim implicated in the murder of the Africanist, Dr. Fungai ra Fumi." "Leading African figures point the finger at President Onim." The list went on.

Fumi focused on a feature by *The Daily Standard*. "Dr. Fungai, who many believe to have died when his offices were bombed many years ago in Zimai, was this week found murdered in cold blood in his home north of Sydney," the paper stated. It went on to explain in detail Dr. Fungai's beliefs on a unified Africa. That is self-reliant, economic independence, free of corruption, where every child is educated, and every adult, male and female, is gainfully employed. Where health care is for all and social support is available for those in need. "In his exile, he continued to support indigenous enterprises, especially in technology and manufacturing. His burial is scheduled for Saturday. *"The Daily*

Standard will keep you informed of further details." The article concluded.

'Let's sleep, you have a long day tomorrow, or is it today? Melissa whispered to Fumi, winking, then kissing him goodnight.

'I need a massage, Chinese, preferably Ms. Ai Chan,' Fumi whispered.

'Me too. I definitely need therapy, preferably African, Mr. President.' Melissa retorted, giggling and snuggling close to him as she clapped twice, killing the lights. Coming through the tinted high windows, the ambient moonlight provided a romantic ambience. The distant sound of the waves breaking onto the rocks adding to the magic of the two lovers.

His alarm went off at 5.30 am. Sitting up in bed, still groggy and not quite awake, he noticed Melissa was gone, no doubt in the Intel Center doing her thing.

'Wake up, Mr. Fumi. It's a new, big day,' Melissa shouted as she came into the room with a glass of apple juice.

'Thanks, Ms. Chan,' he responded. 'News?'

'Young people across Africa have been on the streets, demanding to know who murdered Mr. Fungai. Others are now demanding "change for a better future", "freedom from poverty", "economic empowerment" and "freedom from corruption," they are shouting throughout Africa. "We wait for Nkulu, they shout in Zomba. We want Baba, in Zimai. Tata is coming, they scream in Oko and Baju. We need our Mokozi, they sing in Maisiri, while they claim *Ukumkani* (the King) is on the way in Ukutswani. Even in Sukuta, Onim's hometown, they demand change. News outlets are not sure who is organising the demonstrations that have spread to every city and urban centre in Africa.'

'Who are they asking for?' Fumi asked as he poured his first pure Ethiopian arabica coffee. 'Yes, this is good *oh ...!*' He let out a contented sigh, talking to himself as the caffeine coursed through his system, waking him up fully.

Melissa just laughed off the question. 'You know very well who they are asking for,' she responded.

Fumi continued to watch the information feeds from the array of screens. Social media is in overdrive. Feeds from the major news outlets went deep, covering demonstrations, opinions and interviews across the continent. Yet, no one was sure of the origin of this newfound voice. All that was clear was the murder of the late Dr. Fungai had provided a rallying point for the masses of frustrated citizens of Africa.

The media called him a hero, a founding Father, an Africanist, a person ahead of his time, yet very few people knew him until now. Every African leader was paying homage to the late Dr. Fungai, some with more flamboyant language—adding to his status and mystery.

'Dr. Fungai was a visionary, political architect, a humble person who dreamed of one strong united African nation,' announced President Onim, joining the stream of heads of state from across the globe.

'So, you did listen to Ma Beki?' Fumi verbalised.

The rather secretive group, *Antu* has demanded that President Onim come clean and tell the African people what really happened.

"There is evidence to suggest foul play in the death of Dr. Fungai. Unnamed sources say he was assassinated by a hit squad made up of President Onim's feared Presidential Guards. The Australian authorities have neither denied nor confirmed these rumours," reported *the Guardian*.

"We are informed that President Onim has categorically denied involvement in the murder of Dr. Fungai, who he claims was a friend, implying the CIA are the possible culprits," one social media source stated.

"Behind me are the remains of the late Dr. Fungai's home," an Al Jazeera reporter announced. The camera focused on crumbled bricks and charred timber. "Dr. Fungai was gunned down in his own home, which was later burned to the ground. Who did Dr. Fungai threaten? Why did they kill him? Who is responsible for his death? Is it possible the rumours coming from many parts of Africa are true—did President Onim of Zonga order the assassination of Dr. Fungai?" The reporter asked.

In his new home in Mosman bay, Fumi observed these developments as he prepared for the burial. He had read the thick dossier Mr. Fungai had left behind encrypted on the old Mac computer, not once but three times, understanding more of the hidden messages each time. His father's predictions were playing out to the letter.

Let my death be worthwhile, he had written. *Let it plant the seeds of our dream, awaken the sleeping, destroy what is, and build a new Africa*. People on the streets of more than fifty cities and in villages scattered around the continent, young and old, were demanding change in his name. Somehow, a revolution was brewing—as he had predicted ... or planned.

Fumi had rested and now it was time to be the Chief, the Paramount Chief, *Mokozi* of his people.

Chapter 18:
Fumi - My Blood

t was 11 pm. *I need to replenish,* Fumi decided. From the basement bunker office, he headed to the kitchen for a cup of tea and toast. He didn't make it past the living room.

On the Holo-TV projection, an old woman, standing in front of a small brick-walled house, was speaking in eloquent and heavily accented English. Her holographic image was so real it made Fumi feel a bit disoriented, like he was in the village, looking at the woman a few meters away.

'They murdered our hero. For so long, we have lived in chains, suffering untold pain. The time for change has arrived. The people demand change.' She paused for effect. 'Through death,' she continued, 'Fungai will be, must be … reborn.' Her image looked so real, with her sunken eyes staring at Fumi, coercing him to step up and take action. 'The time for change has arrived.'

Matadi, who had been sitting on the couch, switched off the Holo-TV. The woman faded away, silence followed, a glass-topped table marking where she had stood. Did she just paraphrase Fungai's diary? *"Through death, I will be reborn."* His father had written, remembering the quote vividly, for it had haunted him for some time.

'Who is that woman?' Fumi asked Matadi.

'Boss, I don't know. I would say it's just another old crone with an axe to grind but then again, you really never know,' Matadi responded.

'No, she is someone I'm supposed to know, sending a very clear message,' Fumi stated. 'Find out who she is.'

'Sure, I'll get the tech guys to work on it. The creek has become not just a river but a torrent. In a hundred cities and a thousand villages, they sing of his dream, demand change, an overhaul of the status quo. Mr. Fungai has become a Martyr,' Matadi stated as he headed out of the room.

Like a caged lion, Fumi moved from one end of the room to the other, deep in thought, a frown on his face. Someone is mobilising the masses, igniting their fires. Who? He wondered. A warning in his head told him somehow, *I am part of this seemingly organic movement.*

Fumi felt a tingle in his pocket before hearing the ring tone. Fishing out the dollar-sized Holo-sp5. **Caller unknown**, flashed on the screen. Matadi, now in the living room looked at him with a questioning look and approached. 'Let me talk to whoever it is, boss.' Fumi passed the Holo-sp5 to Matadi.

'Hello! Is this Mr. Fumi ra Fungai?' A polite female voice asked.

'No, who's asking?' Matadi responded with a strong but polite tone.

'You have watched the news, yes? Then you have seen me. Matadi, is it? Pass me to Mr. Fumi now.' The woman spoke in a commanding voice.

'Yes, Ma'am. I will put you on speaker,' replied Matadi.

'You're in grave danger, Fumi, but you must address the people during the burial. Now, that is a conundrum, I know. What do you propose to do?' The woman asked without introducing herself.

Fumi paused for a moment, wondering, *who is this woman?* He had reached the same conclusion but he had not come up with a solution. If he was to be a leader, he figured, he had to show no weakness. But then, he couldn't be a leader if he was dead. He decided to trust the woman, whoever she was, but first, he needed to be sure.

'A very wise man once told me you prepare your garden before the rains. You are of the same mind, yes? How many mango seeds would you plant to get one to grow?'

A slight pause followed before the woman responded with a long chuckle. 'I see you have learned good lessons from the wise man. Seven, I would say. But then you may be able to get all seven to germinate if you use water from the *Black Water.*' With this, Fumi confirmed the woman knew his father and must be one of the leaders of the reclusive group he headed. He also knew where to go.

'I salute you, Ma'am. I gather the garden is prepared, and we're ready to plant?'

'Yes indeed, Fumi, son of Fungai. I look forward to your homecoming, my son.' The woman concluded and switched off.

Melissa, a half-smile on her face and a pinched brow, looked intrigued. 'How many mangoes? What was that about?'

Fumi took a deep breath, ignoring the question, he responded. 'The fog has cleared. I am ready to make my move now. Melissa, please arrange a charter flight to Oko.'

'Yes, boss,' Melissa responded, heading to her office to make the arrangement.

Matadi took note of the new Fumi. He had been a soldier for a long time to realise that Fumi had, right in front of his eyes, transformed into a clear-minded and decisive political leader. *He is not unlike his father and has youth on his side. We might just succeed,* Matadi thought.

'We do have a cell in Oko, yes? Prepare me a sitrep and get the cell mobilised. I want all resources on deck.'

'Yes, boss,' Matadi responded this time with a slight bow of the head.

Change Plan

They took a short break at the Sir Seewoosagur Ramgoolam International Airport, Maurice, Mauritius, while the captain refueled and obtained the necessary departure documents. During the flight to Maurice from Sydney, they had looked at what might happen in terms of security and had prepared plans for the different scenarios. *'Adapt, change, survive'* Fumi remembered his intelligence training. He had a different plan, one that he had not shared with Matadi and Melissa yet.

'In Oko, logistics and security are in place,' Matadi confirmed.

I will have to find time to write my speech and eulogy, Fumi thought as they continued brainstorming.

At 11.40 pm, they lifted off. According to the flight manifest, their destination was Oko, Zonga. That is what the teams on the ground knew.

'A change of plans. We head for the city of Mayi Ndombi, Dembo Republic,' Fungai informed Matadi and Melissa.

'We will be entering Impula airspace in thirty minutes,' the captain announced.

Fumi knocked on the pilot's cabin door. It was immediately unlocked. 'Head for The Hero's Airport in Zimai.' He instructed the captain. 'Maintain radio silence until we're ready to land. Is that clear?'

The captain turned around, frowning with a quizzical expression that seemed to be asking, *why?* 'I thought we were going to Oko. That is what the flight plan says.'

'Yes, I understand but conditions have changed. Oko is no longer the destination. For now, we head to Zimai. By the way, how are we doing with the fuel?' Fungai asked as he looked at the gauge, noticing it was halfway.

'We're good, Sir. Are you sure you want to land in Zimai?'

'Yes,' Fumi said firmly as he turned around towards the cabin.

'We are approaching Zimai. We will be landing at the Hero's Airport in thirty minutes,' the captain announced. 'Expect a bumpy landing, please put on your seat belts.'

'What is this about?' Melissa enquired as Fungai sat next to her. He sighed heavily, knowing he had some explaining to do.

'Can I have a drink? Take one too.' He looked and saw Matadi looking at him and waved him over.

'Now, listen guys. I have changed the plans, courtesy of the old lady we spoke to yesterday,' Fungai said, speaking plainly. 'You remember she talked of *Black Water*?' Black Water translates to 'Mayi Ndombi' in Kibemba. So, we're heading to the Dembo Republic via Zimai.'

'And since when did you learn Kibemba?' Melissa enquired, clearly exasperated that Fumi had changed their plans without informing them. Matadi looked perplexed but not flustered. He had lived with Mr. Fungai long enough to understand the son. *Always expect a change of plans,* the old man had taught him.

'Like father, like son,' Matadi whispered, a smile on his face. 'And what do we do with the Oko arrangements?'

'Nothing.' Fumi responded. 'For security reasons, we're now AWOL. By the way, no comms with anyone from now till we're in Black Water.'

'Good thinking, boss!'

Looking down from the plane, Fumi could barely make out the streets of Zimai. A storm was raging. It was approaching 5 am local time.

The moment they touched down, Fumi approached the captain's cabin, knocking rather hard. The door slid open as the co-pilot was taxing towards the terminal.

'Well done, Captain. Good landing. Taxi to the far end of the strip, the last hangar. We will be picking someone up there before departing.' Fumi could see the captain was not amused.

'I thought you said Zimai was our destination?'

'Sorry guys, change of plans. We will get destination instructions from the passenger we're picking up.'

'I will have to inform the head office of the changes,' the pilot, responded.

'Your boss is already aware that the flight plan was flexible,' Fumi said, fishing out and passing a document to the pilot. 'Here, see for yourself.'

The pilot scanned the document, noticing the triple pay for the crew at the bottom of the page.

'Are we okay with that, or should I call your boss?' Fumi enquired.

'No Sir, it's all good,' the captain responded as he passed the document to his co-pilot.

'This is an emergency pick-up, so make it quick.'

An old woman wearing a hoodie walked out of the hangar, a backpack on her shoulder. She quickly climbed into the plane. In no time, the Gulfstream was in the air again.

'What the hell?' Fumi cursed as he recognised the woman. She had done a good job of hiding her face, fearing someone might be watching.

Fumi felt like standing up but the woman read his intention.

'Do not bother standing up, son,' Mrs. Onim said as she sat down next to Fumi. She closely scrutinised his face, then smiled broadly. 'You are indeed your father's son.' Despite the seatbelt restraint, she hugged him with such force that Fumi felt like he was being choked. She held his hand, as a mother does with their child—full of love and affection. She seemed extremely happy to see him. *Why is this woman, the wife of the man who killed my father, so happy to see me?* Fumi wondered.

'I am assuming you know me as Ma Beki or Bi Onim, yes?' More a statement than a question.

Fumi looked around to make sure Melissa and Matadi weren't listening. He noticed that they had moved to the very end of the Gulfstream jet.

'Yes, I do,' Fumi responded, seeing no need to lie. 'The question is, who are you really, and why are you here now?'

'Instruct the pilots to head for the Mayi Ndombi. That is where Dr. Fungai wanted to be buried. It is not the land of his people, but he wanted a monument that would be a beacon of unity in the future capital city of the Federation of African States.

'Tomorrow, you will meet the other elders of The Seven,' Ma Beki continued. 'There are those who want you to act now. Others will argue that we need to create more chaos before you step in but it will be your decision that carries the day. Do you want to know my opinion, though?' She asked in a whisper.

'Of course, Mrs. Onim, what would you do?'

'Please call me Ma Beki.' She seemed annoyed when Fumi used her married name.

'Well,' she started hesitantly, knowing she had to convince him. 'President Onim wants the demonstrations to end. The mass movement scares him. Other African leaders are also worried about the social chaos spreading across the continent. They blame him for it. You, on the other hand, want chaos to cause the collapse of these governments. You ask me what I would do. I would not want to be the villain that kills presidents. I would rather be the saviour that stopped the chaos and brought calm. Let the masses do the job. They deserve it.'

Fumi thought this made a lot of sense ... *but whose side is she on?* He wondered.

'And what if I chose to strike when the iron is hot?' Fungai asked, wanting to know as much as possible from Mrs. Onim.

'Simply put, the main act will be brought forward. Half of the African countries would be without leaders by the end of the week and chaos will follow. It will be messy and you will not have the name recognition you so deserve. We will not achieve the end goal ... One Africa.'

'Whatever you decide, your destiny is written in the books of your ancestors.'

She just used the words my father used in his memoir as though telling me, I know you, I am with you. Who are you really, Ma Beki? Fumi wondered.

'This is your captain speaking.' Fumi heard over the intercom. 'We will be landing at the Mayi Ndombi airport in thirty minutes. I have not been able to get landing clearance. I don't know what to expect.'

'Go and tell the captain all is arranged. Tell him to taxi to the end of the runway.' Ma Beki instructed Fumi.

As he was about to enter the cockpit, he received a message on his phone, forwarded by Matadi.

Mr. Fumi owns FFR Airlines, Signed CEO, FFR Airlines.

Fumi realised that FFR stood for Fungai Fumi Ramla Airlines. He could not help but burst out into laughter. *Mr. Fungai, you never cease to amaze me, who would have thought?*

Fumi passed the instructions from Ma Beki to the Captain. The 'fasten seat belt' sign came on. The plane started its descent, a line of lights marked the airstrip, a large neon signage, 'Airport FFR', on top of the roof of the barn-like airport's main building, announced that they had arrived at the Fungai Fumi Ramla Airport. *Mr. Fungai owns this airport, too?* Fumi wondered as he glanced at his wristwatch. It was 6.05 am. The Gulfstream disappeared into a hangar at the far end of the runway. He saw a dozen or so security men and women in plain clothes. A couple carried AK rifles.

'Son, I am invisible for now. I leave you here. I will see you soon, hopefully. May your ancestors give you strength.' Mrs. Onim—Ma Beki—hugged him again.

After giving instructions to the captain, Fumi disembarked. An old man came out from an office in the hangar. He rushed towards Fumi, arms outstretched, as though they knew each other. 'Welcome home, sir, I am Obiya Alaneme, a friend of Dr. Fungai for a long time,' he whispered. A dozen security men and women keenly observed Fumi, no doubt wondering who he was. They bowed politely as he passed.

'Welcome, Sir,' their leader said as he firmly shook hands with Fumi. 'I am the captain of this miserable lot,' he said jokingly. 'We're ready and at your service, Sir.'

Matadi and Melissa stood by his side, scrutinising each of the security men and women.

'Keep on walking, boss,' Matadi whispered, quite obviously feeling he wasn't in control of the situation.

'It would be nice to know these ladies and gentlemen who cut their sleep short for me,' Fungai spoke to their leader, ignoring Matadi.

'Yes, Sir, that is very kind of you.'

'Form line.' The leader commanded his unit, taking his position at the head of the line. Fumi looked at Matadi, who was already appraising the security team's movement, distance between each member of the team, stance ... all indicators of training and teamwork. He seemed happy with what he saw, except for the man at the end of the line to the left. He seemed out of place. Their leader noticed the same but kept it to himself.

Fumi looked up, making eye contact with every one of the men and women. Melissa immediately understood what Fumi wanted. She activated a micro-cam which looked like a button attached to his shirt. Fumi heard the click in his micro-ear piece. *It's time to find out who these people are,* he thought to himself.

Approaching their leader, Fumi offered his hand again. 'I'm Fumi, and who are you?'

'Joshua, Sir,' the captain responded. Fumi looked at him as though memorising his facial features.

'Joshua, *eh*! From the South, yes? Luapula? You're Bemba, yes?' He asked as he appraised the captain.

'How did you know that Sir?' Joshua replied, amazed that this stranger could identify where he came from and his people by just looking at him. Fungai just smiled as he stepped to the next man. He made them feel like he knew each one of them, except the very last one.

In the earpiece, he heard Melissa curse. 'That one is not in our database but hold on a minute,' Fumi extended his arm to the man, he looked at him, scrutinising his facial reactions. He saw fear, a tremor in the handshake confirmed it.

'And you are?' Fumi asked.

'Fabrice, sir,' he said in a rather raspy, high-pitched voice as though he was having a panic attack. Fungai looked at the captain, who seemed agitated as though he had failed.

'Yes, Fabrice,' Fungai said as he listened to the earpiece. 'Let me guess, from your appearance, you're from ... the Bami people from the nation of Duala. Yes?' At this point, the man calling himself Fabrice was sweating even though the sun was yet to rise.

'Yes, Sir,' he responded.

'Thank you, Fabrice and everyone for being here for me, I very much appreciate your service.' He looked at Fabrice again, then at Matadi, nodding. Matadi nodded, indicating--understood.

The security team members were very impressed. Fumi noticed they all seemed to have relaxed a bit. A couple had smiles on their faces, no doubt happy that this important man knew not only their names but also where they came from, except for Fabrice, who was still standing at attention and seemed to have isolated himself from the others.

Fumi, he is good, thought Matadi. *He may prove to be as good or even better than his father.*

'Captain, Melissa, ride with me, Matadi will catch up with us later.' A limo and a Toyota Landcruiser left the hanger, heading for an unknown destination.

'He is Onim's man,' Fumi heard Matadi on the earpiece. 'I suggest he goes missing.'

'No, recruit him. We need to identify Onim's men on the ground. Use whatever means to keep him on our side.'

'Captain, your man Fabrice is a spy. You failed us.'

'Sir, Mr. Fumi, I am sorry. He was a last-minute replacement. The man he replaced just disappeared. The FFR Airport management did not have enough time to do background checks.'

He took a moment, breathing heavily, visibly annoyed. Fumi let the captain agonise, no doubt fearing the worst. Fine, but let this be the last mistake you make,' Fumi pronounced each word like a judge would.

Both Fumi and Melissa heard Ma Beki in their earpiece. Fumi looked at Melissa to confirm he heard right. 'Joshua,' Fumi spoke slowly, clearly and with emphasis. 'Presumed hostiles are following us, swap positions with the limo and instruct them to deal with the hostiles.'

Ma Beki relayed their rendezvous location. Suddenly, they heard gunshots behind them. 'Take a left turn, head for Luasa village. Make sure we're not being followed.' Melissa instructed the driver.

Mrs. Onim is indeed on our side, Fumi thought, a smile on his face. A secret weapon right under President Onim's nose? *Mr. Fungai, you're indeed a genius. I hope I can be half the man you were*, Fumi thought.

It was mid-morning when they reached the sleepy village of Luasa on the northern shore of Lake Mayi Ndombi. They passed a group of women crowding a lone fisherman, jesting and haggling over limited fish. No one seemed to notice their vehicle. They left the village behind, driving further north for another forty minutes. "Private property, keep out," a sign read in both French and English. Fumi noticed the two guards who opened the gate were fully geared and smartly dressed in jungle-green army uniforms. Half a kilometre from the gate, the road came to an end.

'We will take a boat from here,' Melissa announced as she stepped out of the car.

Fumi looked around, 'where is the boat?' The captain pointed into a thick bush near the water. He saw it, hidden from sight by thick foliage and green webbing. It would take them about thirty minutes to ride westwards across the grey-blue lake towards what looked like a massive wall, a bluff fifty meters or so high. As they approached the rock face, Fumi barely noticed a narrow opening in the shadows of the cliff face. As they came closer, it became clear that it was a natural entrance to what looked like a cave. A ten-minute ride in the dark underground canal led them into a large amphitheater-like cave.

From his earpiece, Fumi heard Ma Beki's voice. 'Now you meet the Elders.'

Melissa, the captain and his security team took up positions at the entrance of the cave as Fumi climbed up the rough-hewn stone stairs into what could have been a decent boardroom anywhere in the world. Three women and three men sat around a large, shiny, black ebony oblong table.

The six elders stood up and bowed politely even though they were twice his age. Fumi went around the table, shaking hands, one at a time. In their handshake, he could feel their excitement, in their eyes, he saw anticipation.

The Africa Futures: The Organisation
"Attack is the secret of defense;
defense is the planning of an attack"
(Sun Tzu, The Art of War)

Like a spider's web, the centre must hold.

He approached the woman sitting at the far end of the table. 'What the hell!' Mrs. Onim sat at one end of the table. A distinct tribal mark on her forehead now apparent.

'Yes, it's me, my son. I'm sure you're wondering how I managed to arrive before you. Simple. I used your helicopter.'

This is unbelievable, Fumi thought. *Yet it made sense for her to travel separately, discretely.*

She clapped her hands twice, calling for attention. 'Welcome to the Council of Elders Fumi ra Fungai.' She spoke softly in polished American English. 'I paraphrase a saying from the language of my father: *like a spider web, the centre must hold.* We have held together and kept the dream alive, thanks to our leader, Dr. Fungai.'

Fumi was shocked, caught unawares. He remembered his father's memoirs. Is this the woman who literally saved him? Helping him escape his enemy Onim by flying him across Africa? He stood up as though pulled by a magnet, walking across the room, he approached Ma Beki, bent over and kissed her forehead. Ma Beki laughed haughtily, clearly tickled by his gesture. 'You're indeed your ...' She checked herself, 'you're indeed the blood of Fungai, always charming to the ladies.'

The introductions continued. 'I am Moshi Tanga, responsible for natural resources,' said a man next to Ma Beki.

'Asafa Kwame, technology and industry.'

'Linda Abas, finance and commerce.'

'Nzima Ndlovu, military and intelligence.'

'Obiya Alaneme, political affairs and mobilisation.'

Ma Beki took over after the introductions. 'Dr. Fungai was the First of the Seven, the centre of the web. Somehow, he saw the future and provided our vision. He also managed *The Africa Futures*, known just as The Futures Group. How he did this, I don't know.

'He saw The Futures Group as a spider web,' Ma Beki continued. 'The way he put it was this: imagine a spider's web, with six radial strands running from the centre to six locations in Africa and six locations around the globe. Tying this together is a single spiral thread, like the Fibonacci sequence, symmetrically spiralling outwards a total of six times. Connecting the six radial threads through thirty-six nodes, with the centre holding everything together.

Fungai had studied the Fibonacci sequence. '*Math and physics try to explain nature,*' his teacher had said. *But I still don't get it,* he thought.

As though reading his mind, Ma Beki continued. 'This is the way it works.' She looked around the table. 'The six of us are the radial threads. Each has specific assignments in six locations, with a cell at each location, in Africa and around the world,' pausing to allow this to sink in. 'Now, Dr. Fungai was the spiral thread tying the six of us and the centre that held us together. The only one who had full knowledge of everything.

Now, it was clear to Fumi. 'I understand' he said.

'As you know, Fungai, through his businesses, ensured we are one of the richest organisations in the world,' Dr. Linda said, taking over from Ma Beki. 'He was simply a genius. No other word can describe his uncanny ability to predict everything, from politics to financial markets, even wars.' She spoke with so much excitement. 'He started with trading in rare earths, minerals, that only he and The Futures Group could supply, where he got them, we don't know. Somehow, he knew what and when to buy and sell, especially when it came to emerging technologies. The Futures now owns a large share portfolio in all major and emerging technologies and pharmaceutical companies.' Linda finished with a huge sigh, as though regretting the loss of Fungai's capabilities.

Ma Beki looked at Fumi with a kind smile. 'I am sure you will figure this out.'

Fumi thought he saw Linda smile before she continued. 'Fungai, the genius he was, wondered how he could tax all the corruption money held by African leaders. He asked me to come up with a database of all corrupt officials, including their wealth in their bank accounts. Everything. The genius was, he created malware that targeted accounts that had over ten million dollars, withdrawing a 0.5 percentage point every month. He also managed to find a way to get one percentage point for all international transfers over one million American dollars from these accounts.'

Ma Beki burst out in laughter. 'You know what he did with this corruption money, he passed it to the NGO *Support Africa*. We use the funds to provide services such as hospitals, medicines, clean water, schools and education bursaries across Africa. Services that should be given by the same corrupt governments. He would often say, "Give to the people what belongs to Caesar."

Obiya took on the laughter, loud and contagious. 'But the best part is, we are using some of these proceeds to support *Antu*. To destabilise these very governments. Creating political chaos by mobilising the people to demand for change.'

With this statement, it all fell in place. Even Fumi could not resist laughing.

After a short pause, Ma Beki continued in a more sombre voice. 'Now, as you can see, with the passing of Fungai, the people need a leader. Your father's script is playing out as he had planned. By his dying, also part of his script, he has unleashed a storm that even he could not have hoped for. It is now your destiny to take his place. To see through the second phase of his dream or, if you like, his prophesy. Tomorrow, we celebrate the life of our great leader, Dr. Fungai.' They all clapped in unison, cheering for their fallen leader.

'As our leader, where to now?' Ma Beki asked.

Fumi paused for a moment while he looked around the table. Their dedication was unquestionable, now, he needed them to accept him, not just as an heir but as a true leader.

'As our elders say, *"patience puts a crown on the head."* For forty years, Dr. Fungai waited, building, planning and creating a torrent but we must wait for the tsunami that only we can control. I realise that you have been patient for a long time. I ask you for a bit more time. With a bit of help, the governments *will* self-destruct. Then we will pick up the pieces.' Fumi spoke in a calm tone. Somehow, he was sure of this.

He looked around the table. Respect and agreement are all he saw.

Like his father, he is clear-minded and sure-footed, Ma Beki thought. She clapped three times, indicating the end of the meeting. 'Let's have something to eat.'

As they ate, Mr. Ndlovu approached Fumi, pulling him aside. 'Once again, let me say it's really great to meet you in person. We have been waiting for this moment for a long time. Whatever happens tomorrow, have trust in the Six.' Fumi was a bit perplexed by the statement but decided it was better to keep quiet for now. They ate, then left, with a promise to be at tomorrow's burial ceremony at the stadium.

'It is safer for you to stay here. We have prepared accommodation for you, sir.' A woman in a military uniform told Fumi as he was about to ask for his transport.

Chapter 19:
Fumi - Blast At The Burial

"A good star can be seen in the morning."
(African proverb)

Fumi heard the noise, like a swarm of bees. The humming became a cacophony of noises as they approached the city's only stadium. They drove through the gate and heard the voice of a woman, magnified by a sound system that must have been really powerful. *Why is that voice familiar?* He wondered before realising it was that of the woman on the television the other day in Sydney. A security retinue that had been waiting for them quickly walked him to a temporary platform.

Looking out from the raised platform, he saw throngs of men women, young and old. There must have been several thousand. The stadium was at capacity. A step behind him, Matadi and Melissa stood at attention, no doubt scanning the throngs for any sign of danger. Around him were his security personnel, handpicked by Matadi and Melissa. Joshua, the captain of the unit from yesterday, saluted as though Fumi was the president, no doubt happy that he still had a job.

A sense of expectation was in the air. Something monumental was about to happen. Whispers circulated throughout Africa, talking of a messiah who would save his people from the tyrannical governments. Perhaps this was the time and place. Fumi sucked in the energy from the masses. Riding on it, he gathered himself. With both hands high above his tall frame and the mid-morning sun on his face, he was the epitome of power and promise. The humming of the masses died away, silence—anticipation.

He cleared his throat, an orator asking for attention, a trick he had learned from his father, Mr. Fungai. With his booming baritone voice, made more powerful by an excellent sound system, he started. 'Dear friends, let me thank you all for coming to commemorate the life of Dr. Fungai.

'You do not know me, so please allow me to introduce myself.' The stadium went silent, the masses captivated by him.

'I am Fumi, the son of Fungai!' Fumi announced in a powerful, clear voice, bowing to the masses as if saying, *I humble before thee.* He spread both hands in a flourish as though stating—*I have arrived.* The masses went crazy. Screams erupted in the stadium. A group of women started singing. African drums, loud and rhythmic, announced the arrival of the one they had been waiting for.

'Fumi ra Fungai ... the promise is here.' They chanted as they danced to the beat of the drums

'What is happening?' Fumi asked the woman next to him. The one he had seen as a holograph image.

'A good star can be seen in the morning,' she responded, quoting an African proverb. 'Under this African morning sun, it is your time to shine. We have been waiting for this moment for a long time!'

The crowd lifted him, giving him the belief that he so much needed. He continued in his deep voice, now full of emotion. 'I bring you a message from my Father ... Fungai ra Fumi, may he rest in peace.' He paused and took a deep breath. The crowds were with him.

'As though he knew he was leaving us, the great man left me a message.' Fumi pulled out a note and started reading. "My journey has come to an end. From the highlands, I sprang. I have now reached the delta. I enter the ocean to be one with the many who have gone before me."

'He, the great Fungai ra Fumi, wrote, "you Fumi, my son, your time has come, you must carry on the torch."

Raising his fist high, 'I salute you, Fungai the son of Fumi and I pledge this: your death will not be in vain.'

The crowds took over. 'We salute you, Fungai son of Fumi, your death will not be in vain.' The drums picked up speed; the masses moved with the beat.

He raised both hands high, asking to be heard.

'An old wise man once told me, a spring comes from the dark earth, it joins others to become a stream, many streams join to become a river that flows to be one ocean.

'Sons and daughters of this beautiful land, we must spring out of our sleep. Like the Nile, the Congo, the Zambezi and the other rivers of this great continent, we must join together to become the ocean. We must unite!'

Fumi paused, allowing the crowd to take in his meaning. He raised both his hands, like a high priest, he waved, encouraging the masses to speak out and air their emotions. The woman next to him took the mic. In a husky but practised voice, she started.

'Fu-mi ...' she clapped three times '... Unite Africa ...' The masses clapped three times in unison ... It seemed as though everyone in the stadium was chanting, then clapping. Together, they moved as if in a trance, hypnotised by this young man and the loud rhythm of the African drums.

'I didn't expect this. The crowd is going crazy,' he whispered to the old woman. She looked up to him, motherly love in her eyes. 'Isn't it amazing how a messiah can move his people?' Winking, a sly smile on her face.

At that moment, he realised that this very scenario had been in the making for a long time.

Fumi raised his hands again, ready to continue with his speech, this time to eulogise his father, to extol his virtues and visions. But before he could start, a helicopter appeared, circling the stadium. It was too loud for him to speak. He looked up to see a man in military uniform looking down on them. Even at a hundred or so meters above, Fumi could clearly see his face. The man grinned, then suddenly and in a practised movement, threw down an object that exploded in midair, not fifty meters above his head. Grey-green fumes spread out as a canister dropped on the platform he was standing on.

He made to grab the old woman next to him to get her out of harm's way but she had vanished. Matadi sprang into action and grabbed Fumi's shoulder, trying to cover him. Suddenly, a huge explosion rocked the stadium. Fumi heard a single gunshot from somewhere behind him. He saw Matadi fall to his knees, then drop face forward next to his feet. 'Where is Melissa!?' He looked around and saw she was trying to get to him. One of the security men tackled Fumi to the ground as though to protect him. Together with another man, they lifted him and started pushing him towards an exit door. Fumi heard Melissa screaming, calling his name, trying to get to him. He felt a sharp pain on the side of his neck like someone had pricked him with a needle. Realising these were not his men, he made an effort to free himself. His hands would not move, his legs gave in. Then, nothing ...

He woke up to find himself in a van. Sirens in the distance told him he was still in the city. He opened his eyes and realised his head was hooded with a black cloth. His mouth was gagged with duct tape. Discretely, he tested his hands and legs. They were tightly strapped with what he assumed to be tape. All he could do was to listen and smell—dust, grease, gunpowder, sweaty bodies.

Four voices, one on his left, another on his right, the driver plus one in front of the van. They spoke a *Bantu* dialect he did not understand but their tone was relaxed, even cheerful. They seemed to be happy with their job.

'We're going to be rich men,' the driver shouted happily, this time in French, not realising Fumi was awake. Fumi knew enough French to understand what they were saying.

'This is it men. I will go buy myself a nice piece of land, get myself a nice coastal girl, three kids and grow old a happy man. I'll forget about all these bloody greedy, rich politicians.'

'*Pss* ...' the one next to him started. 'You're such an idiot. You think the president will let you live. You're just a loose end. They will silence us the moment we deliver the package. What we need is to find a way to get our money and deliver the package without being killed.'

Bang, bang, bang ... the ringing in his ears was intolerable. Fumi tried to scream, not out of fear but because of the pain and ringing in his ears, but his mouth was gagged. His ear drums felt like they had busted, his brain was on fire, multicoloured stars flickering bright even though his eyes were covered with black cloth. The acidic, peppery, pungent smell reminded him of the fireworks over the Sydney bridge. He realised the gun was fired by the man on his left side. It took what seemed like minutes for the ringing to subside and his heartbeat to slow down. The side of the van grazed onto something before it came to a stop.

'What's happening?' he tried to scream. Still blindfolded, he could only imagine dead bodies.

'Boss, are you okay?'

What the hell ... Jose? What is happening? He wondered even though he could not speak.

'Boss, it is me, Jose. You're safe.'

Jose pulled off the black hood, then, he stripped the tape of his mouth and hands.

'If I remember well, you sold out Fungai for Onim,' Fumi said angrily, rubbing the sore skin around his mouth.

'Boss, I work for you, thanks to Dr. Fungai's forgiveness. Your father gave me a second chance and a difficult assignment—infiltrate Onim's spies in Mayi Ndombi, he had ordered me.'

Fumi looked around, noticing the bodies of the driver and his partner in front of the van. Each had a clean bullet hole at the back of their head. He looked to his right, part of the head of the man who had wanted to marry and settle down was missing. Blood and greyish-white brains splattered everywhere. The gruesome scene was too much. About to vomit, Fumi quickly opened the door, dashed out of the van and vomited on the side of the road. At that moment, a white Toyota Landcruiser pulled behind them. Fumi was about to take off into the thick bush when he heard Jose shouting. 'It's okay, this is us.'

From the back seat, an old woman beckoned him with a wave of her hand. 'Hurry up, my son, we need to move before someone comes by.' He jumped into the back seat while Jose took the front passenger seat. They drove off in a hurry.

'Hi boss.'

'What the fuck! What is happening?' Matadi, who he saw go down covered in blood at the stadium, was driving. 'Don't tell me my father planned your death and resurrection also?'

'No, he didn't, that was Ma Beki's plan.

'Ma Beki, what a surprise to see you here in the bush. I thought you went back to Zimai?'

'Give us privacy, Matadi.' Matadi pressed a button, raising a glass window that isolated the back seat from the front of the car. 'My son, I needed to finish our earlier talk. Then I will let you be.' She heaved heavily as though giving in to a heavy weight.

'Son, we have done a lot of things in our lives but there is one thing that demands a sacrifice no mother should give.' She stopped, apparently thinking about how to progress. Fumi could see from her face she was struggling with emotions.

'Look at me, Fumi, who do you see?' she finally brought herself to say.

Fumi was confused, not understanding the meaning of the question. She held his face close to hers. He looked at her more closely this time. For the first time, he noticed her high forehead and sharp jawline. In contrast to her almost charcoal-black skin, she had light grey eyes with a distinct light brown ring. Involuntarily, he pulled back as though he had seen a ghost. He was out of breath, his heart beat like an African drum. He needed space and time to think. Melissa had once told him, 'you have the eyes of a cat.'

Before he could move, Ma Beki put her hand on his arm to calm him down. 'Look, I know this is a shock to you, yet you need to know the truth that has been hidden away from you for so long. We have all sacrificed so much but when I see you, I realise it was all worth it.' She said this with so much emotion she was almost choking as tears ran down her rather long face.

First, it was confusion, then understanding, followed by anger.

'How can I trust anyone if everyone only tells me half the story?' Fumi asked, fury in his voice.

'My son, I know how you feel. Know this: for your safety, we sacrificed, me the most. I have lived without my son and my love. Your father could not call you son. How much anguish do you think that caused him?'

Fumi's anger dissipated, replaced by an unfamiliar emotion. He started sobbing, tears ran down his face unhindered and then he started laughing. 'All my life, I have wondered who I really was,' Fumi said as he experienced a warm fuzzy feeling. His mind was settled, all his doubts erased. 'Now I know my mother, father and even my great-grandfather. What more could I ask for?' He asked, as though talking to himself. 'You are really my mother!' Fumi spoke in between bursts of laughter.

'Indeed, my son. I am the one you have never known. I left you in Mama Maria's care and arranged for you to go to Boston to live near but not with your grandfather.'

'What? Professor Osman el Nijere is your father and my grandfather?' He broke out into a huge laugh. 'What a day!' was all he could say.

'And Mama Maria who incidentally is still alive is my auntie, so your grandmother,' Ma Beki added.

'What!?'

Underneath the laughter, Fumi was still furious. *All this time, he thought, my grandfather was living right next to me?* The more he thought about it, the more he came to understand the sacrifice both Ma Beki and Mr. Fungai had made. And yet he had a feeling all had not been revealed.

'One day, when we have the time, I will fill you in on the details. For now, you need to focus on the next move.' Fumi took a deep breath. *She is right*, he thought, accepting her explanation. 'You're right ... *Mother.*' She looked up at him adoringly, a smile on her face. 'I like the sound of that but let's keep it to ourselves for now.'

'Your father was a very wise man with super abilities he rarely used. He saw things others didn't. His shoes will be difficult to fill. So, if you have to take his place, you will need to walk where he walked.' Ma Beki said in a somber tone.

Fumi had not noticed that they had left the main road and were approaching a wooden bridge. Matadi stopped the car as a band of five young men in rag-tag clothing, each with a machete and an assault rifle, came out of the bush. Fumi wondered, *what now?*

'Here are your escorts. Remember, we will be waiting for your return, so don't die on us.'

'What's happening? Where am I going?' Fumi enquired.

'To walk like your father, you must follow his steps.' Ma Beki repeated without explaining.

As he stepped out of the car, Matadi handed him a backpack and an old-style walkie-talkie-like smartphone, brand name TFG 5. 'You will need this boss. See you later.' Jose waved, Matadi swung the car around and drove off, leaving him in the bush with the five young men who reminded him of the thugs he had seen in downtown Zimai.

The young men looked at him. His tailored suit, white shirt, black bow tie, shiny pointed four thousand dollars Gucci shoes. Then, they all burst out into haughty a laughter. Fumi looked around, all bush, muddy, a rutted track with thick tropical foliage on either side. His gaze fell on his swish Gucci shoes and his spunky suit. *How outlandish I look*, he thought. He could not resist joining in the laughter. Somehow, he felt at home, even though where he was exactly, he did not know.

They quickly introduced themselves. A lean, tall young man of about twenty-five seemed to be the leader of the band. 'We have a long way to go, brother,' he said, pointing eastwards across a flimsy wooden bridge. 'For five days, we will travel towards the morning sun, and if all goes to plan, we will be in the land of the Tano people. Your people. But first, you will need to change your clothes. You look like a clown.' Contrary to his demeanor and the surroundings, his English was posh, private grammar school type. Fumi opened his backpack and fished out a set of shabby-looking but clean clothes, including a rain jacket. He pulled out the Glock 19 9mm handgun carefully tucked in an inside pocket, checking to make sure it was loaded. *Thank you, Matadi, I need this to feel safe*, he thought. Finally, he flipped open the TFG 5 smart gadget which had a location App. He tapped it, noting the numbers that he knew to be the location coordinates.

'It is important to know where you come from,' he remembered one of his orientation classes.

'We don't have all day. Let's move,' he heard the young man who had introduced himself as Soki shout jovially.

As they headed east, Fumi could not stop thinking of his father, Mr. Fungai. That he had not known him as a father when he was alive pained him. Worse still, he did not have the chance to see him off. For now, he had to put that aside if he was to keep up with these young men—now friends.

Fumi would learn to live off the land, fight like a warrior and do things even Mr. Fungai, would have been proud of. Like his father, he would learn from his ancestors, the Ancients. He will need the knowledge and strength to quell the anger, chaos and anarchy he will find waiting for him.

The End

Characters

Ahmed	Salt trader
Asafa Kwame	Member of the Council of Elders
Baba Mkulu	The Paramount Chief of the Tano tribe
Bekele	Kitchen staff and spy in President Onim's residence
Bekizeli Zendi (Beki)	Born Aminata binti Osman el Nijere, Fungai's close associate
Ben Crawford	Fumi's host 'father' in the USA
Sidai	A young woman of the Tano tribe
Didi	Beki's spy
Mr. Elliot	Colonial Administrator in a colony in Africa
Elysia Broughton	Official, Australian Foreign Affairs
Fabrice	President Onim's spy
Fela	President Onim's security and hitman
Fungai	Who has a dream of Africa
Fumi	A boy from Noah's slum destined for greatness
Habiba	Juma's mother
Ira	Fungai's trainer

Jennifer Crawford	Fumi's host 'mother' in the USA
Juma	President Onim's Aide De Camp and hitman
Jose Tsango	Fungai's security
Joshua	Fumi's security
Linda Abas	Member of the Council of Elders
Mama Maria	Matron, Mama Maria's Women's Refuge
Malika Bi Demba el Sukuta	Mother to Kora el Sukuta (AKA President Onim)
Masika	Fungai's trusted friend and lieutenant
Matadi	Fungai's security and righthand man
Memi	Adoption agent who helps Fumi to move to the USA
Melissa (AKA Ms Ai Chan)	Girlfriend and Security Adviser to Fumi
Mohammed (AKA Mo)	President Onim's security man
Morani	A warrior of the Tano tribe
Moshi Tanga	Member of the Council of Elders
Mulumba Putumayo	Fungai's Lawyer
Mwanza	A young warrior of the Tano tribe
Nzima Ndlovu	Member of the Council of Elders
Obiya Alaneme	Member of the Council of Elders
Mr. O'Rilley	Acting CEO, The Futures Group, Sydney
Paul Osborne	Policeman, New South Wales, Australia

Pedro and Connor	Australian Federal Intelligence agents
President Abawoli	First President of Zonga Republic
President Nima	President of the Republic of Impula
President Onim	Born Kora el Sukuta, President of the Zonga Republic
Professor Osman el Nijere	A Harvard professor, father to Beki and friend of Fungai
Ramla ra Fumi (Bweha)	Fungai's grandfather who inspires him to chase his dream
Sandra Crawford (AKA Sun)	Fumi's host 'sister' in the USA
Sani	A Lieutenant General with President Onim's forces and Beki's spy
Thekisele bi Fumi	Fungai's mother
Vice President Ahmadu	Vice President of the Zonga Republic
Warkara	A shaman

Places-fictional

Baju	A city somewhere in Africa
Dembo Republic	A country in Africa
Dome of the Ancients	A sacred place under the forbidden mountains
Impula Republic	A country in Africa
Iyaka	A border town in Africa
Jola	A country in Africa
Kogi Nijere	A big river somewhere in Africa

Kwamunge Security Jail	A maximum jail in Africa
Luasa village	A village somewhere in Africa
Mansu	A village somewhere in Africa
Mayi Ndombi	Black Water; name of City where Fungai would be buried
Mayi Bula	A deep lake to the south of the Forbidden Mountains
Mayi Siri	A sacred volcanic lake within the forbidden Mountains
Niami	A big city somewhere in Africa
Noah's slum	A slum village in Zimai
Oko	The capital of the Zonga Republic
Sukuta	An old city somewhere in Africa
Tano village	A hidden village on the caldera of the Forbidden Mountain
Zimai	The capital of the Impula Republic
Zonga Republic	A country in Africa